You're an ex-SEAL named Hal Morgan. You served in a desert war and returned to the States with plenty of scars—inside as well as outside. Now you sail charter boats in Puerto Rico, taking the tourists out to sea. You're returning an empty boat to the marina when you spot a daysailer drifting ahead, apparently abandoned and ready to sink. You come alongside and find a young woman in a torn, black cocktail dress, lying unconscious in the cockpit. The daysailer doesn't look as though it will last long, so you hurry the woman over to your boat and do what you can for her.

When she wakes, she finds your gun in the cabin and demands that you go back and get some bag she left on the daysailer. She acts as though this bag means a lot to her—and it does. Because the young woman—Ana Cortez Bolaño—has just left her boyfriend, gangster boss Jaime Rivera, taking all his cash with her. Now you have a choice: you can hand Ana over to Rivera, knowing what he'll do to her, or you can make like a white knight and help her escape. The first decision is easy. After that, well, things get complicated . . . .

D1600053

SMITH

"There are sequences of edgy suspense and artfully done violence. And generous helpings of sex. A chilling story that knows what lurks beneath those superspy romances."
Don Crinklaw, *Booklist*

"Solidly entertaining, with an interesting lead character who has plenty of grit and toughness, Smith is a notable hard-boiled noir that hits the ground running, with guns blazing and knives slashing, and doesn't let up until there are ample corpses piled high."
Nicholas Litchfield, *Lancaster Guardian*

"*Smith* is a promising debut, with tight, no-nonsense prose, convincing dialogue, realistic action, and a character whose problems make our own pale in comparison."
Evan Lewis, *The Virginian-Pilot*

PIRATES

Timothy J. Lockhart

STARK
HOUSE

Stark House Press • Eureka California

PIRATES

Published by Stark House Press
1315 H Street
Eureka, CA 95501, USA
griffinskye3@sbcglobal.net
www.starkhousepress.com

ISBN-13: 978-1-944520-67-0

Book text design by Mark Shepard, SHEPGRAPHICS.COM
Cover illustration and design by JT Lindroos:
JTLINDROOS.CARBONMADE.COM

First Stark House Press Edition: April 2019

FIRST EDITION

DEDICATION
To Meg

ACKNOWLEDGMENTS

Thanks to Steve Dowdy of Bob's Gun Shop for help with "the gun stuff" (although any errors are mine alone).

Thanks to Carmel Corcoran and Guy Holland for reading and commenting on an early version of the manuscript.

Thanks to Lisa A. Iverson, Rick Ollerman, and Warren L. Tisdale, without whose insightful suggestions for revisions the manuscript might not have been published.

Thanks to Marcela Bolland for correcting my Spanish and catching several typos. *Gracias, mi amiga.*

And special thanks to Gregory Shepard and the rest of the "A Team" at Stark House Press, all of whom make the process of publication a pleasure.

PIRATES

Timothy J. Lockhart

CHAPTER ONE

He spotted the boat around nine a.m. She was a dark smudge about two miles off his starboard bow, apparently dead in the water. Something—he didn't know what—told him she was in trouble.

A look through the binoculars confirmed it. She was a single-masted daysailer, a small sloop with headsail gone and mainsail in tatters. The boat rolled slowly in the swells as though she'd taken on water.

The storm must have caught her at sea, he thought. After hearing the weather reports yesterday, he'd decided to remain dockside overnight at the marina and set sail early this morning. The battered appearance of the daysailer confirmed his judgment.

As often happens the day after a bad storm, the sky was clear and bright. There was enough breeze to keep the scent of the sea in his nose and sail his offshore sloop—a much bigger boat—but not so much as to raise whitecaps or make single-handing difficult.

He reached for the handheld VHF to radio the Coast Guard but then saw that on her present course *Sun Chaser* would come fairly close to the daysailer. He decided to call the Coasties when he had more facts.

He locked the wheel and got stiffly out of the helmsman's chair, favoring his left leg, the one with the scars. The movement made his leg throb, but it wasn't the stabbing pain he remembered all too well.

He got the boat hook from the top of the cabin and pulled a dock line out of the canvas pouch hanging from the chrome stern rail. He glanced at the wind indicator atop the tall mast and looked ahead, picturing *Sun Chaser*'s track toward the daysailer.

He returned to the helm and turned the wheel a few degrees to close course with the little boat. *Sun Chaser* responded slowly but easily, being sluggish but forgiving like all the charters that sailed out of Puerto de la Reina, the big marina on the eastern end of Puerto Rico.

Boats chartered from there seldom wound up on the southwest coast. Making a face, the marina manager had told him that the two middle-aged doctors from Chicago and their young, blonde wives had gotten tired of their projected circumnavigation of the island. They'd abruptly decided to leave *Sun Chaser* docked near Cabo Rojo and fly back to the mainland from the closest airport, the one at Mayagüez.

So here he was, bringing the charter back, and there it was—the other boat, perhaps abandoned, perhaps even sinking. Maybe no one aboard, but he had to check.

The daysailer was now less than a mile ahead.

He adjusted *Sun Chaser*'s course again so he could bring the sloop into the wind and stop her as she approached the daysailer. He tried hailing the other boat on the radio but got no answer. When he got within two hundred yards he used the air horn to blow the signal for "what are your intentions?" Still no result.

At what he judged to be the right distance, he came into the wind and loosened the headsail and mainsail sheets. With her sails slack, *Sun Chaser* coasted toward the daysailer, gradually losing speed.

He used the binoculars to take another look and could now see that the daysailer was an old wooden boat that hadn't felt a varnish brush for a long time. He thought he saw a dark shape in the cockpit. The angle was bad though, and he couldn't tell for certain.

Moving carefully, he carried the dock line and boat hook forward to the bow and fastened the line to a cleat. Either he was a better sailor than he thought or Neptune was with him, because when the boats closed they were near enough and slow enough for him to grab the daysailer with the hook.

He pulled her toward him. As the boat gently bumped into *Sun Chaser*'s side, he used the hook to put the loop in the line over one of the daysailer's cleats.

He looked down into the cockpit and saw someone lying there. A woman, judging from the long, light-brown hair splayed out in the several inches of water in the boat. She appeared unconscious—or dead.

He detached the mainsail's halyard and tied a long line to it. Then he took the other end of the halyard off its mast cleat below the winch, tied another line to that end, and took three turns of the halyard around the winch.

He put on a life vest and climbed down to the daysailer's bow, trying to ignore his aching leg, and taking another life vest and both of the lines with him. He worked his way back to the cockpit and stepped into the water sloshing from side to side in the little boat. There was more than he'd anticipated. The storm must have been violent enough to open the old boat's seams. In that case she wouldn't last much longer.

The woman lying in the water was young, in her twenties, and good-looking. Very good-looking. She was wearing a short black cocktail dress, cut low and ripped up one side, and a few pieces of expensive-looking jewelry. She had a bloody gash on her forehead.

Probably standing up when the boom came across, he thought.

Her chest rose and fell slowly in the tight dress, and a little blood seeped from the cut on her head. If the boom had hit her, she was lucky it hadn't knocked her out of the boat. She certainly would have drowned in the storm.

There were also bloody cuts on her manicured hands, which obviously weren't used to handling boat lines.

The woman moved her head slightly and moaned, which was a good sign. The bleeding had almost stopped, and she seemed to be coming around. But he had to get her aboard his boat before he could treat her wounds.

He noticed she was barefoot. He looked around and located one black shoe that was mostly straps and spike heel. He didn't see its mate. He also didn't see a purse, but if she'd had one, it had probably washed overboard. There was nothing else in the boat.

He picked up one of the lines and began tying it to the extra life vest. As he finished, she moaned again and moved her hands in the water covering the bottom of the boat. Then she opened her eyes—brown, a few shades darker than her hair—and looked at him.

He thought his face, complete with black eyepatch, would scare her, and it did. Her eyes widened and she screamed. She tried frantically to scrabble away from him, her hands churning in the water and slipping on the wet wood. Still screaming, she touched the shoe, then grabbed it. She slashed at him with the heel, barely missing his good eye and gouging a furrow down his cheek.

He grabbed her and put one arm behind her head. Then he quickly pressed his other arm to the side of her throat, locked that hand on the arm behind her, and squeezed.

They hadn't required him to take judo, either in basic or in his more advanced training. But like a lot of the guys, he'd learned a few moves because he enjoyed practicing them and thought they might come in handy sometime. He didn't remember the name for this particular hold—something about grasping your sleeve instead of your arm if you were wearing a gi—but he knew it compressed an opponent's carotid arteries, usually causing unconsciousness.

And that's what it did this time. The woman struggled for a few seconds but soon went limp in his arms. Her skin was smooth, wet, and cold.

He put the extra life vest on her, wishing he'd also brought a foul-weather jacket. Then, with a slow, steady pull, he hauled on the other line, the one attached to the halyard near the winch, bringing the halyard taut through the pulley at the top of the mast. Using the mechanical advantage of the winch, he raised the woman out of the cockpit, up *Sun Chaser*'s side, and on top of the cabin. He crossed over after her, stumbling and almost falling into the sea, but saving himself with the line in his hand.

Back aboard his boat he removed both life vests and carried the woman down into the salon, forward along the narrow passageway, and into the main stateroom. He put her on the big double berth, the bed he'd been using.

He took off most of her jewelry, leaving just the rings, and put it in a drawer by the berth. Then he unzipped and removed the sodden black dress. He hadn't expected her to be wearing much underneath but was surprised to find nothing. Her body was as lovely as her face, slim but shapely and lightly tanned everywhere except for the outline of a thong bikini bottom.

He went to the head to get the medical kit and a towel. He covered her body with the towel and used gauze from the kit to clean the cuts on her head and hands.

Once he'd daubed the blood away, the gash on her head turned out to be less serious than it'd looked. He didn't think he needed to stitch it. He disinfected the cuts and bandaged them the way a profane but expert Navy corpsman had taught him a few years earlier.

Then he made the woman as comfortable as possible, putting a pillow under her head, removing the towel, and covering her with the sheet and light blanket. He touched the back of his hand to her cheek. Her skin was warmer now that she was out of the wet dress, and she was breathing more deeply and regularly.

She mumbled something he didn't understand but didn't open her eyes. He raised her head and shoulders enough to try to give her some water. She coughed on the first sip but then was able to drink a little. When she seemed finished, he eased her back onto the pillow.

He left the towel in the stateroom, hung the dripping dress in the shower, and put away the medical kit. Then he moved his sparse gear to one of the two smaller staterooms.

Back on deck, he looked down at the daysailer, which was rolling more heavily now. Won't stay afloat more than a couple of hours, he thought. Well, there's no use towing her. He used the hook to detach the line and push her away.

He raised sail to resume course. As the warm wind bellied the white sails and *Sun Chaser* began to move forward, he glanced back at the daysailer, now falling astern.

He wondered what had possessed the woman, especially dressed as she was, to go to sea in that antique cockleshell in the middle of a storm. She must have wanted to go somewhere very badly. Or to get away from something.

When she woke, he'd ask her which.

CHAPTER TWO

Half an hour later the daysailer was once more a dark smudge on the horizon, and *Sun Chaser* was moving easily through the sea, rising and falling with the rhythm he'd loved since he first set foot on a sailboat. Swiveling the helmsman's chair to sailing position, his back to the wind, he thought again about calling the Coast Guard. But he didn't reach for the radio, wanting, for some reason he didn't quite understand, to hear the woman's story first. He wondered how much she'd sleep.

He didn't have to wonder long.

Down in the stateroom the woman awoke. Her forehead felt as though someone had hit it with a baseball bat. The ache was so bad she almost didn't feel the cuts on her hands or how tired she was. And she was very thirsty.

Even through closed eyelids she could tell that wherever she was wasn't completely dark. She blinked her eyes open and saw a low, narrow ceiling. She was lying in some sort of bed with a thin mattress and the bed was moving as though floating. Was she drunk?

Slowly she turned her head from side to side, groaning as she did it. No, she was on a boat, and it, not the bed, was moving. But it wasn't her boat—not that tiny thing in which she'd almost drowned. This was a much bigger boat. Someone must've picked her up.

She remembered very little about the storm except her terror as the lightning flashed, the wind whipped stinging rain and salt spray into her face, and huge waves threatened to swamp her at any moment. She had watched with horror as more and more water filled the bottom of the boat. There was nothing to bail with, and even if there were, she couldn't steer the boat and bail at the same time.

She knew the basics of sailing, having learned as a child. But out in the storm she'd soon realized she'd made a serious mistake in thinking that she could get away in the boat and that the weather would even help her. When the wind and waves got really bad, she thought she would die. Although she hadn't been to Mass in a long time, she'd prayed as hard as she could to the Blessed Virgin, and now it seemed her prayers had been answered.

But how? Who had rescued her? She remembered nothing since the storm. Had *he* rescued her? If so, she knew she'd soon wish she had died out there. Whatever he had in mind as punishment for her running away . . . well, drowning would undoubtedly have been easier.

She forced herself to raise her head enough to look around the small compartment. The door was open, but no one was with her.

Groaning, the woman eased out of the berth, finding herself naked in the process. She saw the towel hanging from a hook and wrapped herself in it even though the towel barely covered her from breast to thigh.

She noticed the bandages on her hands and lightly touched the larger bandage on her forehead. Who had put them there? Would he have bothered? Maybe. For whatever he had in store for her, he'd want her fully conscious and able to feel as much pain as possible.

She was tempted to wait where she was until someone came to get her, but she was too thirsty. Also, she had to pee—badly. Moving as quietly as she could, the woman tiptoed out of the compartment and found the head.

To avoid the noise, she didn't flush. She saw the medicine cabinet and eased it open. She was in luck—there was a small bottle of aspirin. She shook two into her palm, then added a third, and took them with tepid water from the faucet.

There was no cup, so she held water in the bowl of her hands and drank and drank until she could feel the water filling her belly. Then she splashed water on her face and rinsed some of the foul taste out of her mouth.

Now she felt a little better and more in control, more capable of dealing with whatever she had to face. She saw her dress hanging in the shower stall and felt the fabric, but the dress was too wet to wear.

Still moving quietly, the woman went into the salon and looked around. This boat wasn't his, not his big power cruiser, but there were a lot of similarities—the galley with its single sink and tiny refrigerator, the navigation station crammed with electronic gear, and the long, cushioned settees that could be made into narrow berths.

And drawers. Always lots of drawers to hold supplies and tools and other things. Maybe even the sort of thing that would help her now.

She opened a drawer and, being careful to make as little sound as possible, looked through its contents, not finding what she sought. She opened another drawer, then another, still not finding what she wanted.

But in the fourth drawer, the one under the navigation station, she found it. A black pistol wrapped in an oily rag. She was no expert on guns, but she knew enough to recognize it as a 9mm semiautomatic. From being around him and his men for the past few years, she'd seen a lot like it. Too many, she thought.

She picked up the gun, checked to make sure it was loaded and had a round in the chamber, then crept toward the short flight of steps that led to the cockpit. The hatch at the top was open. She began inching up the steps, holding the gun out in front of her.

When she got halfway there she saw a tall, rawboned man sitting in a metal swivel chair behind the ship's wheel. Dressed in khaki shorts, olive T-shirt, and boat shoes, the man was scanning the ocean in front of the boat and didn't seem to notice her.

She gasped when she saw his ruined face with its mottled skin that appeared to have melted and fused, settling finally into a rough repulsiveness that was as unpleasant to look at as it would be to touch. The man wore a large, black patch over one eye. He had no brow over the other eye, and his head was completely bald, a fact underscored by the eyepatch strap. She wasn't cold despite wearing only a towel, but a chill went through her. The man was scary enough to play a movie killer without any makeup.

Something stirred in the woman's brain. Had she seen this man before? No, she couldn't have—she would certainly remember it. His was a face you would never forget—even though you'd want to.

The man glanced down at the compass and from the corner of his eye caught the white of the towel. He turned to look directly at her, and she came the rest of the way up the steps, still holding the gun—his gun—in front of her.

He hadn't thought to lock that drawer. In the Caribbean you sometimes needed a gun in a hurry. For a moment he hoped that perhaps she didn't know much about guns and would be afraid to fire one, but then he saw she was carrying it correctly, index finger pointed straight ahead, not curved around the trigger. Not yet.

So she knew at least that much. And even if she weren't a good shot, it would be hard to miss at this close range.

He didn't move.

"Quién es usted?" Her voice was high but full like a singer's, and he thought that under other circumstances it would probably be warm and pleasant. But it didn't seem pleasant now.

"Me llamo Hal Morgan."

At the sound of his American accent, the woman relaxed slightly. If *he* had found her, there wouldn't be a gringo aboard.

"Is this your boat?" In English her own accent was heavy but understandable.

"A charter. I'm taking her back to a marina near Fajardo."

"Is there anyone else here?" She didn't think there was, but she wanted to check—assuming he'd tell her the truth, and she wasn't sure about that.

"No, just the two of us."

She relaxed a bit more but still kept the gun pointed in his direction. "So where is my boat?"

"Back there." He jerked his head toward the stern, being careful not to move his hands. "Where I left her after I picked you up."

A look of panic came over her face. "Did you bring the bag?"

"What bag? There was nothing in the boat but you." Remembering how she'd slashed at him, he added, "And one high-heel shoe. I left it on board."

"Then you have to go back—now. I must get that bag. It is in the sail locker."

He remembered seeing the locker door, but he'd assumed there was nothing inside but some spare line, maybe an extra sail, and the usual miscellaneous gear that accumulates aboard boats. He turned to look for the daysailer, and it took him a few seconds to locate her. She was riding low—probably close to half full of water by now.

"She's sinking. You took on water during the storm and sprung some leaks. I doubt we could get back before she goes under."

"No! I must get that bag."

"Look, whatever's in it can't be that important. You can get some new clothes when we get to port."

Her eyes narrowed, and she aimed the gun at his chest. "If you do not turn this boat around, I will kill you."

He paused. She might be bluffing, but he couldn't be certain. As they stared at each other, a wave made the boat lurch. The woman put out her free hand to steady herself. The towel fell to the deck.

Despite his adventurous past Morgan didn't remember having a naked woman aim a pistol at him. But even considering her toned body, even more lovely now in the bright sunshine caressing it, this was an experience he would've been willing to miss.

Especially if it were going to be his last.

The woman didn't seem embarrassed. Maybe she was but hid it well. Or maybe she just knew how good she looked—beautifully fierce, like some Caribbean princess before Columbus showed up.

She didn't move to pick up the towel. Instead, she set her jaw, held the pistol with both hands, and put her finger around the trigger. The professional part of his brain noted that her shooting stance wasn't quite correct. Still, he was pretty sure it was good enough to do the trick.

"Turn the boat around. Now."

He swallowed as she cocked the pistol.

"Okay. But you better sit down. You don't need to get hit in the head again."

He swung the wheel, turned the boat away from the wind, and loosened the headsail sheet. When the woman saw he was making the turn, she put the gun on a cockpit cushion, quickly wrapped herself in the towel, and sat. By the time her rump hit the seat the gun was back in her hand.

Morgan doubted he could've gotten over to her even if he'd anticipated what she was going to do. Maybe before he was wounded but not now.

After he had the boat steadied up on her new course—the reverse of the one he'd been sailing—he looked at the woman. "You know, I sail better when no one's pointing a gun at me."

She said nothing, but after a few moments she put the pistol in her lap, its muzzle pointed toward the deck. She could still shoot him in less than a second, but at least he was no longer looking down the barrel.

"That's better. Now tell me: what makes that bag worth going back for?"

"That is my business. You do not need to know."

"Well, I'm going to know. You can't keep me from looking inside between here and Fajardo. That's assuming we get back to your boat before it sinks."

Instead of replying to that, she said, "Can you not go any faster than this?"

He glanced at the speed indicator. Four knots, about all this breeze would give him. "Well, yes, we might go a bit faster if I use the engine."

She moved the gun but didn't aim it at him again. "Then do it."

He looked at her a moment before reaching down to press the diesel's starter button. Who was this woman? Where had she come from and where had she been going? And what was in this mysterious bag?

Well, she was determined, anyway. And obviously brave, perhaps to the point of being rash. He'd seen that before. And, he admitted, he'd been rash a few times himself.

He kept the throttle low for a couple of minutes to let the engine warm up, then opened it to the three-quarter mark. The boat accelerated slightly, and the indicator said he'd added another knot, perhaps a bit more, to their speed. He looked ahead at the dark smudge, which was visibly closer but even lower in the water. It would be a race to see whether they could get there before she went under.

CHAPTER THREE

As they closed on the daysailer Morgan thought about asking the woman some questions—her name, for one—but he could tell she was in no mood to answer them. In any case the noise of the engine discouraged an extended conversation.

She kept staring at the little boat, leaning forward as though that would make them go faster. Every few seconds she would glance his way just to remind him that she still had the gun and therefore was still in charge. He said nothing to argue the point and didn't move except to steer the boat and trim the sails so as to give them maximum speed.

They needed all the speed they could get. The daysailer was very low now, and they were still at least a hundred yards away. Nevertheless he decided to loosen the sails and go with just the engine.

"Wait!" she said as he slackened the mainsail and headsail sheets. She pointed the gun at him. "What are you doing?"

"Getting ready to come alongside. I don't want to run over your boat, and I'll have more control this way."

She didn't say anything, but she didn't put the gun down either.

"Look. You need to stop fooling with that pistol and get ready to help me. This is going to be tricky."

She hesitated a moment, then laid the gun on the cushion. "All right. What do you want me to do?"

He got out of the chair and handed her the boat hook. Then he retrieved the dock line from the pouch. "Here. You'll need this too."

She watched him move like a rusty machine and tried not to stare at his leg. She wondered how he'd been hurt—he must have been in a terrible accident. One that almost killed him.

"Go to the bow, tie the line off, and use the hook to loop one of the cleats on your boat. Can you do that?"

"Yes, I think so."

"Okay. Then get ready."

She nodded and moved forward, carrying the dock line and hook in one hand, and using the other to steady herself on the life line that ran through the stanchions spaced around the deck edge.

As she bent to tie the line, he throttled down and let the boat slow herself as they closed the last few dozen yards. He had still come in a bit too fast and had to reverse the engine to stop *Sun Chaser* before she ran over the daysailer. As their forward movement ceased he felt their bow bump the sodden wood of the smaller boat.

"Get the line on her!"

He watched as the woman tossed the line down and tried to use the hook to loop the line over a cleat. She made two attempts, dropping the line into the water each time, and he was about to go forward himself when she finally succeeded.

"Lo tengo!"

She had it. "Good." He left the engine throttled down but still running in case they had to maneuver. "Now come back to take the wheel, and I'll climb down to her."

She came back faster than she'd gone forward and put down the hook. "No, let me. It is my boat and my bag. And . . . ."

"What?"

"I can move faster than you can."

"Good for you, but it's too dangerous. The boat is almost under now—she can't handle much more weight. I'll do it."

She smiled faintly, the first time he'd seen her do that. It brightened her face and made her even prettier. "Two more reasons I should go. I weigh less than you do, and if the boat sinks, I can swim back." She gestured toward the swim ladder. "In fact, is that not the best way to go aboard? To swim, not to climb down the side of this boat?"

Morgan glanced back at the ladder. She was right about the swimming. He hadn't thought of that. He used to be a good swimmer, but now, with this leg, he didn't know. That's why he'd been avoiding going into the water. He might not be able to do it anymore.

Well, this was no time to find out. "Let's play it my way. Take the wheel."

"No, do not be so, so . . . what is the word? Obstinado."

Now he smiled, crookedly, the only way he could do it. "Stubborn."

"Yes, that is the word. But we are wasting time. I go."

The woman unwrapped the towel and tossed it on the seat. Without looking at him, she stepped over the stern rail, pivoted like a dancer, and put a foot on the top rung. Then she clambered down the ladder and slid easily into the sea, coming up soon to breathe and slick her hair back. He tried not to think about how the sight of her nude, athletic body made him feel.

"Wait. Let me throw you a life jacket."

"No, I am a good swimmer, and it would only get in my way."

She stroked around *Sun Chaser* and came up to the daysailer, its sides now barely above the waves. He was afraid that to get in, she'd push down on one side and finish filling the boat with water, but before he could warn her, she lay flat, put a leg over the side, and rolled herself into it.

The little boat rocked once but didn't sink. As it probably would have with him aboard, he thought. She'd been right about that too.

She looked up at him. "Give me a . . . a cangilón, and I will take out some of the water."

He had a bucket, but it was below. "That would take too long, and besides you're in a bad spot. That boat could go under any minute. Better get your bag as fast as you can so you don't end up tangled in line or God knows what else in that sail locker."

She made a sound of frustration but went to the locker and pushed her hands down in the water to open the door. She couldn't see what she was doing and had to work by feel. As he watched her search for the door latch, he imagined he could see the boat sinking lower, inch by inch. There weren't many left.

She found the latch and tugged at it. It didn't move. She tugged harder. It still didn't move. She grunted and pulled as hard as she could. "It will not open!"

"The boat frame may have warped during the storm. Or maybe it's the weight of the water. Wouldn't take much on an old boat like that."

She cursed in Spanish and pulled again, her arm and back muscles visibly straining, but the latch didn't move.

"Hang on." He left the chair, seized another piece of line, and hastily tied it to the heavy winch crank. "Hit it with this. But don't lose the crank—I'm not sure there's a spare."

He lowered it to her, and when *Sun Chaser* rolled on a wave, the crank swung toward her head. She snatched the crank just as it was about to hit her in the face. Then she put the crank down under the water and hit the latch with it once, twice, three times.

After the third strike she pulled on the latch. "It moved!" She hit the latch two more times and pulled again. "Abierto!"

She had opened it. She dropped the crank, still attached to the line, took a deep breath, and stuck her head down into the water. Her rear—her charmingly curved rear—surfaced, and he would have enjoyed the sight if the situation weren't so serious.

After several seconds she came up for air. "I cannot find it! The water must have moved it around in there."

"Okay, then we're done. Come on back aboard."

"No! I will not leave without it."

He couldn't believe what he'd heard. "Is the goddam bag worth dying for?"

She paused, looking at the waves that were now beginning to break over the sides of the boat. "No, but I am not dead yet."

"You will be if you get stuck in that locker. You'll go down with the boat."

She glared at him but said nothing more. She took a deep breath, then another, and put her head back under the water.

She stayed down longer this time, a lot longer. He was about to climb down to try to pull her out—even though he knew both of them might drown when his weight drove the boat under—when her head broke the surface and she gasped for air.

"Come back aboard! Now!"

"Wait." She panted for a few seconds. "I have it." She raised a medium-size royal-blue gym bag from the water. She held it as though it were heavy, whether from its original contents or from whatever water had gotten in.

"You can't swim back with that. Tie the line to it. But hurry."

Still out of breath, she simply nodded and reached for the line, which the crank had held in the boat. She made a loop, pushed it through the bag's handles, drew more line after it, and tied a big, sloppy knot.

"Okay, now come back." He wasn't sure that knot would hold, but they were out of time. As she paddled tiredly back toward the swim ladder, he bought the line in, hand over hand, being careful not to snag it on anything or loosen the knot by bumping the bag against the hull. The bag was as heavy as it had looked. Whatever was inside wasn't clothing or makeup.

He had the bag aboard before she got back to the ladder. He lowered the bag to the deck, and as she climbed aboard, he picked up his pistol, decocked it, and put it in the waistband of his shorts.

As she stepped over the rail, he handed her the towel.

"Gracias." She turned away and began drying herself.

He went forward and cast off the daysailer, which had almost disappeared beneath the waves and was now acting as a sea anchor. He watched the boat for a few seconds as she and *Sun Chaser* slowly drifted apart. Then he went back to the cockpit and sat opposite the woman while she finished rubbing her hair and wrapped herself in the towel.

Then she pushed her hair back and looked at him. "I hope you have some more clothes. I do not want to wear a towel the rest of the way.

Even though you have already seen everything there is to see."

"I have an extra pair of shorts and some T-shirts in my duffel. They'll be way too big, of course."

"That is all right. I will—how do you say?—get by."

"Yes, that's how we say it."

But she didn't move to get the clothing and neither did he. They sat there looking at each other while the silence drew out.

She broke it. "I guess you want to know what is in the bag."

"I guess I do. I want to know what would make you risk your life that way."

"And I suppose you are right that I cannot keep you from looking in the bag sometime."

"No, you can't. Not unless you shoot me, and you can see I've taken care of that."

She glanced at the pistol. She didn't seem surprised or especially worried that he'd taken it back. "There are other ways."

"Not if I tie you up. And if I have to, I will."

She paused. "All right. But what is in that bag is mine—mine, not yours."

"I didn't say it wasn't."

"No, and do not change your mind about that. Remember what I said."

"I will. Now open the bag." He took the line off the handles and slid the bag to her.

She looked at him for a moment and then leaned down to unzip it.

Some water ran out when she opened the bag, but not much had gotten in because it was packed so full—stuffed, in fact. Stuffed with money, lots and lots of money in fat stacks of bills banded with paper straps. All of the bills he could see were hundreds.

He was silent for several seconds. Then he said, "Now I know why you went back for it. How much is there?"

"I think about half a million dollars." She tilted her chin, her expression half proud, half defiant.

Yes, that was worth going back for, he thought. Well, whatever she was doing before she set sail in that little boat, it wasn't legal.

CHAPTER FOUR

The woman had gone below, lugging the blue bag with her, to find the clothes he'd mentioned. Morgan was in the helmsman's chair again, having hauled in the sheets and resumed sailing. After running due south for half an hour he judged he had sea room to make the turn to port. He swung the boat in a slow arc and set her on the new course, due east along the south coast of the island. As he trimmed the sails and *Sun Chaser* settled into the degree of heel that would let her make her best speed in this breeze, he wondered what he'd gotten himself into. It wasn't supposed to be like this . . . .

□ □ □

After the marina manager asked him to retrieve the boat, Morgan took the bus to San Juan, spending Thursday night there with friends. The next day he rode along the northern coast and then south through the surfing village of Rincon and the city of Mayagüez, both on the island's west end with the Dominican Republic lying across the Mona Passage. Mayagüez was a faded industrial town with little of San Juan's cosmopolitan flair or the Old World charm of Ponce, the "Pearl of the South."

That didn't matter, though, because he wasn't there to sightsee. The bus got to Cabo Rojo by 2:30, and he took a cab to the marina. He showed the guard the papers giving him permission to take *Sun Chaser* out of the harbor.

He spent the rest of Friday afternoon getting the boat ready for sea, mostly by cleaning up the mess the doctors and their wives had left behind. They'd also left a little food and a couple of bottles of wine, but he still needed to buy groceries and liquor at the marina's little store. After he did that, he stowed the supplies on board and filled the fuel and water tanks. By the time he finished, night had fallen, so he made a simple supper and then read until he fell asleep.

The next morning Morgan checked the standing and running rigging, tested the communications and navigation equipment, and plotted his course on the charts. He left the most important task for last: inspecting the "ditch bag" to make sure the rubber raft held the necessary equipment and supplies.

By noon he was ready to go, but the forecast called for a tropical storm to blow through that night, and he didn't want to fight through it, especially single-handing a big boat.

So he spent a lazy Saturday afternoon reading and dozing in the shade of the cockpit awning. By sunset the sky was becoming overcast, and the wind was picking up.

The ensuing storm rocked *Sun Chaser* until almost dawn, when it finally blew past. The big sloop was safe enough in her snug berth at the marina, but out at sea the daysailer—and the woman sailing her—didn't fare nearly so well.

□ □ □

Tired from the morning's double rescue and feeling both hungry and thirsty, Morgan went below and got an apple and a water bottle from the galley. He heard the woman moving in her stateroom, but the closed door muffled the sound. He put his pistol back in the drawer and this time locked it. The woman seemed to know her way around a boat even though she'd gone to sea in that ridiculous way. Well, maybe the money was the reason.

And maybe, he thought, as he went back on deck, she'd feel like explaining things when she was clean and dressed. He'd just have to wait and see.

Munching on the apple made Morgan think of the night before, when he'd decided to have a good meal before having to eat out of cans while standing watch-and-watch at sea. He'd walked to the marina entrance and asked the guard if there were a good place to eat nearby.

"Un restaurante Americano?" the guard asked, noting Morgan's yanqui accent.

"No, Puerto Rican. Con mariscos." He wanted Puerto Rican seafood if he could find a good place.

"Sí." The guard gave him directions to a small restaurant about half a mile away. It turned out to have no view, no menu in English, and no tourists. The food was excellent.

Sitting over his seafood paella with hot tostones and a cold beer, he noticed the manager laughing with the attractive waitress who'd taken Morgan's order. She'd managed to give him a smile and pretend she didn't notice his face.

"Who's your pirate customer?" Morgan heard the manager ask her. "You must think his eye patch is very dashing."

"Hush," the waitress said. "He speaks Spanish."

"Sure, like a gringo."

"No, some better than that. And he doesn't look so awfully bad. He was probably handsome before."

"Well, if you flirt with him I'll bet you have to do it in English." The manager sounded jealous. "Ask him if he put a fire out with his face."

The waitress gave her boss a cold look and came over to Morgan to see if he wanted another beer.

"Sí, gracia'." He dropped the "s" the way native Puerto Ricans did. He added in Spanish, "The food here is very good—probably too good for a pirate. Please tell the manager I said so."

The waitress had laughed nervously and turned away in confusion. After Morgan had finished his dinner and paid the check, he'd left a generous tip and returned to the boat.

The sun was getting hot, so he took off the eye patch and tied a bandanna on this hairless head before putting the patch on again. Getting used to being bald hadn't been that bad, but he was still struggling with having no eyebrows or lashes.

Struggling with that and a lot of other things, he thought. Like his dreams . . . dreams of fire.

Down in her stateroom—she supposed it was hers now that the man had moved his things to another room—the woman pulled on the shorts and a T-shirt. As he'd predicted, both were ridiculously large on her, but it was better than running around in a towel. Or in nothing, as she'd had to do to retrieve the bag.

Had this Morgan looked at her then, looked at her body? Probably. That's what men did. They'd been doing it to her since she was thirteen, most of them in an open, leering way but a few in a subtle, caressing way. Maybe Morgan was the latter kind—although with that face the only way he'd be able to get a woman would be to pay her.

Something like the way *he* had paid her, she thought, or at least kept her. Well, at least she was honest enough to admit that to herself—now.

She shook her head to clear it of such irrelevant things and picked up the bag. She opened it and dumped the money onto the berth, spreading the stacks out to dry. They weren't soaked, but they were damp enough to mildew if she didn't let them air. And anyway she wanted to get at what was in the bottom of the bag.

The gun. He always put a gun in a money bag. If he didn't need it, the gun was a gift for whomever he was paying. If he did need it, he could get to the gun by offering to show the money. She hadn't learned a lot from him that was useful to her, but this trick might be.

The gun tumbled out with the last of the bills. Like the stacks, the gun was damp but not soaked, so it should still work. As she had with Morgan's gun, she checked to make sure the little pistol was loaded and ready to fire. It was. But she left the safety on for the time being. She put the pistol in her pocket where it would be handy if Morgan tried to take the money from her or . . . do anything else.

She went to the head and did what she could with her hair. That wasn't much—she couldn't find a brush or even a comb. She looked in the mirror and sighed at her appearance. Well, this wasn't a pleasure cruise, and she didn't care what Morgan thought of how she looked. He was certainly in no position to judge others on that score.

She took a bottle of water from the refrigerator and went back up to the cockpit. Morgan watched her holding the bottle in one hand and the waist of her shorts in the other.

He gestured toward the canvas pouch. "There's some small stuff in there that you can use for a belt."

She dug through the pouch and found a piece of light line about a yard long.

"That'll work. Now put it around your waist.."

She threaded the line through the loops of her shorts and pulled it even in front.

"Come here."

She'd noticed how he gave orders, not in a rude, bossy way but simply as someone who was used to doing it. And used to being obeyed.

This Morgan must have commanded men, she thought as she stepped toward him. *He* did the same thing although with a harder edge. And now that it occurred to her, she realized the two men were alike in other ways—both were self-confident and in control of every situation. And Morgan's bandaging her and tucking her into bed showed he could be tender. So could *he*, but, as she knew very well, he could also be cruel. She wondered if Morgan had that dual quality too.

Morgan pulled a bosun's knife from a leather sheaf attached to his belt and jacked open the largest blade. She moved a hand toward her pocket but then willed herself to stop and stand completely still as he took the ends of the line from her and cut off the excess length, leaving her a few inches to tie into a knot.

"Thank you," she said, taking a seat and picking up the water bottle. "That is better."

"De nada." He waited while she drank. "And now I want to ask you some questions."

"Go ahead. Some I may choose to answer and some I may not."

"Okay, we'll see how it goes. First, what is your name?"

The woman hesitated, biting her lip.

"Come on. You know who I am. It's only fair that I know who you are."

"All right. My name is Ana Cortez Bolaño."

"Ana Cortez Bolaño." He liked the way it sounded, rolling softly off his tongue. But this woman was soft only to the touch. She looked—and acted—like someone who'd seen and done some hard things. "From where? Puerto Rico?"

She paused again. "No, the Dominican Republic."

He frowned. "You didn't sail your boat from the D.R. Not all the way across the Passage with no water or compass. And wearing a cocktail dress."

"Of course I did not."

"From where did you sail then?"

"A house. On the shore near Cabo Rojo."

"Uh-huh. And where were you going?

Now she didn't hesitate. "Anywhere away from there."

He paused, thinking. She seemed . . . nervous, almost scared, but very determined. As though she knew what she wanted and wouldn't let anyone keep her from it.

"You sure picked a bad time to go sailing—anywhere. Didn't you know a storm was coming through? I guess not, considering your choice of attire."

"Yes, I knew. I thought the storm might help me to get away."

"Get away and sink maybe—like you almost did. You must have left in a hurry. I noticed you didn't have a chart or any supplies."

"No. I mean, yes, I left in a hurry. There was no time to get such things."

"Well, it's lucky I came along when I did. Apparently the boom hit you in the head, and you were in a bad way. I don't think you'd have made it if someone hadn't found you." He didn't mention the strong currents for which the Mona Passage was famous—or the sharks.

Ana gingerly touched her bandaged head. "Perhaps. Thank you for what you did." She leaned back against the seat. "So you are going to Fajardo?"

"Yes, east past Ponce and then northeast once I reach Punta Tuna."

"When will you arrive?"

"Day after tomorrow, I think. If this favorable wind holds, and it should."

She started to say something, but he held up a hand to stop her. What was that sound? Something in the distance. Something faint but getting louder. The rhythmic beating of rotor blades. He'd heard it too often in the desert not to recognize it.

Now Ana heard it too. "What is that?"

"Helo. A helicopter. Probably looking for you."

Her puzzled look became one of fear. She turned toward the sound and began scanning the sky.

He saw the black speck first. The helo was high and moving parallel to them, apparently in a search pattern. As they watched, the pilot seemed to spot them and juked the aircraft down and toward the boat.

The speck grew larger, and he knew it would arrive in a couple of minutes. He glanced at Ana. Her expression told him that whomever she took that money from wanted it back. Badly.

"Give me your shirt. Quick. Then go below."

She sat frozen, watching the helicopter.

"Come on! You know they're after the money—the money you didn't make waiting tables."

She didn't seem to understand "waiting tables," but his insistent tone snapped her out of her daze. She pulled the pistol from her pocket and flicked off the safety. "They will have to kill me to get it."

At first he thought she'd picked the drawer lock and gotten his pistol again. Then he realized this was a smaller one with a shiny, not black, finish on the barrel and trigger guard.

Shit. It must've been in that bag. He cursed himself for not searching the contents. Well, at least this time she wasn't aiming at him.

"They're probably prepared to do just that. Take off your shirt."

He'd seen her completely naked, so she couldn't imagine why he wanted her topless now. "What for?"

"Goddamn it, this is no time to argue! Do it!"

She didn't want to, but the helicopter was getting close, and this strange, scarred man seemed to know what he was doing. She was afraid of him, but she was more afraid of who was after her. Reluctantly, she pulled the T-shirt over her head and tossed it to him.

"Good. Now hand me the gun and go below."

"Where is yours?"

"I locked it up so you couldn't point it at me again. It'll save time if you give me yours—*now*!"

She gave him an angry look but handed him the pistol. After one more glance at the approaching helicopter, she ducked down the steps and out of sight.

Morgan stuck the gun in his shorts, quickly shook out the T-shirt, and draped it over the transom. The extra-large shirt was just big enough to cover "*Sun Chaser*" and "Fajardo, P.R."

A few seconds later the helo made its first pass, flying bow to stern on the boat's port side maybe fifty feet above the waves. The aircraft was small, with both doors removed.

He saw two men in the cockpit. They were staring at him, one through binoculars. Even with both of them wearing headphones and goggles, he could tell they wanted something. He was pretty sure what it was.

Aft of the boat the helicopter turned and came back slowly to starboard. He saw pilot and copilot looking hard at the shirt-draped transom. When the helo was even with the boat, the helo stopped and hovered about forty or fifty yards away. At that distance the windblast had about as much force as a gust of breeze, and he turned the wheel slightly to correct for it.

He saw that the aircraft had the seating arrangement typical for helos and that the copilot, in the left seat, was facing him and holding a rifle.

The pilot clicked on the external loudspeaker and, barely audible over the roar of the engine and the whirling of the main rotor, said in Spanish, "Channel nine."

Morgan waited a moment, then slowly took the radio out of the holder clipped to the helm station. He turned it on and tuned to nine—the "boater calling" channel.

"Can you hear me?" the pilot said in his ear.

"Sí," he replied.

"All right, head into the wind and lower your sails."

Morgan waited another moment. "Why?"

"Because if you don't, we'll shoot you. We want the money and the girl."

CHAPTER FIVE

"Girl? What girl?"

"Don't be stupid and don't treat us like we are. We saw her just before she went below—topless. Looks like she's getting very friendly with you."

"I don't know what you're talking about."

"Sure you do. There's nowhere else she—or the money—could be. You must've found her in that rotten old boat and decided to keep her and the money for yourself."

"Whose money?"

"Not yours, asshole. It belongs to someone, and he wants it back. The girl too."

"Well, even if I had them, I'm not in the habit of giving girls or money to strangers."

"Fuck your habits. Head into the wind and stop. We'll lower a line. First the money. Then the girl."

"What if I don't cooperate?"

The copilot answered with two shots. They made small splashes a few yards from the boat.

The pilot said, "That's what, dickhead. Only we'll shoot you instead of the water."

"Hard to hit a man from a hovering helicopter. I know—I've tried."

The pilot barked out a laugh of disbelief, and the copilot fired a single bullet that whizzed by three or four feet above Morgan's head.

Pretty good shot, Morgan thought. Too good to call their bluff. Thank God they were amateurs at this sort of thing and didn't know enough to come in with the sun behind them.

He dropped the radio on the seat, pulled out Ana's pistol, and rapidly checked it. It was a stainless-steel Beretta Tomcat, a backup gun small enough to be carried in an ankle holster. With its short barrel the weapon wasn't highly accurate, but this close the helo made a big bullseye, and this civilian aircraft wasn't armored against gunfire.

Bracing himself against the helm and holding the pistol with both hands, he aimed at the fuselage just behind the copilot. He saw the copilot turn to shout something at the pilot, and a curse came from the radio just before he squeezed the trigger. He absorbed the slight recoil, regained his aim, and squeezed a second time.

From the way the pilot jerked the helo up and away, Morgan could tell he'd hit the aircraft at least once. The pilot widened his distance from *Sun Chaser* by another thirty or forty yards and kept the helo moving to present a more difficult target. But that movement, combined with the increased range, made the helicopter almost worthless as a platform for precision shooting.

Morgan could see Ana, still topless, crouched at the foot of the steps, keeping out of sight but looking up at him with wide eyes. He gave her a crooked grin as he picked up the radio with his free hand.

"The next three go in the engine." Morgan wasn't sure he could shoot that well, especially with this gun, but he wanted the helo crew to wonder whether he could. "Think you can swim home?"

There was no answer for several seconds. Then the pilot said, "Okay, you've got a gun and know how to use it."

"Thanks."

There was another pause, and Morgan figured the two men were discussing their options. Unless they had a machine gun aboard—and he knew they didn't or they would've already used it—the situation looked like a standoff.

They must've concluded the same thing, because the pilot said, "We'll leave—for now. But you don't know what you're getting into."

"And what is that?"

"Let's just say you're going to wish you'd given us what we came for."

"Or maybe you'll wish you'd left me alone."

The pilot cursed again as he turned the helo away. The copilot fired again, apparently in frustration, but the bullet went wide as the aircraft banked.

Morgan kept the pistol in his hand until the helo was out of sight. Then he slid it back in his waistband. "Okay, you can come up now," he said, switching to English.

Ana came up the steps, covering her breasts with one arm, and sat in the cockpit. He plucked the shirt off the stern and handed it to her with his left arm, which was damaged but not quite as badly as his leg. She turned away to put on the shirt.

Then she faced him, looking relieved if not exactly happy.

"Don't get too excited," he said. "They'll be back—or their boss will send someone else. Next time it won't be so easy to drive them off."

Her scared look came back. In a gentler tone he said, "Look, you probably want to get cleaned up. And then maybe you better tell me what this is all about."

She seemed about to speak but then merely nodded and turned to go below.

A few minutes later Morgan checked the compass set in the binnacle and brought the sloop one point to starboard. Then he scanned the horizon, on the lookout for the helicopter's return. He could hear the shower running, and he frowned at how much fresh water she was using even though he'd cautioned her.

"No Hollywood showers on this boat," he'd said, but she'd merely looked at him, obviously not understanding. She'd seemed so tired and so eager to wash off the salt that he hadn't pursued the issue. And now he thought that maybe she was trying to wash off something else—the memory of whatever had driven her to risk her life in that little boat on this big, big ocean.

His annoyance made him think of how the marina manager frowned when he learned that *Sun Chaser* had essentially been abandoned on Puerto Rico's west coast.

Hanging up the phone with an irritated gesture, Roberto Cruz had spat out a few curse words and shook his head. Then he'd sighed and looked across his littered office at Morgan.

"Hal," Roberto said, speaking clearly so Morgan could keep up with his brisk Spanish, "take the bus around to Cabo Rojo and bring her back. I'll pay you for travel time as well as the sail home. Think of it almost like a vacation—and you need one."

"I do?" Morgan was surprised to find his boss, friendly but not nosy, giving him personal advice.

"Yes, you do. Living on your boat, never going anywhere. Always working, hardly saying anything." The charter manager smiled slightly to soften the words. "Maybe relaxing a little will bring you out of your shell."

Roberto gave him money for the bus ticket and to buy supplies for the 38-foot charter sloop. Morgan checked the dock lines on the smaller sailboat that was his home and threw some clothes and a few paperbacks into his olive-drab duffel bag.

He hesitated about bringing his pistol, the SIG Sauer he'd bought right after basic training. He doubted that he'd need the gun, but he was going to be single-handing, and anyway he slept better with it around. At least on those rare nights when the dreams didn't come.

So he shrugged and put the pistol and two 9mm magazines, both fully loaded, into the duffel. Then he rode in Roberto's Jeep to the bus station in Fajardo.

"Stay safe, my brother," Roberto said, giving him the Latin embrace to which Morgan had never grown accustomed, despite having lived on the island since 2004—almost three years now.

"I'll try," Morgan said and then got on the bus, picking a seat as far back as he could. On the milk run to San Juan, he read one of his books, despite the distraction of some passengers whispering in Spanish about his face. The comments hurt less than they used to, but he couldn't ignore them completely.

After arriving in the city that afternoon, he took a cab to Luis's house in Ocean Park. His phone call from the bus had alerted Herrera to his arrival, and his friend was waiting with tortilla chips, hot salsa, and cold beer—El Presidente, the Dominican brand both of them liked.

Luis's woman, Karen Ginsberg, was there too, beaming as she kissed Morgan on the cheek. On his right side, he noticed, although she never seemed to see the marks or even the eye patch that everyone else did.

He remembered thinking she'd probably seen stranger things living in New York. Luis had hinted that she'd gotten into some trouble there. Morgan knew that Karen had studied Spanish in high school, so perhaps it was natural for her to relocate to Puerto Rico, where she blended in, with her dark hair and eyes and knowledge of the language.

Morgan offered to take them to dinner, but Karen insisted on cooking. She fixed fresh shrimp with cocktail sauce for the appetizer and then made a big garden salad and arroz con pollo. This furnished house they were renting while they saved money to buy a place of their own had a patio that took up most of the tiny back yard, and Karen served the meal family style out there.

As they ate, the quick tropical twilight came and went, leaving behind a warm, humid June night. Karen lit candles, and they finished dinner in the soft yellow glow. Luis and he had more beer and Karen drank white wine as they talked and listened to the insects and birds and the rustle of the breeze in the palm fronds.

He and Luis washed the dishes while Karen made Puerto Rican coffee, strong the way Luis liked it. When they'd served together in the Navy, Morgan had kidded Luis about having to drink the ship's coffee, which Luis obviously found inferior to the island brands. Now that he was living in Puerto Rico, he had to admit Luis was right.

Morgan slept reasonably well in the guest room, and Karen sent him off in the morning with a good breakfast and another kiss on the cheek. At the bus station Luis hugged him—an embrace Morgan found more natural than Roberto's—and told him not to stay away so long next time.

"You can be comfortable around us, you know," Luis said. "We're not just your friends, we're your family."

He's right, Morgan thought as he rode on the bus down to Cabo Rojo. They were the only family he had left.

CHAPTER SIX

With the autopilot on, Morgan sat in the cockpit, drinking a beer. Ana sat across from him, also holding a beer and looking refreshed from her shower.

Without his asking, Ana had made them sandwiches. Morgan's tuna on whole wheat tasted better than any sandwich he'd ever made. He asked Ana what she'd put on them, and she mentioned a couple of things he didn't even know were in the galley.

"Thanks for fixing these."

"You are welcome. I was hungry and thought you might be also."

"How're you feeling? How's the head?"

"Better, thank you. The shower helped, and I took another aspirin."

"Good. I think you'll feel all right soon, and those bandages can come off in a couple of days."

She was silent for several seconds. Then she said, "Thank you again for saving me from the ocean."

"Don't mention it. Any sailor would've done the same." He noticed that she wouldn't meet his gaze, looking instead at the tranquil turquoise sea shining in the sun.

Probably this ugly face, he thought. Well, he couldn't blame her for having the same reaction as everyone else.

He gave her another moment. When she turned back toward him, he said, "If you're feeling up to telling me now, I'd like to know what made you go sailing in that storm."

She hesitated. "It is a long story."

"We've got plenty of time. A while, at least."

"You do not need to take part in my troubles."

"I think I already have. At least our friends in the helo think I have."

She considered that. "All right. I am Cubana, originally from Havana. My parents died when I was little, and my uncle raised me. My mother's brother. He is still in Havana, but I have lived in the Dominican Republic for the last four years. I am the girlfriend of a man named Jaime Buchanan Rivera. He is a . . . sort of businessman."

"Sort of a businessman?"

"Yes. They call him 'El Bucanero.'"

"'The Buccaneer'?"

"That, or what most people say in English: 'The Pirate'."

"Sounds like a nice guy. What kind of business is he in?"

"Many kinds. He lends money, owns a trucking company, and has interests in several hotels and casinos. Some are in the Dominican Republic because there they often do not enforce the laws. Some are in Puerto Rico because even though here there is the law, he can cooperate with others like him, the ones in . . . ." She seemed reluctant to finish the sentence.

"You can say it: 'the mafia.' So he's that kind of businessman."

She nodded. "Yes, that kind."

"And you're his girlfriend? You mean mistress, don't you?"

Again she nodded. "'Mistress'—that is the word. I act like his wife, but we are not married. He has a wife and two children—well, more than that, but two with her. He spends little time with her though."

"So your job is to be seen with him, take care of him, and . . . help him relax, is that it?"

"Yes." Ana looked him in the eye. "That is what I do, how I live. Do you judge me for it?"

"No, I don't. We all have to live somehow. Maybe I don't want to be judged for some of the things I've done."

He saw her glance down at the leg she'd seen him move stiffly. She started to speak, but, not wanting to answer the obvious question, he cut her off. "What sort of man is this Rivera?"

"Smart, strong—determined to get whatever he wants. He made great success very fast, so he is not that much older than I am, only thirty-eight."

"But still, you can't be more than—"

"I am twenty-three, if that is what you want to know."

Morgan was glad he hadn't articulated his guess, which was a few years higher. Maybe being the mistress of a crime boss aged you. Not that this young woman wasn't spectacularly beautiful—one of the most beautiful women he'd ever seen—but her eyes looked as though they'd seen a lot even though she was almost ten years younger than Morgan.

"I never ask a lady her age."

"A wise policy. But you ask many other personal questions."

"Sorry. It's just that I don't often pick up women at sea wearing cocktail dresses and carrying bags filled with money."

She frowned. "That is *my* money."

"Hey, I didn't say it isn't. If I wanted it, I could take it. I have all the guns now."

"You would have to kill me. Or throw me over the side and leave me to drown."

"Yes, but I won't. So don't worry about me—I won't try to take the money away from you." He scanned the horizon again, seeing only the calm ocean. "But Rivera will. And soon."

Ana sipped her beer and said nothing.

"Tell me more about him."

"Why?"

"I want to know what I'm up against."

"Jaime is the son of a Dominican . . . uh, I am not sure of the English word—in Spanish, 'puta'."

"Whore. Or, more politely, prostitute."

"Yes. His mother told him that his father was an American businessman, but of course Jaime does not know for certain. That is one reason he dislikes Americans."

"He probably has others."

"Ah, an honest yanqui. Good—many of the American tourists I have met would not admit that. Yes, he has others. But it is mostly because he is—what is the word? When the parents are not married?"

"Illegitimate."

"Yes. Being such a one, especially as the son of a prostitute, causes him shame, so no one ever speaks of it. Jaime is smart, as I said, but maybe not as smart as he thinks. He has been successful because he does what he wants, takes what he wants, and others are afraid of him. He has killed several people, some with his bare hands but most with a gun or a knife."

She looked at him again, studying his face as if to gauge his reaction. "Jaime likes to use the knife if he can get close enough."

Her gaze made him uncomfortable, and he shifted in his seat. "Thanks for the warning. I'll try not to let him get that close. How did you meet this charming fellow?"

"It was in Cuba. My uncle introduced us. He does business with Jaime."

"Is your uncle that sort of businessman too?"

Ana paused, thinking of her uncle Francisco Torres Bolaño. Tío Paco. He worked for Cuba's General Directorate of Intelligence—DGI, as the Cubans called it, usually in a whisper—and had been trained by the KGB during the Cold War. Jaime collected information for Tío Paco and on occasion did certain types of jobs for him. In return Tío Paco steered certain kinds of deals to Jaime. But she didn't want to tell this yanqui about that.

"No, he works for the Cuban government. The Ministry of the Interior." It wasn't completely untrue—DGI was part of MININT.

Morgan gave her a long look. "I see."

She wanted to ask what he meant by that but decided not to. She didn't know anything about this man with the scary face except that he was good with boats and guns and hadn't tried to rape her—yet.

So she continued her story. "After we met, whenever Jaime was in Havana on business he would come to see me, bring me presents, take me to dinner. Then I started spending weekends with him in Santo Domingo, and after a while he asked me to live with him."

"What did your uncle say?"

Again she paused, not wanting to tell this Morgan that Tío Paco had said she could go, could get away from her dreary life in decaying Havana and live in luxury in Santo Domingo, if she would, in effect, work for him. Keep him informed about what Jaime and his associates were doing. Carry messages and small packages—all sealed in ways that would reveal if anyone had tried to open them—back and forth when she returned to Cuba to visit her family and friends. That sort of thing.

"He told me I could."

"I'm surprised—especially if he was acting as your father."

She frowned again. "What do you know about it? Or him?"

"Nothing. But I don't think that's the answer I'd have given my daughter, if I had one."

"Please keep your opinions about my family to yourself."

He shrugged. "Fine. Apparently things didn't work out the way you planned. I mean, considering how I found you."

"For a long time, two years at least, Jaime was kind to me—as kind as he knows how to be. He treated me like a reina, a queen. He gave me clothes and jewelry, had me live in the hotel penthouse with him, and introduced me to all his friends. He often took me with him when he traveled, so I have been many places." She looked at him and said proudly, "Even the United States."

Morgan thought Rivera might have used a boat or private plane to sneak Ana past Puerto Rico's U.S. Customs officials, but he couldn't see him doing that on the mainland. "How? They wouldn't let you in with a Cuban passport."

She gave him her faint smile. "I have also one from the Dominican Republic. Jaime knows people in the government, and they owe him favors."

"I see. It sounds very pleasant for you. So why did you leave?"

"It gradually became . . . unpleasant. Jaime got used to me, perhaps

even tired of me, and he would shout when he got angry or frustrated
in his business. He began to criticize me for little things and then started
slapping me when we were alone. Over time he began hitting me in
front of people—his men, who seemed to enjoy it. At least they said
nothing against it."

"No, they wouldn't, not if he's the sort of man you say he is."

"Once I packed my things and tried to leave, but he caught me before I could get away. He beat me so badly the doctor had to come. After that he locked me in the penthouse whenever he was gone or always
had someone watching me. He would send a man with me whenever
I went shopping. I think even my maid is his spy."

"So how did you get away?"

"Yesterday afternoon Jaime took me to a party at a beach house near
Cabo Rojo. Several of his business friends were there, including the one
they call El Viejo."

"'The Old Man.'"

"Yes, like that actor in the gangster movie, the one with the wedding."

"*The Godfather*. You're talking about Marlon Brando as the mafia
chief?"

She nodded. "Jaime loves that movie. He watches it often. The Old
Man has been at this business longer than any of them. They all pay
money to him, and some of the money in the bag was for that, for Jaime
to give the Old Man his share. Some was for other people, men Jaime
needed to pay for things they had done."

"In other words, you stole the payroll."

"Yes, that is one way to say it. Another way would be that Jaime gave
me very little money and would not let me leave with all my clothes and
jewelry, so I took what he owes me."

"I'm sure he doesn't see it that way."

"No, I am sure of that too. Anyway, they all had a lot to drink, including the few other women there, but I drank very little. After dinner there was a . . . show. Two girls." She paused. "You understand?"

"Sure. I've been around—I even saw a copy of *Playboy* once."

Her cheeks flushed the color of pale roses. "So while they were watching that, I was able to slip away. I went down to the beach and found
a boat. My uncle used to take me sailing when I was little, and I remember some of how to do it."

"I guess he didn't teach you not to go sailing in a tropical storm."

"I knew a storm was coming, but I did not know it would be so bad.
In any case I had no choice—it was my one chance to get away, and I

took it."

"Okay, I understand, but you're not home free. I'm pretty sure you're going to see Jaime again, and he'll want it to be up close and personal."

She leaned forward, an anxious look on her face. "Please, will you help me? At least put me back on land and get me some clothes so I can go away and hide?"

"Go where?"

"To Miami, if I can. I have relatives and friends there."

"Is your passport in that blue bag?"

"No." She sighed. "I could not get to my purse before I left. So I do not have a passport or any other identification. But with enough money . . . something could be done, no?"

"Something could be done, yes, if you know the right people."

"Do you know such people?"

Morgan thought a moment. "I might."

"And you will help me get a U.S. passport?"

"I might."

"I will pay you, of course." Ana saw him looking at her. She glanced down and saw her nipples clearly outlined against the thin T-shirt. She cleared her throat. "But perhaps you want something more than money?"

He waited several seconds before saying, "What if I do?"

She didn't hesitate. "I think you will have to be satisfied with money. And find some other woman to—"

"Don't worry. I'm not in the habit of committing rape."

He sounded sincere, and she believed him. She told herself she hadn't really been worried, but still, a woman never knew, especially with a man like this Morgan. Because of the way he'd dealt with the helicopter, she'd thought he'd try to help her, but she hadn't been sure at what price.

"I did not think you were. But I—I have sold myself long enough. I will never do it again."

"Good. I hope you can stay alive to keep that promise."

She thought of Jaime, and despite the warmth of the sun, a chill came over her. "I hope so too."

CHAPTER SEVEN

Jaime Rivera was on the phone in his Puerto Rico office, the location of which he'd chosen carefully. The office was in a San Juan hotel casino that, although not the largest or newest or most expensively decorated, definitely was the most . . . flexible when it came time to wash some money and hang it out to dry.

The Dominican woman, growing tiresome, was thanking him for the large check he'd sent to the orphanage. She thought he'd done it to help the little kids who had no homes.

Well, okay, maybe that had been part of his motivation. After his mother died he'd spent time—long, dreary days and scary, lonely nights—in a place much like that orphanage. He'd tried hard to forget that time, but he knew he'd never be able to. Not completely.

Not even when he tried to forget everything except how relieved he'd felt after escaping at fourteen and beginning to live life on the streets. Meeting boys who were older and stronger. Boys who knew how to steal, intimidate, do what they wanted.

Stronger, yes, but only for a while, only until he grew a bit older himself. They were never smarter—he'd shown them that enough times. And never tougher. He'd shown them that too. He had a few scars to prove it.

But really he'd given the money in his quest to become respectable. He hoped to buy a place in Santo Domingo society. Make polite, well-mannered people forget who he'd been and how he'd made so much money. Or at least ignore those things when he threw lavish parties or contributed to their favorite charities.

The woman finally ran out of thank-yous and invited Rivera to come by the orphanage to see for himself all the good his generous gift was doing. He lied, promising to check his schedule and get back to her. Then at last he was able to hang up the phone.

He immediately cleared all other thoughts from his mind and focused on the problem at hand. He'd slept in the car on the two-hour drive from Cabo Rojo and now felt relatively fresh despite partying the night before and, after Ana vanished, staying up far later than he'd planned. First to look for her and then to try to deal with the fact that she had gone, taking the money with her.

But now he could concentrate on getting both back. He began by staring down at the chart of the Mona Passage that was spread out on the large oak table he used as a desk.

He'd found it useful to have a big desk—one big enough to put a man on, if things came to that, as they sometimes did.

Those situations seemed to arrive more often now as his younger competitors became bolder. Perhaps they thought El Bucanero was past his prime, beginning to slip a little. This business with Ana would only encourage them to think that way. He had to get her back.

And the money of course. He'd tell his business partners it was the money. The money was important, but really—he'd acknowledged the truth when he'd looked into the mirror that morning—it was mostly her.

He wasn't going to let the little bitch get away with humiliating him in front of the Old Man and the others. No, he was going to make her pay. Thinking of her face, so striking that it stopped men on the street, he touched the switchblade in his hip pocket. She'd pay for the rest of her life—if he let her live. Right now he wasn't sure he would.

The thought of El Viejo made him remember the deadline: three days. That's how long the Old Man had said he'd wait for his money. When he'd found out that Ana had disappeared with the money—Rivera hadn't wanted to tell him, but of course he had no choice—the Old Man hadn't shouted, threatened, or even gotten visibly angry.

He'd just let Rivera's words hang in the air, then looked at Rivera with his cold, deep-set eyes. Dios mío, the coldest eyes Rivera had ever seen. Looked at him as though he could see all the way down inside Rivera, down to where his deepest fears lay hidden, the ones he never showed to anyone, not to Ana and certainly not to his men.

But this old man could see them.

Then El Viejo had said in his gruff voice made even harsher by many decades of rum and cigars. "Tres días." He'd paused to let the words sink in. "Tres días—no más."

He'd didn't have to explain what would happen if he didn't have his money by the third day. Rivera knew. He knew all too well. And even though Rivera had forced himself not to show any fear, he'd certainly felt it.

And still felt it. He knew that if he didn't pay El Viejo by the end of the three days . . . well, then he'd personally have a problem much more serious than a runaway girl and a missing gym bag.

The clock was ticking.

He tapped his finger on the chart at the position the helicopter had radioed in. The distance from Cabo Rojo seemed about right, and there was a woman on board. He couldn't be sure, but maybe . . . .

If the man with the pistol, whoever he was, had found Ana, he was going to wish very soon that he hadn't. He might even wish he'd never lived.

Rivera's men stood at a respectful distance while he studied the chart. Respectful or maybe just careful. They knew he was angry. They also knew about the knife—sharp and always ready for use.

Rivera glanced up at them. They were all wearing what the well-dressed Caribbean gangster should wear: dark dress slacks, sharply pressed, with loose white shirts, several gold chains, and light sports coats cut to accommodate their guns and shoulder holsters. Shoes black with a mirror shine or spotlessly white.

They looked like what they were: predators in search of prey.

Just as he was about to speak, one of the casino's prettiest cocktail waitresses—and they were all very pretty—came into the room. She was wearing a black dress cut almost as high on her long legs as it was low on her large breasts. Rivera's men took on wolfish expressions and almost licked their chops.

She knew who led the pack. She went straight to Rivera and, standing close, asked if he wanted a drink. Although she was a bit scared of him, having heard the stories, some of which sounded unbelievable but were sworn to be true, she forced herself to look into his eyes and give him her beauty-pageant smile.

After a moment he smiled back, not as broadly but trying to put some warmth in it. "Yes, scotch with three ice cubes. Please."

"Certainly." She knew she could remember the order, but she leaned forward to write it on her pad so he'd get a good look at the top halves of her impressive breasts.

Her surgeon did a fine job, Rivera thought. They look almost natural. After he had done what he was going to do to Ana, maybe this girl . . . .

She took drink orders from the rest of them. Then she left, knowing every man in the room was watching the smooth roll of her hips beneath the short dress.

El Segundo came over as the waitress closed the door behind her. "What're you thinking, chief?"

Rivera knew Garcia was asking on behalf of the men as well as for himself. He was their spokesman as much as he was Rivera's deputy, his "number two."

"I'm thinking she could be on that big sailboat the helicopter found.

Maybe that shooter came across her and has decided to keep the money for himself. What do you think, Benito?"

"She's there. They didn't find any trace of her boat, and they caught a glimpse of a woman who looks like Ana on his. I think you're right about the money. Why else would he risk his life by firing at the helicopter?"

Garcia, almost as tall as Rivera but more slightly built, was smart—one reason Rivera had made him El Segundo even though he was barely out of his twenties. Another was that, unlike Rivera, he never lost his temper. He always looked at things in terms of profit and loss, not letting emotion interfere with his thinking. At least not visibly.

Rivera believed that sometimes acting on his anger had helped him get where he was and that showing it occasionally kept the men in line. But Garcia had done almost as well without that, and Rivera knew he would have to watch El Segundo with a close eye to keep him in his place.

"That makes sense. The question is what to do next. Or rather how to do it."

"Let's send the helo back, and this time give them a machine gun. They can kill that bas—*man* on board, lower the copilot to the boat, and see if she and the money are there."

Rivera knew what Garcia had been about to say before realizing the danger. Garcia had been in the casino the night Rivera killed a man for calling him that.

Rivera remembered how the word had cut like a whip and how he'd thrown his drink in the speaker's face. While the man rubbed his eyes, Rivera's men crowded around so no one could see. Rivera stabbed the man in the gut, thrusting the knife in and up. He watched the man slump, then stabbed him again. They took the body out the back way, put it on a boat, and tossed it to the sharks.

No one had called Rivera a bastard to his face since or even used the word in his presence. He doubted anyone would be brave enough to do so in the future.

"No, we can't chance having the helicopter shot down and the damn Coast Guard investigate it." Rivera smiled at his deputy—coldly, despite the white teeth flashing in the tanned, handsome face. "Besides, I'm going to handle the bitch myself. And her new friend."

Garcia frowned. "From the helicopter? That sounds risky, chief."

"Always cautious, eh, Benito?" Rivera laughed. His men relaxed somewhat, smiling at each other, and loosening muscles they didn't know they'd tensed.

"No," Rivera continued, putting his hand on Garcia's bony shoulder and pointing at the chart. "We're going to fly down to Ponce, get a power boat, and go after them. We can be there in less than an hour, and in a sailboat they can't have gone very far. Call the airport and have them get my plane ready. Then call downstairs and have them bring one of the cars around. On the way to the airport you can phone that marina in Ponce, the one we've gone fishing from, and see about a boat. I want the fastest they've got."

He was thinking of the deadline the Old Man had given him, but he didn't want anyone to know about that. Especially Garcia, who might think—correctly—that it was influencing his judgment.

El Segundo chose his words carefully. "Jaime, you don't need to do this thing yourself. You should stay here and run the business. I'll send Pablo and a couple of the boys. They can handle it."

"We'll take two men but not Pablo," Rivera said in a low voice. "I have other plans for him. He was guarding Ana last night, wasn't he?"

This time Garcia could guess what his chief was thinking, and he knew better than to interfere. "Well, he was supposed to be."

The cold smile again. "Yes, that's a better way to say it. Go in the next room to make the calls. I'll take care of Pablo in here."

Garcia also knew better than to argue when Rivera smiled that way and used that tone. "Okay." He turned and left, thinking he was glad Pablo didn't owe him any money.

The waitress returned and distributed the drinks. When she was finished, Rivera walked her to the door. As she left, he patted her broad but firm ass, getting a little wiggle in return. Then he locked the door and went back to his desk, where he sipped his scotch as his men drank too.

After he'd given them a couple of minutes to relax further, he put his glass on the desk and walked over to where they were clustered. "Pablo?" he said in a normal tone.

"Yes?" A skinny man with a dandy's mustache stepped forward, drink in hand.

"You were watching Ana last night."

A cloud came over the man's narrow face. "Yes, chief."

"What happened?"

"I don't know. She said she had to go to the bathroom, so I went to get a beer. When I came back, she was gone."

"How long was it before you came back to check on her?"

"Not that long. A few minutes."

"How long?" Rivera's tone changed, becoming as hard as the look on his face.

"Only fifteen minutes. Maybe twenty."

"Maybe thirty. Or more. Long enough that by the time you finally told Garcia that she'd disappeared, she'd gotten away in that little boat."

Pablo didn't want to answer, but Rivera just waited. "I guess so."

"And how did she get out? No one saw her leave." Rivera already knew—Garcia had told him the night before—but he wanted to hear it from Pablo.

"Uh . . . ." Pablo looked intensely uncomfortable. "The bathroom window was open, and the screen was outside on the ground. I think she crawled through the window."

"I see." Rivera looked into the other man's eyes. "While you were getting a beer."

Pablo backed up a step. "Yes, chief, but who'd have figured she'd crawl out a window? I mean, wearing that dress she could hardly walk in? And those shoes?"

"That must've been part of her plan—make you think she couldn't and wouldn't go anywhere. So you let your guard down."

Pablo said nothing.

"And the blue bag? All that money? You just let her steal it?"

"She'd never even looked at the bag," Pablo said defensively. "How was I to know she was going to take it?"

"Because that was your job, Pablito. Because you've been with me a long time, and I trusted you to do it right." Rivera stepped very close, and Pablo would've backed up farther, but his chief put his arm on Pablo's shoulder. To an outsider the gesture would've seemed friendly, but Pablo knew better.

The rest of the men formed a loose circle around the two of them, watching. They were very quiet.

"But you didn't do it right, did you?" Rivera's voice was soft, as though he were speaking to one of his children.

"I did the best I could, chief. That little hellcat—you know how she is. You get too close, you piss her off, and the next thing you know she's trying to scratch your eyes out."

"So you were afraid of her?" His voice was still soft, but now there was an edge to it.

"Yes—I mean, no. But I didn't think I had to watch her every second.

I mean, Jesus, even when she went to the bathroom?"

"She tricked you, my friend. Ana is clever that way. I see now she is too clever for you. That was my mistake."

Pablo let out the breath he hadn't realized he'd been holding. Maybe Rivera wasn't going to hurt him after all. Maybe—

Rivera made a slight, quick movement. Pablo heard a "snick" as the switchblade opened, and gasped as the steel slid between his ribs. Slightly to the left side, over his heart.

"I won't make that mistake again," Rivera said. "Neither will you."

For a moment the blade was ice cold. Then it was burning hot, and Pablo felt the thick, warm liquid oozing out over the knife and smelled the metallic tang of his blood. He looked at Rivera, whose eyes were flat, dead. A shark's eyes.

Pablo blinked and dropped his glass, which shattered on the floor. Slowly he put his hands to the wound. His fingers touched the knife, and the blade cut them as Rivera pulled it out. The extra blood didn't matter—Rivera's hand was already covered with it.

Pablo sank to his knees and watched his life run out onto the floor. Oak, not carpet, he thought as his brain began to go dark. That'll be easy to clean up. The chief thinks of everything. Then he slowly pitched forward and lay still.

Rivera stared at the dead man. "You can't work for me unless you have balls and a brain." He looked up and glanced around at the others. "Understand?"

"Yes, yes," they all murmured, looking everywhere but at the body or Rivera.

"Good. Then clean up this mess and get him out of here. Feed him to the fish."

He watched as they brought towels from the bathroom to mop up the blood and sheets from a nearby bedroom to wrap the body in. He snatched a towel from one of the men and carefully wiped off his hand and the knife.

When he had both of them clean, Rivera threw the towel down where one of his men was wiping up the final traces of blood. For a moment he watched as they rolled Pablo in the sheets.

Then he closed the knife without making a sound, put it back in his pocket, and left the room.

CHAPTER EIGHT

"Find the girl," El Viejo said to the man standing in front of him. "Find her and get the money. You can do what you like with her—as long as she disappears, permanently—but I want my money."

"And Rivera?" The man's low voice sounded rough, even rusty, as though he didn't use it much—which he didn't. That was why others called him El Callao, slang for The Silent One, although never to his face. He was of medium height, obviously fit and, as the Old Man had witnessed on two occasions, even stronger then he looked.

The only unusual aspect of his appearance was the old knife scar that ran from an ear to jawline. Everyone knew the scar had to be old, gotten in youth, because this hard-looking man would never let someone do that to him today.

No, now he was the one who gave others scars—or worse. Although he never said much, he had a way of making others talk. Even—or especially—when they didn't want to. That was why he always carried the pair of needle-nose pliers the Old Man could see weighing down a side pocket of his jacket. And the Old Man knew that the thing weighing down the other pocket was a gun. The switchblade, honed to surgical sharpness, would be in an inside pocket.

Good. If anyone could get the money back—assuming Rivera failed to do it— El Callao was the man for the job.

"It depends. If you can find the money, I may let him live. His mistake will cost him, of course, but he has his uses, so I may not kill him . . . yet. Otherwise, yes, he's a dead man."

After a moment the rough voice came again, grating like a wooden bucket being dragged up from an abandoned well. "I'll follow Rivera—that's the best way to find her."

"That's the way to start. But I've put the word out, and people are watching for her. If I get a tip about where she is or where she's going, I'll let you know."

"Anything else?"

"If Rivera finds her first, don't interfere. Just watch and report to me. I want to see how he handles things. Understand?"

The man merely nodded.

"Good. Now get going. Find that money."

He nodded again and left.

The Old Man watched him go. If Rivera failed to recover the money and if for any reason this soldier couldn't do it, Rivera was going to wish he'd never been born. The Old Man would see to that.

The silent one and his pliers would make Rivera scream for a long time, he thought. A long, long time.

❑ ❑ ❑

"I want you to steer." Morgan had already turned off the autopilot. He grunted as he stood to let Ana into the helmsman's seat.

"Why?"

"Because we might need you to do that if your boyfriend sends someone else after us."

"You think he will do that," she said, not putting it as a question.

Morgan paused. He didn't want to lie to her, but he didn't want to scare her either. "Probably. But maybe we can make him wish he hadn't. Here, take the helm."

He held the big vertical wheel with one hand until she was settled, then told her to put her hands where his had been. Their fingers brushed as she took the wheel, and she looked up at him.

That face . . . that dark, grim face. She found it hard to look at, but she could see the strength in it. Maybe something else too, obscured by his disfigurement. Or hiding behind it?

"Keep her on our present course." He tapped the paper chart in a large clipboard that he kept near the helm in case the boat's electronics went down. "Due east."

Ana looked at the chart and saw the line he'd drawn on it, paralleling the island's south coast. Then she peered at the binnacle. She could read the compass but had no idea what to do with any of the knobs and switches mounted near it.

He sensed her hesitation. "Just watch the compass and stay on this heading. Understand?"

"I know how to do it," she snapped. "More than that, I know enough about this boat—especially its captain—to want to get off it as soon as I can." She let that sink in for a second, then added, "And I know enough about guns to have one in my hand when you did not—twice."

"Touché, tough girl." He threw her a mock salute. "You've got me there."

She looked at him again. "I am not stupid. Even if I do speak with an accent you will make fun of later, when you are around your Anglo women."

"Okay, spare me the sarcasm. I didn't say you were stupid. I just want to keep heading east, okay? Away from your hotheaded friend and his pals."

She was pleased to have provoked a reaction in him. "Now who is the sarcastic one?"

Morgan didn't reply. He gathered their plates and empty beer cans and took them below. He put the disposable things in the trash and cleaned up the galley. He took his time, hoping that steering the boat would distract her from worrying about what Rivera might try next.

When he came back on deck he had his pistol in one hand and the extra magazine and a small towel in the other.

The sight of the big yanqui coming up the steps with a gun frightened Ana, and she hoped she hadn't pushed things too far. Then she realized how he must have felt when she appeared in the same way. Well, almost naked, but still.

He saw her face and gave her his crooked grin to let her know she needn't worry. She told herself to remain calm and wait. She was beginning to trust this Morgan—but only so much.

He spread the towel on a seat cushion and put both pistols and the magazine on it. Ana glanced at him but remained focused on her task. She did a good job, keeping *Sun Chaser* on course almost as well as he could have.

Seeing that she was getting comfortable at the helm, he turned to his task. He wished he had his kit to clean the guns, but he didn't, so he decided not to worry about it. He'd cleaned his pistol recently and hadn't fired it since then. He didn't know when Ana's—Rivera's—pistol had last been cleaned, but he'd just have to chance it.

He ejected the magazine from the SIG Sauer, looked it over, and snapped it back into place. He looked at the other mag to confirm that it was also full. He didn't have any of the .32-caliber ammunition that fit the Beretta, but he knew there were some cartridges left in its magazine, and he checked to make sure they were properly positioned. She watched him, noting the quick, sure movements despite his big, awkward-looking hands.

He put the pistols and the extra magazine in the canvas pouch hanging from the forward side of the helm and then checked his bosun's knife. He'd learned the hard way—from badly needing to cut a fouled line and not having a knife handy—that a good sailor always carries a knife at sea. The blade was sharp enough to draw blood on his thumb, so he figured it would be sharp enough for hand-to-hand if things came to that.

He knew he was a lot slower than he had been, but he might still be faster than someone with no training. And even on a large sailboat like *Sun Chaser*, he wouldn't have to move very far.

He wiped the blade on the towel and slipped the knife back in his belt sheaf. As he folded the little towel and tucked it into the pouch, he saw Ana watching him.

"There," he said. "Now we're ready for whatever happens."

"And you think something will?"

"Yes. I don't know what or when, but I don't think Rivera is just going to let you go, especially considering what's in that blue bag."

She wanted to disagree, wanted to speculate that Jaime might leave her alone, but she thought she would merely sound naive. She was afraid, and the fear hung like a cold stone in the pit of her stomach. However, she was determined not to show her fear either to Morgan or, if she did see him again, to Jaime Rivera.

Morgan saw the look on her face. "Don't worry—we'll be fine. I've been in a few tight spots before and always come out okay."

Not always, she thought, not looking like that. She forced herself to return his smile, knowing it wasn't much but the best she could do at the moment.

"That's the spirit," he said. "We'll spit in his eye."

He was pleased to have gotten even a slight smile out of her. He decided to leave things right there, so he picked up the binoculars and settled onto the port side cushions, facing forward. He didn't tell her that on their easterly course that spot was the best place for him to see someone coming for them.

They stayed that way for an hour or more. She didn't say much, merely asking him sailing-related questions now and then. Her questions were intelligent and concise.

He liked that. He didn't mind listening when someone had something meaningful to say, but he didn't welcome a lot of chatter.

That quality had cost him a few women, he supposed. Most women seemed to like to talk—a lot—and have a guy around who would throw in a remark once in a while to show he was listening. Morgan wasn't very good at that. Sometimes, especially if the talk was about clothes, jewelry, or celebrities, he wasn't listening.

But he had other qualities women appreciated. For one thing, he was good at killing spiders.

Without being obvious about it, he kept a close lookout, watching the horizon and occasionally using the binoculars to scan above it. He hadn't forgotten what the helo could have done with a machine gun aboard.

Once in a while he allowed himself to glance at her. As much as he loved to look out over the sparkling sea on a sunny day like this, he enjoyed the view of her profile more. But he was sure she knew how pretty she was, and she didn't need him to tell her. Plus he had nothing to gain by doing it. Not now, not with this face. So he just kept silent and kept watch.

Finally he saw it. A black dot moving low above the northern horizon. He knew it had to be the helicopter, and although it was too distant for him to tell for certain, he thought it was coming toward them.

Ana noticed him staring at something in the sky and turned in the same direction. She sucked in her breath.

"Is that—?"

"Looks like it. You're not surprised, are you?"

"No." She continued to stare at the helicopter. "No, I am not surprised."

"I didn't think so." He decided to steel her for what might happen next. "You must've known Rivera would send someone after you—or come himself. You took quite a lot of his money and shamed him in front of his men. Didn't you realize how angry that would make him?"

"Yes, but I did not care. I had to do it."

"I see. Well, actions have consequences, and now we have to deal with them."

She turned to look at him. His remarks made her angry—at him for implying she needed his help and at herself for knowing she did. "You did not have to do this. You could have left me in my boat or given me to them when they came the first time."

Morgan didn't reply. He was still watching the helo, which was closer now and definitely heading toward them.

"Is that not so?"

After a moment he said, "No, it's not so. I couldn't have done either of those things."

"Why not? This fight—it is not yours, it is mine."

"Maybe I want the money."

"Yes?" She raised her chin. "Then you are foolish. It is my money, and I will not let you take it."

"You think you can stop me?"

"I know I can try." She looked pointedly at the pouch hanging from the other side of the helm.

"Right." He got out the pistols and the extra magazine, put the mag in his pocket, and stuck the SIG Sauer in his waistband. The Beretta he held out to her.

"Here, now each of us has a gun. But don't shoot me until we've dealt with your friends."

Hissing a curse in Spanish, she snatched the gun. "They are *not* my friends."

"Your enemies then."

"They will become yours, if you fight them."

"Yes, I suppose so." He looked at the helo, which had closed to about a mile and was hovering a few hundred feet above the water.

Holding the pistol in one hand and steering with the other, she thought, well, this is it. She was casting her lot with this strange man and his boat. She just hoped that together they could keep ahead of *him* and whatever he had planned. "You do not seem to be worried about that."

"Well, Ana, I've never been smart about picking my enemies. Or my friends."

She wasn't sure what he meant by that last remark. He couldn't be talking about her—he barely knew her. She certainly didn't consider them friends. They were just two strangers thrown together in a dangerous situation, one that she knew they would be very lucky to get out of. And despite his obvious attempts to keep her morale up, she knew that he knew it too.

Then it struck her: he had called her by name for the first time. She liked the way "Ana" sounded in his deep voice, so different from the way Jaime said it. Jaime's pronunciation was more correct, but his tone was not as—what? Warm. That was it. This man said her name as though he enjoyed saying it.

"You may be many things, Morgan, but stupid is not one of them."

If he caught her use of his name, he didn't react to it. Or maybe he did, but his face made it hard to tell. "Thanks. I can see I have you fooled."

"Stop joking." She gestured toward the helicopter. "What do you think they are going to do this time?"

He turned back to the aircraft, which didn't seem to have moved. "It doesn't look like they're going to get any closer. I think they're spotters now, not shooters."

"'Spotters'? What does that mean?"

"They're watching. Radioing our position and our course and speed to a boat on its way to intercept us."

She didn't speak for a moment. Then she said, "A boat. Do you think Jaime will be on it?"

"You tell me. You know him, I don't. But I think it's likely. After that failed first attempt, he'll probably want to handle this himself."

Yes, she thought, he probably would. She didn't want to look at the helicopter again, but she couldn't help herself. It was still there, black as a spider, hovering about a mile north of them.

Morgan looked too, using the binoculars. "Yep, too far away to shoot—or get shot at. They're tracking us, letting others know where we are. Leading them to us. Too bad we seem to be the only sailboat in this part of the ocean."

Ana thought hard, trying to come up with something that would help. "Should we cover up the boat's name again?"

"No, it would just look suspicious if we did it a second time."

"What can I do?"

"Just steer for now. You're doing a good job. I'll handle . . . whatever."

Morgan reached for the radio, tuned it to channel 16, and handed it to her. "Here. I've set it on a channel the Coast Guard monitors. If something happens to me, call them. Say you're being attacked by pirates and tell them to send a helo from the base at Aguadilla."

She took the radio reluctantly.

"The Coasties can be here in half an hour. Tell them to home in on our friend hovering out there. Then turn on the autopilot—you just press this button—go below and lock yourself in a stateroom."

Ana stared down at the radio. He could tell what she was thinking.

"I know. You don't want to get the Coast Guard involved, especially since you're Cuban and would have a hard time explaining what you're doing out here with no passport and a bag full of American money. But you may have no other choice—except to go back with him. And you don't want that either, do you?"

She shook her head.

"Okay, then. Let's hope I can keep them away."

He stood to search the horizon. The helo continued to float low over the waves, trying to stay off air-control radar. The wind carried most of the churning noise away from him, but he could still hear the sound that had become so familiar in the desert.

Then he heard something else. A higher-pitched engine noise that was barely audible over the sound of the helo but soon grew louder.

The sound seemed to be coming from the east, out ahead. Morgan took the binoculars to the top of the cabin, grunting as he seized the stays and hauled himself up.

He saw a speedboat, low and sleek, racing at full throttle. The boat bounced over the waves, its big twin outboards throwing a rooster tail of spray. He could see three—no, four—people in the boat.

He knew they'd be hard men, armed and dangerous.

He looked back at Ana, who was gripping the wheel, her knuckles white. He could tell she heard the speedboat. Soon she'd see it.

She looked up at him, a question in her eyes. He didn't know the answer, but he nodded to her as though he did. Yeah, he was tough too—or used to be. And he was armed. He'd find out whether he was still dangerous.

CHAPTER NINE

The speedboat kept coming, heading straight for them.

Morgan put down the binoculars. There was no doubt where the boat was headed. He turned to look at Ana. "You better go below. You'll be safer there."

"No!" She struck the wheel with her palm. "I will stay here. I will not let him intimidate me. Not anymore."

"That's good. But it's all right to feel . . . nervous. These guys mean business."

"Are you afraid?"

He thought about that. He could feel a surge of adrenaline but little fear, and he knew why. "Let's just say I don't have a lot to lose."

She wanted to ask him what he meant. Later, maybe—if there was a later. "What do you think we should do?"

He got down from the cabin and crossed the distance to her in long, painful strides. "*I* am going to try to keep them off this boat. *You* are going to get below and stay below. Don't use your gun unless I can't keep them away."

Anger flashed in her hazel eyes as she looked up at him. "Two people can keep them away better than one."

"Not necessarily. If you're on deck I'll be worried about you instead of trying to protect myself."

She wanted to argue but knew it would be futile. "All right, I will hide. But I am coming up if you need me, and I will not let them take me without a fight."

"Better get moving then—they're almost here."

Ana yielded the helmsman's chair to him and scooted down the steps but didn't retreat far into the salon. Instead, she knelt on the steps and leaned forward, holding her pistol out in front of her. Morgan liked the resolute look on her face.

The speedboat closed on them, its powerful engines drowning out all other sound. The man at the helm kept on a collision course—constant bearing, decreasing range—until the two boats were only a dozen lengths apart. Then he turned slightly to starboard and passed on *Sun Chaser*'s port side, close enough to examine her but not close enough to make an inviting pistol target.

The helo must've warned them, Morgan thought. But he knew they'd get closer after they'd looked the boat over some.

All four men aboard the speedboat were staring at him. Morgan stared back, easily picking out Rivera: the trim, handsome man who seemed to be in charge. He was sitting by the helmsman and was the only one not wearing sunglasses.

He wants to show his eyes, Morgan told himself. To intimidate anybody looking at him. Probably works most of the time.

As the speedboat passed *Sun Chaser*'s stern, Rivera turned and said something to the slender helmsman, who nodded and moved his hands. The engine noise dropped several notches and the boat slowed, losing her train of white water.

Now Morgan could read the name on her transom: *El Halcón de la Mar*. That fit—she looked like a sea hawk.

The speedboat's wake reached them and rocked *Sun Chaser*. He braced himself on the life rail and Ana clutched the main hatch opening for the several seconds it took for the wake to pass.

As the waves diminished and the rocking slowed, then stopped, the speedboat made a tight turn and slowly came up behind *Sun Chaser*. He could see the men reading her name and "Fajardo, P.R." on the stern.

El Halcón de la Mar came abeam of *Sun Chaser* on the sloop's starboard side and paralleled her course from about fifty feet away. The helmsman had to throttle the engines down almost to idle to keep the sleek craft from outpacing the much slower sailboat. Morgan saw that although Rivera wasn't carrying a gun, all of his men were, the short, stocky one cradling a semiautomatic rifle. Morgan set the helm on autopilot to leave his hands free.

"Hello, my friend," Rivera called in Spanish. Morgan could hear him all right over the muted engines. "Out of Fajardo?"

Morgan could see Rivera staring at his face and body. He imagined that Rivera, like everyone else, wondered what had happened to him. "Sí."

"Looks like a charter."

"Does she? Well, she's easy to sail—except when power boaters who should know better get too close and make her ride their big wakes."

Rivera gave him a hard look but kept his tone even. "Seen a little wooden boat with a girl on board? Got caught out in last night's storm?"

"You're looking for her?"

"Yes, she's a friend of mine. Have you seen her?"

"Have you tried calling the Coast Guard? Maybe they've spotted that boat."

Despite the distance, Morgan could see Rivera frown. Rivera said, "You sound American, my friend, not Puerto Rican. But you understand me, no?"

"Yes, I understand you very well."

"Good. Then stop fucking with me by answering every question with a question."

Morgan said nothing, just watched the men on the boat. The man with the rifle uncradled it and held it loosely, barrel pointed just ahead of *Sun Chaser*. Morgan knew the man could point it at him very quickly.

Rivera waited a few seconds, then continued. "You've got a couple of things that belong to me—the girl and the money. I want both of them back. Now."

Morgan still said nothing.

Rivera's frown deepened. "Listen, friend, give me what's mine and I may let you live."

He's negotiating, Morgan thought. Rivera surely realized Morgan could just throw the money over the side, and the helo crew must have told him Morgan had a gun. "And if I don't?"

Rivera smiled, and Morgan felt the chill of it even across the distance between them. "Then I will take them anyway, and instead of sailing back to Fajardo, you will sleep with the fish."

Morgan laughed. "Is that supposed to scare me? Better think of another line—one that isn't from *The Godfather*."

Rivera said something to the man with the rifle, and he swung it up into shooting position. As Morgan drew his pistol, the man with the rifle aimed it at *Sun Chaser* and squeezed off a shot.

The bullet shattered the cabin window closest to Ana. She yelped, and Rivera's pleased expression showed that he'd heard her.

"Well, my friend, it seems you do have a woman on board—and I know which woman. Tell her to come on deck."

Morgan said nothing. After a few seconds Rivera spoke softly to the man with the rifle, who aimed it at Morgan.

He knew he couldn't shoot the man pointing the rifle at him before being shot himself. Without looking away from the man, he whispered to Ana in English, "They know you're aboard. Come up into the cockpit, but keep your head down. Maybe we can talk our way out of this."

Ana nodded and came up the steps. She knelt on the cockpit sole and slowly raised her head over the gunwale to look at the other boat. Rivera saw her and grinned. Morgan thought he looked like a hungry wolf finding a stray lamb.

"Ana! There you are. It's good to see you again—I've been worried. Are you all right?"

She glanced at Morgan and hesitated. "Yes. Yes, I'm all right—here."

Her remark didn't cause Rivera to lose his grin. "And my money? Is it safe too?"

"I have the money."

Rivera waited, but she didn't add anything.

"Okay, I will come alongside. Get the money and come with me." She shook her head. "No."

Rivera's frown returned. "What? I don't think I heard you."

"You heard me, Jaime. I'm not coming back with you—and I'm keeping the money."

"You can't do that, Ana. You know you can't."

She glanced at Morgan again. "No, I think I can."

Rivera gave Morgan an angry look, as though the situation were his fault.

Morgan shrugged. "The woman can do what she wants, and I don't think she wants to go with you. The money's hers, as far as I know, so she can keep it if she likes."

Rivera slapped the speedboat's topside. "Ana! What are you doing with this stupid, ugly gringo? Come home with me."

"No, I've had enough beatings, thank you. And more than enough of being kept prisoner."

"You must come back and bring that money with you. I'm a patient man, but I'm running out of patience."

"You—patient?" She laughed. "I'm keeping the money. God knows I earned it by what I had to take from you. Anyway, you got it illegally, so it's only justice that someone steals it from you."

Morgan remained silent. Watching Rivera's face, he sensed what was coming. He shielded the pistol with his body and cocked the hammer.

"Kill him," Rivera said to the man with the rifle, his anger making him speak loudly enough for Morgan to hear.

"Get down!" Morgan said to Ana as he dropped to his knees in the cockpit. The rifle cracked, and the bullet whizzed a few inches over his head.

As the man adjusted his aim for another shot, Morgan raised and fired. He didn't hit the man, but he came close enough to make him throw his second shot wide.

Morgan ducked again. Rivera's other two men pulled out their pistols and sent a fusillade of bullets toward *Sun Chaser*. A few passed over the boat, but the rest hit her cabin and the hull above the waterline.

The fiberglass didn't stop the bullets, but it slowed them enough to be stopped by whatever they hit next. One round hit the teak frame of the main hatch, splintering it and driving a sharp fragment of wood into Morgan's arm. He winced as he withdrew the bloody piece of teak but was glad none of the bullets had hit Ana or him—yet.

He looked at her, crouched even lower than he was. She was clearly frightened but still had that shiny little pistol in her hand and looked ready to use it.

After a few seconds Rivera said, "Stop." The crash of gunfire gave way to silence. "You can't hit him that way, and we don't want to sink the boat. Not for a while."

As his ears stopped ringing, Morgan let out the breath he'd been unconsciously holding. The breeze brought the stink of cordite to him, overlaying the fresh salt smell of the sea.

Rivera said, "Stand up, you. I want to talk."

Morgan didn't move. "Go ahead. I can hear you all right."

Rivera muttered some obscenity Morgan couldn't make out. "Give us the money and the woman or we'll come aboard and kill you."

"If I give them to you, you'll kill me anyway." Morgan cautiously raised his head over the side—and raised his pistol so Rivera could see it. "Go away, Señor Rivera, or this will be *your* last boat ride. Your men may get me later, but first I'll get you."

"You think you're good enough to hit me at this distance, especially from a moving boat?"

"I'm good enough to try. Want to bet your life I can't do it?"

Rivera glared at Morgan, seeming to weigh the odds.

"The bell—one shot," Morgan said. With its longer barrel, the SIG Sauer was more accurate than the Beretta, but the bell was a much smaller target than the helicopter. He steadied the pistol in both hands and aimed, timing *Sun Chaser*'s roll and praying for luck. He squeezed off a shot at the speedboat's showy brass bell.

The metal clanged, and Rivera and his men ducked.

When Rivera stood again, he said, "Not bad. Who are you anyway?"

"Nobody. Just a guy."

"Just a guy, huh? Where did you learn to shoot like that?"

"I've had a lot of practice. I used to be a SEAL."

Rivera's helmsman said, in a voice Morgan had to strain to hear, "A Navy man. That must be how his face—"

Rivera cut him off with an angry gesture. For several seconds he seemed to consider what Morgan had told him. Then he said, "The woman is nothing to you. Give her to me, and you can keep some of the money—ten thousand—and your life."

"No."

Rivera looked surprised at the quick answer. "You want more money? Okay, twenty thousand—but that's it."

"No."

Now Rivera seemed frustrated. "Why the hell not? We can certainly kill you if we want. Isn't it better to have some money and live than die here—for someone you don't even know?"

Morgan glanced at Ana, who was looking intently at him. He could tell she wondered if he was considering Rivera's offer. He gave her a bit of his crooked grin.

"Maybe, but I don't like the way you shot up my boat."

"We'll do some more shooting if you don't give me what I want."

"Then so will I." Morgan pointed the pistol at Rivera.

The crime boss shifted slightly but said nothing. Morgan knew he wouldn't show fear in front of his men—that's why he wasn't holding a gun.

"After I kill you, I'll hit your engines, and the sparks will ignite the fuel. Ask your men if they know how to fight a fire on a boat."

Rivera's men looked at one another, then at Rivera. One of them whispered something to him.

Morgan guessed they might not have a fire extinguisher on board or at least might not know where it was and how to use it. These guys probably didn't know much about boats, probably hadn't checked their safety equipment before leaving port. A scene from the movie *Hombre* flickered through his mind—the Mexican bandit telling Paul Newman that the other robbers brought whiskey, not water, on their raid because they thought it would be easy.

After a long pause Rivera said, "Okay, you win this round. But I'll see you again, and soon. When I do, you're going to wish we'd ended it here."

Morgan said nothing.

Rivera gave him a moment, maybe to see if he'd reconsider or maybe just to see if he was stupid enough to gloat over the victory—small and temporary as it was. When Morgan remained silent, Rivera made another angry gesture at the helmsman.

The man opened the throttle and the speedboat pulled away. Rivera, eyes full of hate, stared back at Morgan until the boats were far apart.

CHAPTER TEN

Morgan stuffed his pistol and the extra magazine back into the pouch and took the helm off autopilot. After checking their course, he glanced around the horizon.

"Look." He pointed at the sky. The helo was departing to the northeast.

Ana, who had gotten up from the bottom of the cockpit, turned to follow his finger. "It is leaving. Why, do you think?"

"Rivera must've radioed the chopper to refuel and be ready to look for us first thing tomorrow. He knows that, regardless of what course we steer, we can't go very far very fast in this boat."

He paused, wondering whether he should tell her. After a moment he decided she should know.

"If the crew reports we're still at sea in the morning, Rivera will come back, probably with two boats so he can straddle us. Definitely with a lot more firepower, and then it'll be over. But now we have a little time to figure out what to do."

She sank onto a cushion and put her pistol beside her. She breathed deeply as she fought off images of what Jaime had done to others who'd crossed him—and not as badly as she had. Then she looked at Morgan.

"I was very frightened when they started shooting. Were you?"

"Sure. Despite what I said earlier, only a fool wouldn't be scared once someone starts shooting at him. The trick is not to show it—and you didn't. That makes you brave."

She smiled weakly. "I do not feel very brave, but thank you for saying that. And thank you for getting—no, wait, it is 'standing'—standing up to Jaime. I did not mean to involve you in my problems."

"That's okay. What's done is done." He adjusted his eye patch to a more comfortable position. "I've learned to accept that in life."

She looked at him for a moment. Then she said, "You told Jaime you were an animal—a seal, I think. Why did you say that?"

"Not an animal, S-E-A-L in all capital letters. A Navy SEAL. It comes from 'Sea, Air, Land.' Special operations guys who conduct clandestine missions."

"Clan—what?"

"Sorry. Secret missions—reconnaissance, counterterrorism, stuff like that. Basically, you sneak ashore in rubber boats or maybe parachute or helo in. Then you blow stuff up or protect high-value targets, which could be people, buildings—almost anything. Sometimes you spy on bad guys or even capture or kill them."

"That is how you learned to shoot the way you do."

"Well, as I told Rivera, I practiced a lot. And did it for real a few times."

"Where was that?"

"First Afghanistan, then Iraq."

She hesitated for a moment. "Is that where you were . . . ?"

He looked at her. "Where I was what?" For some reason he wanted her to say it.

"Hurt. Where you lost your eye."

"And got all this . . . decoration?" He said it lightly, but the joke sounded flat, even to him.

She held his gaze. "Yes, where you got that."

"Pretty ugly, huh?"

Again she hesitated. "No, not ugly. Instead—ah, I do not know the English word. In Español it is 'feroz.'"

"Fierce."

"Yes, fierce, like a lion. That is why I thought you said you were an animal."

For several seconds he remained silent, steering *Sun Chaser* through the rippling blue-green sea. Then he said, "Fierce, huh? Well, I guess there are worse things."

She was pleased that she hadn't offended him. "Many worse things, and some of them I have seen."

He remembered what she had told him about Rivera. "Yes, I guess you have."

Ana took their water bottles below to refill them. Gazing out the galley porthole, she realized that if Morgan hadn't found her, she'd either be dead or Jaime would have her now—and she knew which of the two would be worse. She shuddered.

She suspected that Jaime cared more about the money than he did her, and she knew that he was angry at the way she'd embarrassed him in front of El Viejo and the others. But if he'd been angry before, he must be furious now, having been shown up by Morgan with his men looking on. He probably thought of Morgan as a one-eyed crazy man too foolish to understand what he was getting into.

She'd thought the same thing. And she would've described him as ugly—very ugly—before she'd seen him in action. First with the helicopter and now with Rivera and his men.

Morgan was feroz, just like a lion. She'd meant what she'd said. A lion mauled, maybe almost killed, in an earlier battle but willing to fight again.

As she picked up the water bottles, she saw a bullet hole in the galley bulkhead. She remembered how the bullets had hammered into the boat and how she'd been terrified that one would punch through where she was crouching, shatter her skull, and spray her brains all over the cockpit.

That must be what war is like. Morgan must have known that awfulness was coming, but he accepted it. Why? For the bag full of cash? Or . . . something else?

She didn't know. What she did know was that Morgan's prediction for the next day scared her. She also knew he was right—if this boat were still at sea, Jaime would return with more men and guns. And she knew he would kill Morgan, perhaps kill her too, and take back the money.

She didn't know what to do. She hoped Morgan had some sort of plan.

Back in the cockpit Ana handed one of the bottles to Morgan, who thanked her and took several long swallows of water.

"That's good. Tension always leaves you dry."

She drank too. "Did you learn that in the war?"

"Yes. That and a lot of other things."

She sat next to him and looked at his face. Without realizing it, she'd chosen his "good side," the one still capable of expression.

"Will you tell me about it? Please?"

He glanced at her. "Why?"

"Because I want to know." She didn't say what she was thinking—that she wanted to know him better. She added, "I have never known anyone who fought in a war. Well, no one but my Tío Paco, and he will not talk about it."

"Most people who've been in one don't want to talk about it. Where did your uncle fight? Africa?"

Ana knew that between his KGB training and his work for the Cuban government, Paco had fought in many places around the world, including Africa and Central America. Mostly as part of—how had Morgan described it?—"special operations." But she still didn't want to tell Morgan too much about her uncle, so she said only, "Yes."

"And he's never told you anything?"

"Very little." That was certainly true, she thought, making her feel better about holding things back from the man who'd probably saved her life twice in one day.

"Then he must've seen some things he thinks are too . . . unpleasant to share. I imagine he's trying to protect you."

"Yes, but should one be protected from the truth?"

Morgan thought for a moment. "Perhaps not. As an adult, anyway. Of course, knowing the truth doesn't mean you have to say what you know. Silence is different from lying."

His comment was so similar to what she'd just been thinking that Ana wondered if he could read her mind. But it had to be coincidence.

"Yes, you are right. I do not want to hear lies about what he has seen—or what you have seen. But now I would like to hear . . . something more than silence."

"You're sure?"

"Absolutamente." Something, maybe her desire to convey all the emotion she could with a single word, made her speak in the language she knew best.

"Okay. I can tell you what I know, which is just a little piece of a big war." He drank more water, remembering the chemical taste of the tepid water he'd carried in his canteen. "We infiltrated Iraq from a neighboring country. I can't tell you which one because I think that's still classified."

"Infiltrated?"

"Went in very quietly so the Iraqi Army wouldn't know."

"Okay. But how?"

He grinned. "If I tell you, I'll have to kill you."

Ana's eyes widened.

"Just kidding—it's a line from a movie. Well, let's say that another way SEALs get places is by fast-roping from helos. That's sliding down a rope really fast, using a seat harness and braking with your hands, like wringing out a towel. You can't brake with your feet because it would chafe the rope."

"It sounds dangerous."

"Not as dangerous as what we just went through."

"Perhaps," she said, and he was struck again by how lovely she was. Sitting there with no makeup, her tawny hair tied in a ponytail, his shorts and T-shirt hanging off her curved frame, she was still stunning. And now he had spent enough time around her to learn that she was also smart and brave.

He could see why Rivera had wanted her, maybe still wanted her even after she'd stolen from him and made him look like a fool. But he knew that no matter how much Rivera wanted her, the man would, if he got the chance, make her suffer for what she'd done. Maybe by doing to her face or even her body a little bit of what the war had done to Morgan's.

"Anyway we were in-country a few days ahead of the invasion force. There were a lot of us, over two hundred, scattered around in small groups, usually five or six men. Our main job was to conduct reconnaissance of the Iraqi military. Spy on them, basically. See who was where, what they were doing, what their state of readiness was. Also, we planted demolition charges to blow things up—mostly command-and-control targets—once the war started."

"What things?"

"Headquarters buildings, radio towers, stuff like that. A few of us protected things, especially port facilities and oil refineries, even a dam. To keep the Iraqis from destroying their infrastructure the way they did the Kuwaitis' in the Gulf War. Avoid the economic and environmental damage."

"That is what you did?"

"That's what my group did. A chief petty officer, three other enlisted men, and me. I was a senior lieutenant—same as a captain in the other services. Our job was to protect part of this big oil refinery down near the Gulf. We did okay until a couple of days after the war started. Then things went to hell."

She leaned toward him. "What happened?"

"We were going to be relieved by some Army troops in the morning, so it was our last night on watch for a while. In fact, the Army radioed us that they were setting up a perimeter to protect our position, but the Navy told us to stay until we actually saw the soldiers.

"We were dead tired, had barely slept since we got there. It looked like the area was fairly secure, so I told the other men to rest while I took the mid watch. That's midnight to oh-four-hundred, four in the morning."

"Yes, I understand."

"We were dug in, two foxholes, Chief Herrera and two of our sailors in one and me and another sailor about thirty or forty meters away. We were about twice that distance in front of some big storage tanks, oil or maybe gasoline. Our map of the facility wasn't all that accurate, and none of us could read the Arabic signs posted around. We just knew we were near something the bad guys wanted to blow up if they could.

"Anyway, around oh-two-thirty I heard something moving out in the darkness. I wasn't sure what it was. I used night-vision goggles but still couldn't tell. I thought it was probably just a stray dog, but I woke up the other man to cover me while I went to check it out."

Morgan paused, remembering. "Going out there, as thinly manned as we were, was probably a mistake. I found what was making the noise—two bad guys moving toward our position with a mortar. I got both of them."

He didn't mention how the two Iraqis had looked lying on the sand, one shot in the chest, the other in the head. So much blood he could see it even in the starlight. Bits of skull and brains blown from the second man.

A feast for the flies.

"It had taken me some time—too much time—to work my way near enough. As I was doing that, some other guys had closed on our foxholes. Maybe my shipmate fell asleep or maybe they were just very quiet. Anyway they got close enough to charge. That woke my men up, and they started shooting. The bad guys shot back, of course, and it was a real firefight.

"I had a submachine gun, so I ran back and attacked from behind. We got all of them, but they killed one of my sailors and wounded two others. And something—a stray round, maybe a grenade—started a fire."

Ana held her breath. She was pretty sure what was coming.

"Not from one of the big tanks, fortunately, or we'd all have been blown to pieces. It was a smaller tank, about the size of a fifty-five-gallon drum, with a hand pump on top. It had wheels and a handle, so I guess they used it to drain other tanks or haul samples of oil or gasoline around. The pump or the hose must have leaked onto the top of it.

"Anyway, this portable tank was on fire, close to the storage tanks. The chief was moving toward it, but I got there first and pushed him away. I yelled for him and the rest of the men to get out of there, and then I grabbed the handle to pull the rig back from the storage tanks. I'd gone maybe ten or fifteen yards when it exploded.

"That's all I remember. I woke up in a military hospital, looking like this. Well, a lot worse then, but I know it's still pretty bad. And probably as good as it's ever going to get."

There was nothing to add to that, so he fell silent and looked out over the endless ocean. The day was far gone, the late-afternoon sun an orange ball rolling down the flaming western sky, throwing shadows forward from the life rails and mast.

After a few seconds he felt a hand on his knee. Ana was looking up at him, glints of moisture in her eyes.

"That sounds so . . . . It is hard to say. Awful, terrible, whatever the right word is."

He was tempted to touch her, put his hand on hers or even stroke her hair. But it'd been a long time, and he was reluctant to risk her drawing back.

So he didn't move except to say, "I don't think there is a right word. No one word anyway."

Just "hell," he thought, and even that isn't enough.

CHAPTER ELEVEN

They sat like that for a minute or two. No sound but the creak of the spars, the thrum of the rigging, and the hiss of the bow cutting through the water.

Then Ana took her hand away and leaned back. "Thank you. I know it was hard for you to tell me that."

Morgan said nothing.

"I think you are very brave. I have seen it today, and you had to be brave to risk your life to save your men."

"I didn't save all of them."

"But it was war, yes? In war people die. You cannot save everyone." She paused. "Perhaps now it is time to forgive yourself and forget about it."

"I'll never forget about it. I can't—I've tried."

"Not think about it so much then. Or about how you look."

He frowned. "I'm not that vain. It's not how I look—well, okay, maybe that's part of it. What I really hate is what I can't do anymore. I used to be an athlete. I could run, swim, climb, do lots of things. Now I can barely sail this boat."

She looked at his body, long and lean with muscles bunched under the skin. But also with those marks of war. She could see how once he must have been quick and strong. Also handsome. Not now, true, especially with that face. Still, he had a certain quality, a certain confidence that made him attractive once you looked past the wounds.

She doubted she could ever fall in love with him, but she could see how other women might.

He interrupted her thoughts. "Speaking of the boat, I think we should get off her. We're too easy for Rivera to find."

"But do you not have to take this boat back to Fajardo?"

"Not if I'm going to get killed doing it, and you along with me. I know a cove up ahead, about an hour from here. We can anchor there tonight and leave the boat. Rent or steal a car, go to San Juan, and hide in the city."

"Then what? Jaime will keep looking until he finds us. I know him—he does not give up."

"I don't either," Morgan said. "You don't have a passport, and they're hard to counterfeit. But maybe we can get you a fake Puerto Rican driver's license, and with that you can fly from San Juan to Miami and just disappear."

He picked up his phone and found Herrera's number. He could see the shoreline to the north, and the signal-strength indicator on the phone confirmed that they were in range to make a call. When his friend answered, he said, "Luis, it's Morgan."

"Hal! Where are you? On the boat?"

"Yes. I need a favor."

"Sure, man, anything. What is it?"

"I need a driver's license—unofficial—for a friend who needs to get off the island, fly to the States."

"What's her name?"

"Why 'her'?"

"For you to do this, my friend, it would have to be a 'her'—probably a very good-looking 'her.' No?"

"Well, yes, but she's in trouble."

Luis laughed. "If she's with you, I'm sure she is."

"Seriously, can you help?"

"Depends on what kind of trouble."

"She's running away from a guy—a Dominican named Jaime Rivera."

"Jaime Rivera . . . not *that* Rivera? The one they call 'El Bucanero'?"

"Yes, that Rivera."

"She's his woman?"

"Well, one of them anyway. Plus she has something he thinks is his."

"What's that?"

Morgan glanced at Ana. "Some money."

Luis whistled softly. "Thank you, my friend, for coming to me with this problem. I'm going to hang up now. If you want to commit suicide, please call someone else."

Morgan waited. After a moment Luis said, "Okay, okay. I'll try to help, but a fake driver's license? Not something a casino security supervisor should be doing."

"No, but I'll bet you know people who think they should be doing it."

"Sure, some who are good at it and some not so good. We see their work all the time."

"Then you know who can make one that will pass inspection."

His friend paused. "Maybe."

"Well, can you help? She can pay whatever it costs."

"Really? That would make it a little easier." He paused again. "Okay, for you, shipmate, I'll talk to someone I know."

"Great. Should I take her picture with this phone and send it to you?"

"No, the quality would be shit, and besides, she should look differ-ent if she's trying to avoid someone."

"Good point."

"Why don't you let Karen work on her? Change her hair, makeup, all that stuff?"

"You think it would make that much difference?"

"With Karen doing it? Sure. When can you be here?"

"Tomorrow, maybe by noon."

"Okay. I'll tell Karen, and both of us will take the day off. Stay safe, man." He hung up.

Morgan put the phone on the cockpit cushion and looked at Ana. "I've got a friend in San Juan who can help you get a driver's license. His girlfriend is a hair stylist and can change your appearance."

For a moment she thought about his plan. It sounded crazy, but she didn't have any other option.

"All right. It might work. I will pay of course. How much do you want?"

"You should pay Karen for whatever she does. Luis will need some money for the person who makes the license, and you should add some-thing for Luis's trouble—and risk."

"What about you?"

"I'm already being paid to bring the boat back."

She studied his face. He looked away. "Why are you doing this?" she asked.

"Doing what?"

"You know—helping me. Risking your life."

"Maybe I miss having a challenge. Or maybe I just don't like Rivera."

She smiled. "I think that is it, that you do not like him. Are you per-haps jealous?"

His face froze. He set his lips in a thin line and said nothing.

She realized her words had been ambiguous—maybe he assumed she was referring to Jaime's looks. Ay, Ana, she thought, you have gone too far. Clearly he does not like your teasing him in that way. "I am sorry. I did not mean it the way it sounded. I was not talking about—"

"Forget it." His tone was sharp, and he busied himself with check-ing their course and making a minor adjustment to the mainsail sheet.

She thought about apologizing again but knew that would only make things worse. "Let me make us some dinner."

He said nothing but nodded as he looked out over the ocean. In the east the colors of sea and sky were beginning to soften and run together as afternoon faded into evening.

She went to the galley and got busy. She hadn't been hungry earlier, but now she was, perhaps because the danger was past. For the time being, she thought.

She took her time, wanting to prepare good food and show him that she was not simply some gangster's girlfriend. When the meal was ready, they ate silently in the cockpit. Not knowing whether he liked wine, she'd poured some from an opened bottle she found in the galley, and he accepted the plastic cup from her.

"Thanks. I didn't mean for you to wait on me this way."

"I know. That is why I do not mind doing it. It is a chore only if you think someone expects it."

"Does Rivera expect it?"

"He did. Now he will have to find someone else to wait on him." She smiled at the thought but only for a few seconds.

Maybe he won't catch me, she thought. And if he does . . . . She touched the pistol in her pocket and a chill came over her.

"I am a little cold. Do you have a heavier shirt I could wear?"

"There's a sweatshirt in my duffel. Help yourself."

"Thank you." As she stood she palmed the phone and hid it in her hand.

Ana went into the head, closed the door, and sat on the toilet lid. She punched into the phone the U.S. number Tío Paco used. She thought he was in Havana now but wasn't sure.

She knew he wouldn't answer a call from a number he didn't recognize. She murmured a brief message identifying herself and saying she'd call back in a couple of minutes.

Then she rooted through Morgan's duffel bag, looking for the sweatshirt. To get at the shirt she had to take out his books—a couple of novels and a history of the Spanish-American War. Looking at their covers, she realized that in his place she'd have brought two or three bags of clothing but probably nothing to read.

She was bright enough to have learned early not to reveal to men that she was smarter than most of them. But somehow she'd never developed a taste for reading, and certainly Jaime had never encouraged her to. Tío had chided her about it, saying books, or rather the ideas they contained, were the most important thing in the world.

He nagged her until she'd read his favorite, *The Old Man and the Sea*.

But he'd never been able to get her to finish many other books. Certainly not the dreary *Das Kapital*, which he'd pressed on her once, saying that any niece of his should be familiar with the literary foundation of Communism.

Looking at the books Morgan had brought along, she determined to start reading more. Maybe once she was settled in Miami, she could go back to school. Take some college classes, perhaps even graduate.

The thought pleased her until she remembered the odds against her getting there. Then she sighed. Well, maybe.

Keeping her T-shirt on, she shrugged into a dark-blue sweatshirt with NAVY on the front in big yellow letters. Then she stuffed everything else back into the duffel and returned to the head.

She called Paco again. He answered on the first ring, and she rapidly whispered a summary of her situation. She finished by saying, "So I need your help."

"Yes, I think perhaps you do."

"Can you meet me in San Juan tomorrow?"

"I'll have to reschedule some appointments, but I can be there. Your plan is to go to Miami?"

"Yes. I haven't thought any further than that."

"You probably won't need it, but I'll bring you a U.S. passport just in case."

"You have time to do that?"

Sitting at his desk in Havana, Paco smiled. His niece underestimated what the DGI could do when necessary.

"Certainly, my dear. Will I be able to reach you at this number?"

"No, it's not my phone. I'll have to call you."

"Do you know where you'll be staying in San Juan?"

"I think with friends of Morgan's, a couple named Luis and Karen. I don't know their last names or their address, but I think I can find the phone number. Wait a second."

She searched for the last number Morgan had called and recited it. "Can you find me with that?"

"Yes, even if it's a mobile. Don't worry, I know my job."

"I know you do, Tío. Okay, I'll see you soon."

She went back to the cockpit and sat on a cushion. Dusk was well along now, and overhead the sky was deep blue with the first stars showing. The western sky was royal blue shot with crimson and gold and a hint of green. Venus, shining brightly, hung low on the horizon behind them and would soon follow the sun down behind the darkening waves.

Morgan had steered the boat closer to shore. He kept checking the chart and the compass and peering intently at the shoreline.

Ana waited until he was looking away before she put the phone back on the seat. "How much more to go?"

"Just a few minutes. I hope I spot the place before it's full dark. We'll have to motor in."

"How can I help?"

He glanced at her. "Steer while I drop the sails. Then act as bowman."

"As what?"

"Go stand on the bow and tell me if I'm about to hit something."

"Like a rock?"

"Yes, or a floating log. Anything that could bang up the hull or dent the propeller."

"Okay." She hoped she'd be able to spot any obstacles in time to avoid them.

She sensed Morgan wasn't in a mood for conversation, so she kept quiet while he sailed the boat and looked for the cove. The evening air was much cooler, and she was glad she'd put on his sweatshirt. She'd heard somewhere that people with extensive burns feel temperature changes more than other people, so she was surprised that he didn't seem cold.

Maybe he doesn't feel it, she thought. Sometimes he seems made of stone. Or maybe he does feel it but won't let that show. A strange man in many ways . . . .

"There it is." His comment snapped her back.

"Where?"

He pointed. "A mile off our port bow."

In the gathering darkness she could barely see the entrance to the cove. She was glad Morgan had spotted it.

"Let's drop the sails. After I head up, you take the wheel and hold that course."

He started the engine, leaving the throttle low, and swung the boat into the wind. He plucked some sail ties from the pouch at the helm and stuffed them in his pocket. Then he loosened the sheets, allowing the sails to luff in the breeze.

He motioned with his head, and she took his place at the wheel. She held the course while he worked his way forward.

As she watched his stiff movements, she thought about his description of that night in the desert. Based on what he'd told her, she thought he was lucky to be alive. She wondered if he thought so too.

He wound up the headsail and let the mainsail fall. He gathered up the mainsail's folds and used the ties to cinch the sail onto the boom.

Obviously he'd spent a lot of time on sailboats. Ana wondered whether he'd been alone most of that time. She knew she was really wondering if he'd had a woman with him, and she shook her head at having such an idle thought at a time like this.

Once he had the sails secured, Morgan returned to the cockpit. He went below for a flashlight and a life preserver and handed them to her.

"Here. I'd rather no one sees us, so use the light only if you have to. If you fall off, swim to shore. It'd be hard to pick you up in the channel in the darkness."

She stuck the flashlight into a pocket of the baggy shorts. "I will not fall off."

"Good. Put the jacket on anyway, just in case."

He'd seen that she was a good swimmer, so she thought for a moment about arguing with him. Then she shrugged and put on the life preserver.

"Okay," he said, "now I'll steer and you be the bowman."

"I will go to the bow, but I am not a man."

"Yeah, I noticed. All right, bowperson, just holler if we're about to hit anything."

□   □   □

He took the helm, nudged the throttle up, and turned the boat toward the entrance to the cove. She went to the bow, moving carefully and holding onto the life lines. The boat bucked some now that it was powering through the waves instead of sailing with them.

At the bow she spread her feet and braced herself on the rolled-up headsail that led from the deck to the top of the mast. She peered ahead, not seeing anything in their path but not sure she could see it in the vanishing light even it were there.

The entrance to the cove grew slowly in front of her. Morgan kept the boat in the middle of the channel that led through the entrance. The bucking slowed, then stopped, as the boat eased onto the shallower and smoother water.

As the boat approached the narrowest part of the channel, Ana used the flashlight sparingly to look for rocks. She didn't see any, but she did see a large tree limb floating ahead of them. She turned and called to Morgan, raising her voice just enough to be heard over the engine.

He said, "Get the boat hook and try to push the limb away. It probably won't hurt the hull, but I don't want the prop to hit it."

She got the hook and, leaning over the bow, was able to shove the limb to one side. The waterlogged piece of wood turned out to be bigger and heavier than she'd expected, most of it invisible below the surface.

Still holding the boat hook, she made another quick scan with the flashlight. "I do not see anything else in our way."

"Good."

Morgan brought the boat through the entrance to the cove, and an expanse of water about half as big as a football field opened in front of them. The surface, black now that night had come, was completely calm except for the ripples of their wake. The dark mirror of the water reflected the bright tropical stars and was silvered by the quarter-moon rising in the east.

He put the gearshift into neutral and let the boat glide closer to the shore. He switched off the engine, and the sounds of the Caribbean night closed in around them.

He opened a locker under a cockpit seat and lifted out a small anchor, a "lunch hook." He tied the anchor line to a stern cleat and threw the anchor out behind *Sun Chaser*. The boat gently stopped after it had coasted a few more yards toward the narrow strip of sand that separated the water from dense foliage.

He went to the bow and showed Ana how to deploy the main anchor. The bigger anchor made a bigger splash when they dropped it over the bow. He let out a length of line equal to about four times the boat's length, and the boat slowly drifted to a point making a triangle with the two anchors.

"There. That should hold her pretty well even with the suction through that entrance when the tide goes out."

As they moved back to the cockpit she said, "How do you know about this place?"

"I came here once on a fishing trip out of Ponce. We beached our power boat and walked up to a little town about three miles from here."

They sat across from each other in the cockpit. There was just enough light from the moon and stars for her to see him looking at her.

"There's a small guesthouse, not very nice but quiet. I thought we would stay there tonight."

He seemed to be waiting for her reaction, and she wondered if she thought he could sleep with her. She knew she was quite capable of telling this big, gruff man to stay out of her bed but somehow felt nervous about the prospect. She wasn't sure what his reaction would be, and she knew he could be violent. She'd seen that herself.

Then she wondered whether he wanted to sleep with her and whether she'd let him if he did. She'd started off by not liking him much, but now that she'd spent most of this long, dangerous day with him, she wasn't sure how she felt. And she certainly didn't know how he felt—or whether he felt anything at all about her as a person.

Her cheeks grew warm as the thoughts ran through her head. She hoped that in the darkness Morgan couldn't see her blush.

She didn't know what else to say, so she said, "All right."

CHAPTER TWELVE

When he got off the phone with his niece, Bolaño closed his eyes and thought. He had learned over the long, hard years to think before acting—at least if there was time to think. In this case there was time. Not much, no, but enough.

He'd always felt a bit uneasy about Ana's living with Rivera. She was a grown woman, so she could do as she pleased, but he knew he'd pushed Ana toward Rivera for his own reasons. And he knew what Rivera could be like with women. He'd seen it often enough, both before Rivera and Ana got together and since then, at times when Ana wasn't around.

He'd never told Ana that Rivera had other women—he thought she probably knew and just looked the other way. Another compromise he'd made with his conscience. As a spy for Castro's Cuba, he'd made many such compromises, each a little easier than the last. By now there had been so many he couldn't remember them all, but their cumulative weight rested heavily upon him.

Well, apparently things were over between his niece and Rivera. He would have to find someone to replace Rivera in his espionage network, and Rivera would have to find another . . . mistress. He didn't like thinking of Ana that way, but there it was.

He sighed and glanced around his office. He wasn't a sentimental man, but over the course of his long career he had accumulated a few mementos. There was the picture of him with Castro—an obligatory picture for anyone who was senior in the Cuban government or ever wanted to be. A couple of pictures of him in Africa, one where he was wearing camouflage and another where he was dressed in khakis, neither uniform showing his rank or even his name.

What had the Africans called him? Something he couldn't pronounce, but they said it meant "jungle snake." Based on their resentful expressions when he'd barked at them for screwing something up, he thought it probably meant "foreign prick," but he hadn't bothered to check. All he cared about was finishing their training, leading them on a few patrols to see how well they'd learned their lessons, and getting the hell out of there. Alive.

Which he'd managed to do. And earlier he'd done his own training with the KGB, learning the Russians' tradecraft with codes and ciphers, dead drops, and evasive driving. And, of course, poisons, a specialty of theirs.

God, the winters were cold in Moscow! So were most of the KGB instructors who sneered at his poor Russian even though their Spanish was no better.

So there was the picture of him in Red Square at midnight. Him with Vasily, the one instructor with whom he'd become friends, and the two women—slim, hard-eyed blondes—Vasily had brought along for their vodka-fueled dinner of borscht, beef stroganoff, and cabbage. Then they'd had blini for dessert. Well, the first dessert—the women had turned out to be the second.

The cop who'd taken the picture with Vasily's camera had apparently figured that out, giving him a broad wink as he handed the camera back and wishing the ladies and gentlemen a "sweet ending" to the evening.

It had been sweet, something to savor, even though the woman who ended up in Bolaño's bed tried to pump him for information about Castro, the DGI—anything that she could take back to her KGB bosses. But Bolaño had simply smiled, put a finger to her lips, and whispered, "Shhh," which clearly annoyed her, but he went to work and was able to supplant her pique with a much different and more pleasant feeling

His gaze turned to another picture, the one of which he was most proud. There he was, wearing a well-cut civilian suit and standing next to a Florida congressman, in a hall of the Pentagon. He'd posed as a Cuban immigrant who loved the United States almost as much as he hated Castro and ingratiated himself with the not-overly-bright House member from a district with a large Cuban American population.

Although that visit had revealed little about the U.S. military that he didn't already know, he considered his wrangling a tour of the Pentagon as one of the highlights of his colorful career. It was as if a CIA agent had been given a tour of the Kremlin. He didn't know whether that had ever happened, but he had a photo to prove a DGI agent could penetrate the headquarters of America's armed forces.

His boss had arranged for Bolaño to give Castro his report in person, and he'd made sure to bring a copy of that photo, which he presented to the Bearded One with a flourish and a slight bow. When he told Castro the story behind the picture, the dictator laughed so hard that tears came to his eyes.

"This is priceless. I should send it to that asshole Reagan with a note—'Love from your friend Fidel.' Here, sign it for me."

Bolaño had taken out his pen, the one that doubled as a camera, thought for a moment, and then written "Para El Comandante. Con lealtad eterno. Francisco Bolaño."

Castro liked that expression of undying loyalty. Castro had framed the picture and kept it in his office, pointing it out to Bolaño on the one other time the agent had been summoned into the presence of the great man.

Finally Bolaño looked at the three family pictures. There was Ana, of course, looking young and innocent on her quinceañera, already at fifteen almost as lovely as the beautiful grown woman she turned out to be. His parents, both dead now, when they were younger than Bolaño was today, his father's face worn and stoic, his mother's almost as worn but venturing a slight smile as though she thought there might still be happiness somewhere in the world if not on this island prison.

And Bolaño with his sisters, one older, one younger. The older one was still alive, a widow now to whom Bolaño sent money every month, not much but all he could afford and almost all she had to feed and clothe herself.

The younger sister, Ana's mother, the one to whom he'd always been closer . . . well, she was gone and nothing would bring her back. Fingering the small silver cross that he kept hidden under his shirt, Bolaño wondered if he'd see her again in the next world. If there was a next world.

The priests said there was, but what did they know? To them, evil was abstract, something present only in the Bible. On the rare occasions when he allowed himself to attend Mass, always alone and always outside the country, he had heard them read about evil and then speak about it, condemning it, of course, but doing little to stop it.

But then, they had never seen the devil as Bolaño had. Seen the devil sometimes in Cuba, especially in the political prisons that were simply a slow form of execution. But seen him more frequently in the benighted places in Africa and Central America where Castro's government sowed the seeds of Communism for people desperate for some form of worldly salvation, some respite from the hell that was their daily lives.

There the devil walked among the people, and Bolaño—now cursing himself as he thought back on some of the things he'd done, the things he'd tried without success to forget—had sometimes walked with him.

Bolaño sat slumped in his chair, the late-afternoon sun slanting in through the dirty windows. He forced himself to clear his head, to stop thinking about the past and focus on the problem in front of him. How to help Ana get out of the mess that he'd helped to get her into.

After a few minutes a plan came to him. It was risky and dangerous, but it might work. And he could think of no good alternative.

He picked up the phone and made the call.

□　□　□

Stepping back into the cockpit, Morgan said, "I'll zip up the boat. You gather whatever you want to take with you."

Ana gave a short laugh. "All I have is the money, a gun, and these clothes of yours. I do not even have shoes."

Morgan paused. "I hadn't thought of that. You'll need some if we're going to get anywhere. Let me see what I can find." He went below and rooted around in drawers and lockers until he found a pair of men's flip-flops the charter sailors had left on board.

"Here." He handed them up to her. "I know they don't fit you any better than my clothes, but they'll have to do until we can buy you some things."

She liked hearing him say "we"—in fact, she was surprised at how much she liked it. She slid the sandals on, stood, and lifted each foot experimentally. "They will be fine for now. I can keep them on my feet."

Next he handed her the blue bag, which she took without comment even though their eyes briefly met.

Morgan spent a couple of minutes straightening up the salon, head, and galley. He was neat by nature, so it didn't take long. He stuffed a water bottle into the duffel bag and put his wallet, keys, phone, and a small flashlight into the pockets of his shorts. Then he put on a light squall jacket.

He climbed back into the cockpit and put the duffel on a seat. He closed the main hatch and locked it, more for the form of the thing than because he thought it might deter thieves.

Ana noticed the jacket. "Do you think it will rain tonight? The sky is clear."

"It doesn't rain much here along the South Coast, which is almost like a desert. Not like around El Yunque." The mountain named "The Anvil" was in northeastern Puerto Rico and surrounded by a rainforest.

He knew the real reason for her question. "No, I don't think it's going to rain." He pulled his pistol and the extra magazine from the pouch and tucked them into the jacket's inside pockets. "But the gun will show if I stick it in the waist of my shorts, and if I put it in the duffel, I can't get to it fast enough."

She paused, looking at him. "You think you will need it?"

"Yes—if they find us. If they find us, I'm sure I'll need it."

Ana said nothing to that.

He untied the rubber dinghy that was on top of the cabin, lowered it to the water, and secured its mooring line to a cleat. After helping Ana into it, he handed her their bags and climbed down himself.

The leg and arm made him clumsy, and he almost fell over the dinghy's side. She clutched his sleeve and helped him steady himself.

He sat and looked at her. He knew he should thank her, but he was too self-conscious about needing help. And he knew she knew it, which made it worse.

He took the paddle out of its Velcro holders, freed the line, and pushed away from the boat. Neither of them spoke as he quietly paddled ashore, then tied the dinghy to a palm tree and began cutting a number of small, leafy branches. When Ana saw what he was doing, she took the branches and draped them over the dinghy.

After they had finished, he said, "Well, that blaze orange doesn't help, but it's hidden about as well as it can be. Maybe it'll still be here if we need it again."

He looked back at the cove. *Sun Chaser* was pretty obvious, but there was nothing he could do about that. In fact, she looked lovely anchored there in the moonlight, he thought. He was surprised at having such a romantic notion.

Then he looked at Ana. He thought she was lovely too. The baggy clothes didn't detract—perhaps they even added to the picture. She looked like a delightfully rumpled castaway on a desert island.

She saw him looking at her. She was used to men looking, staring, making her feel as if their eyes were crawling over her body. When they looked at her like that, she could tell exactly what they were thinking.

But this Morgan looked at her differently. Not like she was a piece of meat, just something for him to enjoy. No, he looked at her like he might look at—what? A sunrise, perhaps. Or the way he'd looked at the boat just now.

What a strange man—brave and smart but often so silent. She'd been afraid of him before but not now. He wouldn't hurt her or even take the money. At least she didn't think so.

Morgan had picked up some palm branches and was wiping their footprints out of the sand. Trying to help would just make more footprints, so she watched him work.

He would be handsome but for his wounds, she thought. She wondered if he'd had a woman and she left him after he came home from the war. Maybe that explained his silence. Well, such a woman hadn't known what she was giving up.

□ □ □

Speaking very little, Morgan and Ana slogged through the forest to a narrow paved road with crumbling edges and numerous potholes. He turned to parallel the road and she followed him.

Walking along the road was much easier than pushing through the underbrush. There was little traffic, and they could spot the few cars soon enough to scramble back into the forest.

Other than the infrequent headlights and a few lamps twinkling in scattered houses on the hills around them, there was no illumination except that of the nighttime sky. But there was more sound than just their feet crunching on the edge of the road and the cars passing by. There was a constant low murmur of insects and the louder, intermittent croaking of thousands of coquís. The little frogs began making their distinctive "ko-kee" calls at sundown and continued all night long. He'd read somewhere that only the males sing, presumably to attract females.

"Just the opposite of humans," he said to himself.

"What?"

He hadn't meant for her to hear him. "Uh, I was thinking that the coquís are the opposite of most people. The males are loud, and the females are quiet—the frogs, I mean."

"You are saying that women talk too much?"

"No. I just mean—well, it's true that most women talk more than most men."

"Maybe we have to. If we waited for men to talk, no one would ever say anything—at least nothing important."

She didn't sound annoyed, but he glanced at her to make sure. In the moonlight he could see her slight smile. He liked the way it looked on her.

"Maybe you're right."

CHAPTER THIRTEEN

Walking to the little town took over an hour in the heat, which night-fall didn't seem to have reduced much. He stopped twice so they could rest—and he admitted to himself that he needed the breaks as much as she did. Both times he got out the water bottle and they drank, each careful to leave some for the other.

Finally they topped the last hill and saw the town at the bottom. Some lights showed, but the place looked mostly shut up for the night.

"The guesthouse is on the main square. As I said, it's no luxury hotel, but it's a place to sleep."

"Good. I have never been this tired in my life."

"Well, you've had a pretty long day—two long days, actually. I don't wonder that you're tired."

He dug into the duffel and came up with a baseball cap and a pair of sunglasses. He took off the bandana and eye patch, stuffed them in his pocket, and put on the cap and glasses. He saw her quizzical look.

"People remember an eye patch. I know that with the way I look I'll still be memorable as hell, but at least the description will be different."

"You look . . . fine."

"I wish that were true. Still, it's kind of you to say so. Now I need some money from your bag."

Ana hesitated.

"We need a car. Cash will get us one faster than anything else."

She thought about that for a few seconds. Then she reluctantly opened the blue bag and handed him a pack of $100 bills.

He broke the paper band, counted off ten bills, and put them in a pocket of his shorts. He stuffed the rest into another pocket.

She watched him, saying nothing.

"Okay, let's see what we can do."

The guesthouse looked even more dilapidated than Morgan remembered. A few lights were on inside, but the door was locked. Morgan had to knock several times before someone opened it. An old man's unshaven face, made darker by the contrast with his white whiskers, appeared in the gap allowed by the safety chain. Morgan didn't recall seeing the man the other time he'd been here.

"What do you want?" The tone of his Spanish showed his annoyance at having been interrupted. The rum on his breath told Morgan that whatever the man was doing involved drinking, apparently a lot of it.

"A room, if you have one."

The man looked them over with bleary eyes, carefully noting Morgan's sunglasses and scars and Ana's ill-fitting clothes. "You have cash? I don't take credit cards."

"Yes, we can pay in cash."

After a moment the man said, "All right," and opened the door.

Morgan negotiated the cost of a room for one night, knowing that because of the way they looked, the old man was charging them more. The man asked for the money in advance, which was fine with Morgan. Paying now would let them leave anytime they wanted, and he knew they might have to leave in a hurry. He gave the man $200 and waited for his change.

Handing Morgan some bills and the key, the man said, "The entrance is outside and to your right as you face the building."

"Thanks. By the way, we could use a car. We'd like to drive to Fajardo early in the morning." Morgan saw Ana blink at "Fajardo," but she said nothing.

"No place to rent one around here."

"That's too bad. We do need a car. In fact, I'll be willing to buy one, if necessary. I can pay cash." He showed the man five $100 bills.

The man eyed the money. "You must really want to get there."

"That's right."

"Well, for a few hundred more my brother might sell you his car. It's pretty old, but it should get you anywhere you want to go on this island."

"Okay, please call him and tell him I'd like to see the car early, at seven o'clock."

"Sí, señor."

That was the first time the man had called him "sir." The money must have made me respectable, Morgan thought. It could do that for people—Rivera, for instance.

Remembering that the guesthouse didn't serve breakfast, he gave the old man $20 to have some rolls, fruit, and coffee for them in the morning. Then he took Ana to the room.

Standing in front of the door, he took out his pistol. He didn't think there was any real possibility Rivera had predicted they would come to this place and arranged for the old man to send them to this room, but he'd seen men die from betting their lives on false assumptions.

"Stay here," he whispered to Ana. He worked the lock as quietly as he could, then flung open the door and followed his gun inside. There was no one in the shabby little room. He checked the tiny closet and the dingy bathroom. Nothing.

He lowered his pistol and looked around in the stuffy heat. There was no air-conditioner, but there was a ceiling fan that looked like the newest thing in the room. He yanked the chain to turn it on and went back to the door. "Okay, you can come in now."

Ana handed him the duffel and picked up her bag. "Did you really think they might be here?"

"No, I didn't, but I might have been wrong. Rivera strikes me as being pretty resourceful."

She frowned, not seeming to understand. "You mean . . . ."

"I mean I don't want to underestimate him."

That word she knew. "No, he is not someone to take light."

"Take lightly."

Her frown deepened. "Perhaps I should assist you with your Spanish, which is far from perfect."

"Very far. Come on in and let's close the door."

The first thing Ana saw as she entered the room was its one bed. She looked at Morgan but didn't say anything.

He saw the question in her eyes. "Don't worry. The bed's yours. I'll sit in this armchair and watch the door."

She liked that but not quite as much as she'd have predicted. "All right, but you will get little sleep."

"Maybe, but that's not the point. Go to bed. You're tired, and you're going to have another long day tomorrow."

She looked at him a few seconds more. Then she nodded and went into the bathroom, closing the door behind her.

He took off the cap and swapped the glasses for his eye patch, not bothering with the bandana. He sank into the sagging chair, which was even more uncomfortable than it looked. He too was tired but didn't want Ana to know.

He heard the toilet flush and then the shower running. A shower would feel good, but he didn't want to give Rivera a chance to catch him in there, naked and defenseless, especially at night. He decided to wait until morning.

He stuffed the cap and glasses into the duffel and rummaged in it until he found a pint of whiskey. He drank from the bottle once, twice, and then sat staring at the bed, the bottle on his knee.

After a few minutes she came out of the bathroom, dressed only in his T-shirt, which came almost to her knees. Her hair was wrapped in a towel that once might have been white.

Although the shirt was loose on her, the damp cloth clung to her breasts. He said nothing but took another drink.

She looked at him a moment, then said, "Is there any for me?"

"Sure." He held out the bottle.

She looked around for a glass but didn't see one, so she put the bottle to her lips and tilted it. The whiskey was cool in her mouth but burned going down. She coughed.

"You probably prefer rum," he said.

"Yes, or wine. Actually, I am not much of a drinker."

"I guess I am. Well, I seem to be lately."

"Is that right? Tonight I will join you, my friend."

He liked how she said that, "my friend." He hadn't thought of them as friends, but perhaps that's what they were now. What was that saying—"the enemy of my enemy is my friend"?

She tilted the bottle again and didn't cough this time. "Umm, that feels good—all warm inside. It makes the tired feeling go away."

He said nothing, enjoying the sight of her. Her face and figure were lovely, but her real beauty came from her eyes, something in their bright expressiveness.

He caught himself. Hell, pretty soon he might start spouting poetry. He held out his hand for the bottle. "One more and then it's lights out."

When she gave it to him, their hands touched. He glanced up and saw her looking at him. She seemed about to speak but didn't say anything.

He had his drink, then held up the bottle inquiringly. She shook her head, and he spun the cap on.

As he put the bottle away, she pulled off the towel and shook out her long hair. Wet, her hair was darker and tangled. She ran a hand through it.

"Is there a comb in your bag?"

He touched his bald head. "Nope, sorry. Not much use for one."

"I am sorry. I should have—"

"No, don't be sorry. It was a perfectly natural question. I'm not offended."

"Good. I would not want to hurt your feelings."

"Oh, that's hard to do. I'm a pretty tough guy."

"'Tough guy'—like in the movies?"

"Yeah, but not nearly as good-looking."

She sat on the bed and slowly rubbed her hair with the towel. "To a woman how a man looks is not as important as you might think. We care more about what is in his heart."

"Is that right?"

"Yes, as you know very well. You know about women, I think."

"Well, you're the first woman who ever thought so."

"Or maybe I am just the first one to tell you." She put down the towel. "Do you . . . do you have a woman?"

He laughed. "What kind of question is that? I mean, why do you want to know?"

She gathered some strands of her hair and looked down at them.

"I am curious. You know much about me, but I know little about you."

"Consider yourself lucky then. Come on, it's time for bed."

She leaned on her elbow and looked at him between the bedposts. "All right, I will ask you again some other time. But you do not need to sit in that stupid chair all night. This bed is big enough for both of us to sleep—and you know I mean only to sleep."

He smiled, trying to keep his face from being crooked. "Yes, I know. I'll be fine here. Now please get under the covers."

She looked at him, her eyes growing heavy as the whiskey took hold. "You are very . . . stubborn, Morgan. Do you know that? And see, I remember the word."

"Yes." He wasn't sure to which remark he was replying—maybe all of them.

"What is your first name anyway? I cannot keep calling you 'Morgan' in this stupid manner."

"Hal."

"'Hal.' I like that. Is it a nickname?"

"Yes, short for 'Harold.' My father liked history, so he named me after an English king."

"See? Now I know something about you. That is good."

"Yes, and so is sleep. Why don't you get some?"

"All right, *Hal*." She yawned. "But you must turn out the light before I can go to bed." At his puzzled look, she added, "I do not like to sleep in clothes, so I want to take off this shirt."

A variety of thoughts whirled through his head, and he didn't move for a long moment. Then he stood and walked over to the light switch. He turned to look at her. She was plainly enjoying the effect of her words.

He flipped off the light and went back to the chair. In the dark he heard the rustle of the covers and the squeak of the bedsprings. Then, straining for the sound, he heard the whisper of her pulling the shirt over her head.

He wished he hadn't put the bottle away.

The springs squeaked a little more as she lay down and got comfortable. After a moment he heard her say, speaking softly in the darkness, "Good night, Hal."

He spoke just as softly. "Good night, Ana."

Then there was silence except for the faint swish of the fan and the muffled sounds of the Puerto Rican night. He tried to think of nothing, but it didn't work, as he'd known it wouldn't.

So after a while he thought of Susan.

They'd been seeing each other for about a year before he went to Iraq, living together in his rented townhouse the last two months. For security reasons nobody on his SEAL team used civilian e-mail at the beginning of their deployment, so Susan had written him long chatty letters about their friends, what she was doing from day to day, and the things she wanted to do with—and to—him when he got back.

He wrote back on the rare occasions when he had time to do so. He had a lot more time during the long months in the overseas hospital—that is, once he was able to write again—and he tried to prepare her.

Finally he came home.

He believed Susan had honestly tried to make things work after his medical discharge. She'd even helped him change the dressings the way the doctors said, and she'd tried not to look away when she did it.

She could rarely bring herself to look at his face although she'd still kiss the right side of it—but only with her eyes closed. They made love a few times, but it was graceless because of the dressings and his pain, and she couldn't bring herself to do more than lie there beneath him. They silently agreed not to do it anymore.

One day he came back from physical therapy and she was gone. She'd left a note. It was a lot shorter than her letters.

Late that night, a night much darker than this one, he'd sat on his deck, drinking and thinking. After a few drinks he was trying not to think. Eventually he'd piled the letters in the barbeque grill and put the note on top. He'd taken one last drink and then unsteadily poured the bottle's last half inch over the stack.

He'd tossed in a match and sat there, watching the flames leap up. The fire blazed for a few minutes before dying into ash.

A week later, after he'd sold or given away almost everything he owned, he flew to Puerto Rico. He'd trained at Naval Air Station Roosevelt Roads before the Vieques controversy led to the closing of the base in 2004, not long before he moved to the island. He remembered long, lazy weekends sailing from the big marina called Puerto de la Reina. And he remembered there were always live-aboard boats for sale.

He leaned down and pulled the bottle out of the duffel. He had another drink, a big one. Then he sat there during the long night, listening for Rivera and trying not to think anymore.

CHAPTER FOURTEEN

Roosters were still crowing as Morgan looked at the car. Almost twenty years old with three mismatched colors of paint, much of that scraped off along the sides, it was a beater, even by P.R. standards.

He popped the dew-laden hood, wiped his hands on the trousers he'd put on that morning, and asked the old man's brother, apparently his younger brother, to start the engine. It clicked and coughed—complaining, Morgan thought—but finally caught and ran about as rough as he'd expected. Still, it was transportation, and he didn't think Rivera would be looking for them in a car like this.

"Okay, seven hundred," Morgan said in Spanish.

A regretful expression came over the brother's leathery face. "Sorry, sir. This car is an old friend of mine. I could not possibly sell it for less than one thousand dollars."

"Well, I guess we can't make a deal then. Thanks anyway." He looked at Ana. "We'll find another car." She nodded and they started to walk away.

"No, wait." The man held up his hands, then stroked his chin. "I suppose I could let you have it for nine hundred."

"Eight."

"Eight-fifty."

"Deal. Here's the money."

He counted it out. Ana watched him hand the bills to the brother, who took them with evident satisfaction and no sign of remorse at parting with his old friend.

The old man and his brother walked toward the front door of the guesthouse. When they were several paces away, Morgan said quietly to Ana in English, "Let's grab our things and get out of here. With me so recognizable, we've got to keep moving if we want to stay ahead of Rivera."

Minutes later they were on the road, headed north. The old car didn't ride any better than it ran, so every bump in the pavement—and there were many—jolted its way from their backsides up their spines. But neither of them complained.

"I'm going to stick to back roads and older highways as much as I can and stay off the autopísta. It'll take us a lot longer to get to San Juan, but it'll be safer. The tricky part will be getting past Ponce."

"You think Jaime is there?"

"Probably. I think that's where that speedboat came from yesterday. They might figure we'd leave the boat, which is easy to spot from the air, and try traveling by land."

A chill came over Ana as she remembered the gunfire. She didn't want to go through anything like that again. She hoped Hal would be able to keep them away from Jaime and his men, but she knew there was no certainty of it.

She looked at the bag on the floor between her feet. She'd thought getting away with the money would be worth the risk. Now she wasn't so sure.

Both of them were tired, so they didn't talk much for a while. He hadn't slept at all, and she hadn't slept well, being in a strange bed and wakened a few times by bad dreams.

Each time she woke up she looked over at Hal and saw him sitting in the chair. Although he sat completely still, she could tell from his erect posture that he was awake. She thought he'd probably heard her moving in the squeaky bed, but he hadn't looked her way.

She now regretted saying so openly that she slept in the nude. She could've simply slipped out of the T-shirt underneath the covers. There was no need to tease him that way. No, be honest, she thought. There was no need to tempt him.

He hadn't seemed very tempted. For some reason that fact bothered her too although she hadn't wanted to make love to him. Sleeping in the same bed would've been fine—comforting, in fact. But she didn't know Hal well enough to think of him as a lover. She was, however, very glad to have him as a friend. Especially with Jaime after her.

But not just for that reason, she thought. Also because she trusted him . . . and liked him. Even that crooked grin of his. Thinking of it made her smile.

That morning she'd waited until he'd gone into the bathroom before getting out of bed and getting dressed. The old man brought their breakfast, and they ate quickly before going to look at the car.

She'd heard the man mutter to Hal, "Very beautiful." She knew he wasn't talking about the car. Hal had made no reply.

She wondered if he thought she was pretty. She wasn't vain, but she was confident about her face and figure. She knew that many men— all right, most men—found her attractive, and she'd always been happy to accept the good things her appearance brought her. But she didn't trade on her looks, didn't try to get what she wanted by flirting.

No, be honest, she thought. Sometimes she did. But not very often.

She looked at Hal, who was focused on driving. He was wearing the cap and glasses again. He sensed her gaze and glanced at her.

"Are you okay?"

"Yes. A little tired perhaps."

"Me too. When we get to Luis's place in San Juan, we can rest."

"And his woman will be there?"

"Karen? Yes, she should be there."

"Karen is not an Hispanic name—she is an Anglo?"

"Yes." He glanced at her again. "A gringa from New York."

"I did not use that word."

"No, but were you thinking it?"

She hesitated. "Perhaps. But I did not mean it in a bad way."

"I understand."

She paused, then said, "Do you like Hispanic women? As much as your blonde Anglo women? Or do you think of us as 'spics'?"

"I like all kinds of women, all colors too and not just their hair. But I don't use that word."

"I should not use it either. But I have heard some rich tourists say it in the casino. When they did not know I could hear them."

"Some rich people are idiots, just like some poor people."

"Yes, that is true." She paused again. "Do you want to be rich?"

"I don't want the responsibility—or doing what you have to do to get the money in the first place. No, I like living simply. My main goal right now is to get a new set of sails for my boat."

"Really? They looked fine to me."

"Not for the charter boat. I mean *Blue Rover*, the boat I live on."

"Oh, you live on a boat? That must be fun."

"I like it, at least for now."

She thought he would naturally follow up, say something about what might come next in his life. But he didn't, and the pause went on so long she remained silent as well. They bumped along that way for a while, watching the island go by.

As they approached Ponce she saw him looking closely at every car that passed them in either direction. She followed suit, hoping that she wouldn't recognize Jaime or any of his men—or that if she did, they wouldn't recognize her in this old car with Hal at the wheel. She wished she had something for a disguise—a hat, a scarf, anything. But she didn't.

When they stopped at an intersection, she noticed a white SUV waiting to cross in the opposite direction. The vehicle looked familiar and so did the two men sitting in it.

Then she gasped—she did know them, and they looked as though they'd gotten a tongue-lashing from Jaime before they set out. She fell to the seat just before men turned their gaze on the old car.

Morgan had seen where she was looking. He didn't move except to ask from the side of his mouth, "Know them?"

"Yes." She whispered even there was no need. "They work for Jaime."

"Shit. They may still spot you."

"Perhaps not if I am on the floor."

She scrunched on the floorboard and rolled into a tight ball, thinking of what Jaime had done to certain people who'd crossed him. She knew that even if he let her live, he'd hurt her so badly that death might seem preferable.

Morgan rubbed his chin, covering his mouth with his hand. "They're checking us out," he said, his voice muffled. "Too bad this light caught us."

She said nothing but curled even tighter as sweat beaded out on her forehead.

"Okay, the light changed. Here we go."

She felt the car lurch into motion, jarring her on the floorboard. Dust swirled into her nose, but she willed herself not to sneeze even though she knew the sound would make no difference.

They gathered speed, but Morgan said nothing. She wanted to ask him what was going on, but her mouth was so dry she couldn't get the words out.

After a few more seconds he said in his normal voice, "We're past them. They gave me a long, hard look but must've decided I'm not their guy, especially when they didn't see you."

"Thank God."

"Yes, and your quick thinking to get down."

The comment pleased her, but she wanted to be honest with him. "I moved because when I saw them, I was suddenly afraid."

"That's okay. Sometimes fear keeps us alive."

She climbed back on the seat and looked at him, remembering the story he'd told her. "I think you know what you are talking about."

He was silent for a long moment. "I guess so."

"Then I am not ashamed to say I am afraid of him—or what he is capable of."

"No need to be ashamed. I'm beginning to get a pretty good idea what that crazy boyfriend of yours will do if he catches us." He glanced at her as he said it and, seeing her sharp look, added, "Okay, former boyfriend. How's that?"

She thought about that. "Now he is simply someone I want to get away from and never see again."

He nodded. "Then we have something in common."

They drove through Ponce in silence. The sun was higher now, and they felt its heat through the dirty windshield and the warm wind that whipped through the open windows.

"It'll be cooler once we're north of Ponce and higher above sea level."

She dabbed her forehead with the back of her hand and nodded.

They climbed the mountains that were the east-west spine of Puerto Rico, the old car wheezing every mile of the way. The engine-temperature gauge climbed too, and as they approached the top, Morgan noticed that the needle had gone into the red.

He found a place to pull over and parked as wisps of steam began coming from under the hood.

"We're over-heating," he said as he switched off the engine. "Let's stretch our legs while she cools."

"Can we still get there?"

He heard the anxious tone in her voice. "I think so. The engine won't have to work hard as we go down, and then it's not far into San Juan."

They got out and stood on the crest. Looking south they saw the placid Caribbean sparkling in the sunlight. To the north they saw the Atlantic, also sparkling but rougher, with whitecaps racing to shore.

And they saw the sprawl of San Juan to the northeast, the city spreading out from the harbor that was its main reason for existence. The enormous maze of buildings and roads looked like an ugly gray stain on the island's splendid green carpet.

Morgan looked at her, admiring her hair, the shining brown of buttered toast, as it was blown back by the wind. "Have you ever been to San Juan?"

"Yes, several times. Jaime has business associates there. He even keeps an office in one of the casinos in The Condado."

"The touristy part of the city."

"That is all I have seen. The hotels and casinos and beaches. A few of the shops."

"You're never been to the old city—Viejo San Juan? With the pastel buildings and blue cobblestones?"

"No, I have seen it only in pictures."

"Well, that's too bad. It's a fine place. There's no time now, but perhaps in the future . . . ."

"You mean if Jaime does not kill us."

He paused. "Yes." He seemed about to add something but then paused again and said only, "Let's go."

□ □ □

As they drove down the mountains toward San Juan, Morgan phoned Luis to let him know where they were. Two hours later they parked on a quiet residential street not far from the ocean. Ana looked around.

"This is nice. Which house is it?"

"None of these. It's a few blocks from here. I'm trying not to make it too easy for Rivera in case he got a description of this car."

They got out. She noticed he left the car unlocked.

"Are you not afraid that someone will steal it?"

"I hope somebody will—and take Rivera on a wild-goose chase."

She frowned. "I do not understand about the wild goose."

"It's just an expression. It means Rivera will waste his time looking for someone else. At least if someone steals the car—I'm not sure anyone will want to. I'll take the key in case no one steals it and we have to move it."

They took their bags and walked to Luis and Karen's house. Before Morgan could ring the bell, Luis opened the front door.

"Hey, man, I've been waiting for you. Quick—come in before someone sees you." They squeezed past Luis, and he locked the door behind them. "It took you long enough—it's almost one now."

"I was driving the oldest car in Puerto Rico, and we kept to the back roads."

"Scared of Rivera, huh?" Luis softened it with a chuckle.

"Yes, and I'll bet you are too."

"No bet—you know I am!"

While the men were talking, Ana and Karen were looking at each other. Morgan saw it and said, "I'm sorry. Karen, this is Ana, Ana Cortez Bolaño. Ana, Karen Ginsberg."

Ana inclined her head. "I am very pleased to know you," she said in careful English.

"And I you," Karen replied in Spanish. Both women smiled.

"And this is Luis Herrera, a Navy friend."

Luis turned to her. "Bienvenida a nuestra casa, Ana."

"Thank you. I am very sorry to be so much trouble."

"I'm sure you won't be half as much trouble as this one usually is," Luis said, gesturing toward Morgan.

"Oh, Luis," Karen said. She kissed Morgan on the cheek. "It's good to see you again, Hal. You didn't stay long enough last time."

Ana watched Karen standing so close to Morgan and felt—what? Not jealousy. Nor envy. Perhaps just a desire that Morgan not prefer Karen's company to hers even though she knew they were close friends.

Karen saw Ana watching her and stepped away from Morgan. "Ana, you must be tired from your journey. Please let me show you where to freshen up."

Half an hour later the women reappeared. Ana was dressed in a short cotton skirt, a camisole, and sandals. She had combed her hair and put on a touch of makeup.

Both men stood as the women entered. Karen saw their expressions and glanced at Ana, who was keeping her face carefully neutral. Still, Ana was pleased to be able to make an entrance again.

"I'll fix lunch." Karen started for the kitchen. Ana followed to help.

Luis waited until they'd left the room, then looked at Morgan, raising his eyebrows. "Now I see why you're willing to take on Rivera."

"Well, I never planned to. She sort of fell in my lap, and he came looking for her."

"Yeah, but I never figured you for a knight in shining armor."

Morgan glanced at his friend and then looked toward the kitchen. "Neither did I."

CHAPTER FIFTEEN

Over lunch Morgan gave Luis and Karen the highlights of what had happened since he'd found Ana adrift. Ana didn't say much, and when Luis questioned her about a couple of details, Morgan quickly changed the subject.

After the meal Luis and Morgan loaded the dishwasher and cleaned up the kitchen while Karen studied Ana's face and hair. "I didn't know what I'd need, so I brought several things home from the shop. If you want to look really different, I think we need to cut your hair as well as color it. Is that okay?"

"Anything that keeps me away from Jaime Rivera is okay."

"He sounds like quite a guy—but not in the good way."

"He is. He certainly is."

"Come on. Let's wash your hair first, and you can tell me about him."

Later Karen cut Ana's hair. Karen had spread newspaper on the floor of the living room and placed a chair in the middle of the paper. Ana sat erect in the chair, a blue bath towel wrapped around her neck.

Luis had never seen Karen practice her trade before, so he watched with interest. Morgan sat by the window, reading a well-worn copy of *Dead Calm* he'd pulled from his duffel. At least once a minute he glanced down at the street.

"With your long hair you have that runway model thing going on, so I'm going to give you a short, sassy look. That'll change things more than you might expect." Karen's hands deftly manipulated the scissors and comb.

Ana watched her hair fall to the floor. She was clearly not thrilled about it but didn't say anything.

"Then we'll color it. Blonde would suit the cut, but that might attract too much attention. I'm thinking dark red or jet black. What about you?"

"You are the expert."

"Thanks. I'm glad you said that before you see the final result." Karen laughed. Ana joined in but stopped sooner than Karen did.

When she'd finished the cut to her satisfaction, Karen held a mirror in front of Ana. "Well, what do you think? I told you—short and sassy."

Ana was surprised at the difference shorter hair made. She'd be hard to recognize at first glance. She was also surprised that she liked the look. Shorter hair made her appear more—how to put it? Confident, in control, assertive.

"I like it—I really do. You did a great job." She turned to Morgan. "What do you think?"

He cocked his head and looked at her. "Pretty good disguise. Rivera will have to look twice to make sure it's you."

"Definitely," Luis said. "There's quite a difference."

She realized she'd been hoping for a compliment. She looked at Karen, who shook her head.

"Don't mind them. They're just men. They don't notice our hair unless we go bald. Maybe not even then."

Ana smiled. "Is that right, Hal?"

He looked at Ana, then at Karen, who was watching him with a bemused expression. "Sometimes, maybe. But not right now."

Karen chuckled. "Okay, back to the bathroom for the color and maybe change your makeup a little. Luis, you clean this up, okay?"

"Sure, honey." He winked at Morgan. "And I'll get us a couple of beers while I'm at it."

Luis put the chair back in its place and swept up the shorn hair. Then he crumpled the newspaper, dropped it in the kitchen trashcan, and put the towel on the washing machine. On the way back he got two beers, and he and Morgan had almost finished them when the women returned. Ana's short hair was now as dark as midnight, and Karen had done something to make her eyes and mouth appear larger.

"Wow," Luis said. "You look like a completely different person. I didn't realize Karen could change you that much."

"Thanks for the vote of confidence," Karen said, playfully hitting him on the shoulder.

"Hey, you know what I mean. You really did a good job."

"Yes, I'm sure that's what you meant."

Ana looked at Morgan. "Well?"

He looked at her longer this time. "As I said, good disguise. And, yes, you look fine—quite pretty in fact. Not that you didn't before."

Ana felt herself blush. She noticed Karen looking at Morgan, then at her.

Luis broke the silence. "Okay, are we ready to take ID photos?"

"Yes," Ana said, glad to change the subject.

Luis got his phone and posed Ana against a cream-colored wall. He took several close-ups of her face and then showed them to her.

"Which one do you like best?"

"Mmm, this one, I think." She tapped the screen with a fingernail. Morgan came over. "Let me see them."

Luis scrolled through the pictures again.

"That one." Morgan pointed to a different shot.

"But that is the worst!" Ana said. "I am not smiling and my face looks strange."

"Then it's a typical ID photo and looks less like you than the pictures Rivera and his men may be showing around. At the airport, for example."

After a moment she said, "All right. I understand."

Morgan looked at Luis, who nodded.

"Okay, I'll go see this guy I know. He works out of the coffee shop a few blocks from here. He should have the license ready tomorrow." Luis hesitated, looking at Ana.

"He'll want some money up front," Morgan said.

"At least half," Luis said.

Ana went to the blue bag. She handed a packet of bills to Luis. "Take what you need."

She saw him looking at the bag full of money. She glanced at Karen and saw that she'd halted in the middle of putting her implements into a carrying case and was staring at the bag, eyes wide.

"I guess he has two reasons to be looking for you," Karen said.

Ana didn't reply. Luis counted off several bills and handed what remained of the packet back to her. She took out five $100 bills and handed them to Luis.

"For your trouble. And for taking the risk."

Luis looked at Morgan, who nodded. Luis shrugged and said, "Thanks, Ana."

Then she counted off another $500 and held it out to Karen.

"Thank you for your work. I appreciate your helping me."

Karen put a bottle of hair dye into the case. "That's okay. You don't have to pay me."

"I want to. You took the day off, brought those things home, took time to do all this." She gestured at her head. "It would not be fair otherwise."

"Take the money, Karen," Morgan said. "I told her both of you deserve to be paid. Ana's not looking for a free ride."

Ana nodded. "That is right. I know I have put all of you to much trouble."

Karen let Ana put the money in her hand. She looked down at it. "But this is too much. Half this would be more than enough."

"Please accept it as a gift. You must let me do something to thank you for inviting me into your home, and right now I cannot get you anything appropriate."

Karen hesitated, then tucked the money into her pants pocket.

"If you ladies have sorted that out," Luis said, "I need to get going."

"Go on," Morgan said. "We'll be here when you get back."

"It shouldn't be too long." Luis gave Karen a quick kiss on the cheek, picked up his keys, and left.

□   □   □

Rivera walked slowly through San Juan's Luis Muñoz Marin International Airport, looking closely at every woman about Ana's age. Some ignored him and some turned away from his searching gaze, but some smiled at the tall, attractive man in expensive, well-cut clothes.

When the helicopter reported no sign of the sailboat that morning, Rivera had decided Ana had gone ashore—probably bringing her new friend along—and might be trying to get off the island. Flying out of San Juan was by far the easiest way to do that, and Rivera knew Ana had plenty of cash for a ticket and was clever and bold enough to steal or buy some sort of ID.

So Rivera had gone to the casino to gather a few more of his men, who were now scattered throughout the airport. Every few minutes he checked with one of them in person or by phone to keep them alert. He was about to call one of them when he saw something that made him pause.

A wiry man of medium height was moving through the airport. He wore a light-colored, tropical-weight suit and a white, open-necked shirt. He was carrying a small, black overnight bag. He had the half-tired, half-expectant look of someone who'd just gotten off a plane.

Rivera turned so that the man wouldn't be able to see more than his profile. He watched from the corner of his eye as a young, pretty woman in a pantsuit went up to the man, seeming surprised to have encountered him. They kissed each other on the cheeks and talked animatedly for a couple of minutes.

Soon the woman glanced at her watch and showed it to the man. She pulled what looked like a ticket envelope from the briefcase hanging from her shoulder. The man nodded, and they appeared to be saying goodbye.

As they kissed again the woman discreetly put a small package into his hand. Rivera thought she must've taken it out with the ticket, hiding it behind the envelope. Without looking at the package, the man slipped it into the outer pocket of his bag.

The woman gave the man a wave and walked toward the security checkpoint that led to the departure gates. He returned the wave and began moving toward the exit nearest the taxi stand.

Rivera knew the man and thought he knew what the package contained. The man was Francisco Torres Bolaño—Ana's uncle. Rivera had met with him several times since becoming involved with his niece, usually to give the Cuban intelligence officer information about what was going on in the Dominican underworld. On a few occasions Bolaño had given him packages of money to ferry part of the way—twice all the way—to one of the several revolutionary or terrorist groups that the Cuban government supported.

In his office Rivera had a framed picture of himself, Bolaño, some other Cuban officials, and a gorgeous Hollywood star. The photo had been taken in Havana when the woman had come to Cuba to protest something about U.S. policy—Rivera couldn't remember what, and the star herself had seemed pretty vague about the details.

She had, however, enjoyed the drinks and music at one of Havana's tourist nightclubs. She'd danced with Rivera, repeatedly pressing her thigh against his almost painful erection. In turn, he'd moved his hand up and down her back and cupped her ass, confirming his impression that she wore nothing beneath her short, tight dress.

Bolaño had just sat there, sipping mineral water, and saying little, a faint smile playing beneath his neatly trimmed mustache. Later, when Rivera had asked him what he was thinking about, Bolaño had said only that he was enjoying the show.

He knew Bolaño was surprised that his niece had apparently fallen in love with Rivera and moved to the Dominican Republic to be with him. He was pretty sure Bolaño had intended only for Ana to be a contact between the two men, a contact who, because everyone would assume they were lovers, would arouse no suspicion about the true nature of their relationship.

But Bolaño, a calculating man, had made a mistake—something he rarely did—by failing to allow sufficiently for the chance that his young niece might find Rivera, with his money and fast, fashionable life in Santo Domingo, very attractive. Rivera thought that was the one time he'd gained an advantage over the Cuban spy.

Rivera tapped on his phone. "Benito, get the car—quickly! Bring

Chavez and meet me at the taxi stand. We're going to follow someone."

"The girl?" said El Segundo.

"No, her uncle, the Cuban. He just flew in and may know where she is."

"You want anyone else?"

"No, leave the rest of the men here to keep looking for her. We'll see where Bolaño goes. Did you bring some line from the boat?"

"Yes, I figured we might need it."

"Good."

Rivera walked toward the exit, keeping Bolaño in sight but not crowding him. The Cuban went outside and joined the line of people waiting for a cab.

Rivera also went outside. He didn't see the watchful man behind him.

El Callao had followed Rivera and his men from the casino to the airport. At first he thought Rivera might be trying to flee, to get away from the wrath of the Old Man who was sitting in Cabo Rojo without the large sum of money Rivera owed him. But then he saw that Rivera was looking for someone—undoubtedly the girl, who probably had the money with her.

He was surprised when Rivera began following the man in the light-colored suit. He didn't know who the man was, but Rivera seemed to.

Rivera strolled a few yards from the taxi stand. Standing there, half turned away from the queue, Rivera acted as if he were checking his phone, but every few seconds he glanced over at the man in the light-colored suit.

El Callao thought hard. Clearly the guy in the taxi line was leaving, and it seemed likely that, having followed him in the airport and then outside, Rivera would continue to follow him.

El Callao went outside himself, making a sharp left and keeping well away from Rivera. He hurried back past two exits in the arrivals section of the airport to where he'd left his car, flashing a fake private-investigator ID at a security guard and bribing him with a hundred-dollar bill to let the car sit there for a few minutes.

As Bolaño neared the head of the line, Garcia pulled up in a gold Mercedes. Rivera slid into the front passenger seat. Chavez, short and with muscles beginning to go to fat, sat in the back.

"There—see him? The slim man in the light suit. The one next up for a cab."

"Yes, I see him." Garcia paused as the lead taxi inched forward and Bolaño climbed into its back seat. "Here we go." He swung the Mercedes out into traffic and began following the cab.

Intent on watching the cab, Garcia didn't notice the gray Nissan that pulled out behind them, the hard-looking man at the wheel.

"Try to keep a couple of cars between us," Rivera said. "I don't want him to know he's being followed."

"Okay, but he probably wouldn't figure that out in all this traffic."

"Just do it." Rivera's irritation was plain. "This guy's good—he's been trained for situations like this."

"Trained?" Garcia glanced over at his boss. "By whom?"

"The Cuban government. I never told you, because you didn't need to know, but Bolaño works for the DGI."

Garcia became annoyed, partly at having gotten involved with Cuba's sinister intelligence service and partly at having been kept in the dark. "You mean he's a spy? Some fucking James Bond?"

"No, that's just in the movies. He's an intelligence agent."

"Then why have we been dealing with him? Man, he could blow our whole operation."

Rivera glanced at Chavez, then gave his lieutenant a hard look. "*I* have been dealing with him because it benefits me to do so. He has steered me to some good things—several opportunities with the Colombians, for example. Besides, he has no interest in exposing us. We are no more friends with the American authorities than he is."

Garcia waited several seconds before saying, "All right, *chief*, but I don't like it."

Rivera caught the emphasis. "You don't have to like it, my friend." He spoke quietly. "You just have to do what you're told. Right, Carlos?"

"Yeah, that's right, chief." Chavez didn't say the word the way El Segundo had.

Garcia set his jaw and concentrated on driving. The taxi led them west from the airport, past The Condado. Rivera looked at the large hotels along the beach, several with glittering casinos. He had business in most of them, some of it legal.

They ended up in Ocean Park, a residential area of older houses. Some of the larger ones on or near the beach had been turned into guesthouses.

"This is where the queers come, isn't it?" Garcia glanced at Rivera as they drove slowly down a narrow, shaded street, keeping well back from the taxi. "I mean, to stay at the beach?"

"That's what I've been told."

"So, is this Bolaño queer?"

"No." Rivera had often seen Bolaño with women and once with two women, one blonde, one brunette, both stunning. That had been on New Year's Eve in Havana. Bolaño and the two women had left the hotel party shortly after midnight, walking up the cracked marble staircase, Bolaño in the middle with a woman on each arm, very courtly.

"I know he's not queer. And look—he's not going to a guesthouse. The cab's stopping. Quick—turn into this side street."

The taxi came to a halt as Garcia swung the Mercedes into an even narrower street. Rivera jumped out, went back to the corner, and peered around a building. He cursed under his breath as a gray Nissan drove slowly down the street, passing the idling cab on its left and momentarily blocking his view.

By the time the Nissan was a block away, enough time had passed for Bolaño to pay the driver. He got out of the cab, carrying his bag. He glanced up and down the street but didn't seem to see Rivera.

Bolaño waited until the taxi had driven away. Then he started toward one of the houses. As he walked up the steps, he pulled a gun from his pocket and held it down by his side.

Yes, that's what she gave him, Rivera thought. He watched Bolaño ring the bell, wait a moment, and then walk into the house, the gun still at his side.

CHAPTER SIXTEEN

Rivera stood on the street, weighing the options. Garcia and Chavez walked up to him, Garcia stuffing the car keys into his pocket.

"I parked in the alley right over there. No one can see the car and we can get the fuck out of here if we need to."

"Good. Bolaño went into that house. Carrying a gun."

Garcia and Chavez glanced at each other. Then Garcia looked at Rivera. "Okay, what do you want to do?"

Rivera thought. He didn't know why Bolaño had gone into that particular house or why he'd gone in armed. Rivera and his men had their guns, of course, and it would be three-to-one against Bolaño, but perhaps Bolaño had friends inside.

"Chief?"

"Quiet! I'm thinking."

As they stood there they saw a man coming from the opposite end of the street. He had dark skin, a buzz cut, and the quick, confident step of a cop or maybe an ex-military man. He was carrying a sack of groceries. As the man passed the house next to the house Bolaño had entered, he began digging for his keys.

"Come on," Rivera said.

The three quickly walked up to the man and surrounded him. The man didn't panic. He stood very still and looked at Rivera, who was facing him.

"Who's inside?" Rivera said.

"Who are you?" the man said.

Rivera pulled out his knife and flicked open the blade. "A man with a knife. Who's inside?"

The man looked at the knife. "Some friends of mine."

"What friends?"

The man said nothing. He looked at Rivera again, and now his eyes were hard.

Rivera held the knife close to the man's face. "What's your name?"

"Luis Herrera."

"Okay, Luis, I'll ask you again. Who are your friends?"

Luis said nothing.

Rivera said, "Benito."

Garcia grabbed the sack from the man and threw it on the ground. A jar of salsa spilled out and broke on the street, staining the pavement dark red. A couple of cans began rolling downhill.

Luis put out his foot to stop one of the cans. When he moved, Garcia punched him in the stomach as hard as he could. Luis doubled over.

Garcia and Chavez seized Luis from each side and stood him as straight as he'd go. Rivera leaned close. "Now, Luis, who are your friends?"

Clutching his stomach, Luis cursed them but said nothing else.

Rivera sighed. "Why do you want to make this so hard?" He put his knife to Luis's throat. "If you want to live, my friend, you'll answer my questions."

Luis cursed them again but not so violently.

"All right," Rivera said, "if that's how you want it." He flicked the blade along Luis's neck. Luis winced and blood began seeping from the cut. "The next one will be deeper. Now tell me: who's inside?"

Luis swallowed hard. "Hal Morgan, a friend of mine. He's got a girl named Ana Bolaño with him."

Garcia said, "This Morgan must be the man who was on the boat with her. The one who shot so well and stopped us."

Rivera gave his lieutenant an angry glance, then looked back at Luis. "No one else?"

Luis hesitated, and Rivera sliced his neck again. Blood flowed freely from the second cut and began soaking into Luis's shirt. "Who? Talk, damn you!"

Luis inhaled sharply as the pain swelled. "Nobody, just them."

"That's it?" Rivera glanced at his men. "What about Francisco Bolaño, her uncle?"

Luis looked confused. "Her uncle? I don't know him."

"All right. Thank you, my friend." Rivera's eyes glittered like bright stones. "You were stronger than most. Goodbye." He slashed Luis's throat, and blood spurted out, almost hitting Rivera.

Garcia and Chavez held Luis for the half minute it took him to die. Rivera wiped his blade on Luis's sleeve and closed the knife. "Put him in the trunk. Quickly, before anyone drives by. But first give me his keys."

Garcia fished the keys out of Luis's pocket and tossed them to Rivera, who began flipping through them one by one. Grunting, Garcia and Chavez picked up Luis's body, carried it to the car, and dumped it into the trunk. They walked back, checking their clothes for bloodstains.

"Okay," Rivera said, "let's go in. I want Ana, the money, and Morgan. If you have to, kill Bolaño."

Garcia said, "Kill Bolaño? Won't that piss off the Cubans, send them after us?"

"They won't know who did it. They'll probably think it was the CIA."

Garcia didn't seem convinced. Rivera said, "Maybe we won't have to kill him. The important thing is to get Ana and the money. And that asshole Morgan. Ready?"

Garcia and Chavez looked at each other and then nodded at Rivera. All three men readied their guns.

"Good. I think this is the house key."

Rivera slid the key into the lock and turned it. The door began to open. Quietly he said, "Here we go."

He pushed the door open and went inside, followed closely by Garcia and Chavez. As they walked in, he saw a woman with short, black hair. Something about her reminded him of Ana, but he wasn't sure what. That Luis must've lied to him, saying there was only one woman inside.

This one was sitting on the sofa next to the man from the boat, the one-eyed shooter called Morgan. Bolaño was seated in a chair perpendicular to the sofa and facing the door. He must have put away his gun, because Rivera could see his empty hands. He used one of them to tap a small booklet on the coffee table.

The three of them looked as though they'd been having a serious but friendly talk. The opening door hadn't put them on guard, so they must have thought Luis was coming in.

But then the woman glanced up, saw Rivera and his men, and gasped. Her wide eyes became even wider. Noticing her reaction, Morgan and Bolaño also glanced up and then went for their guns.

Figuring Bolaño was faster, Rivera shot him in the chest. Then he swung his gun at Morgan, who was bringing up his pistol more quickly than Rivera had predicted.

Still, Rivera had the drop on him. "Move and you're dead, motherfucker." His Spanish was so quick Morgan could barely understand it, but the context made the words clear enough.

The black-haired woman reached her hand toward Bolaño and half-rose from the sofa. Without swinging his pistol toward her, Rivera said, "You too, bitch. Watch her, Benito." The woman put her hand to her mouth and sank back on the cushion, tears beginning to roll down her cheeks.

Morgan looked at Bolaño, now slumped in his chair, a red stain spreading on his upper chest. Bolaño was bleeding, so he was alive, but he was bleeding so much he wouldn't live long without medical care. Slowly Morgan put the gun on the sofa and raised his hands to shoulder height.

"Good," Rivera said. "I see you don't want to die—not yet." He used his free hand to gesture to his men.

Garcia and Chavez flanked Morgan. Garcia put Morgan's gun in one pocket and pulled a three-foot length of boat line from the other. Chavez pulled Morgan up and shoved his hands behind him. Garcia tied his hands and Chavez pushed him back on the sofa. Then Garcia stepped over to Bolaño and scooped the man's gun off the floor.

From the corner of his eye Morgan saw Karen, face stark white, peer into the room from down the hallway. She'd obviously had the good sense not to charge into the room. He didn't look directly at her, so Rivera and his men didn't notice her either. After a second her face disappeared.

When Morgan's hands were tied, Rivera relaxed slightly. "That's better." He walked over to Morgan, bent down, and backhanded him hard across the face. "That's for shooting at me, asshole."

Seeing Morgan's look of hatred, he laughed. "Yeah, and you'd like to do it again, wouldn't you? I'm sure you'd shoot to kill this time." He hit Morgan again. "But there won't be another time—for you."

Morgan said nothing. He flexed his wrists, feeling the line dig into his skin. The knot was too tight for him to do anything right now. Maybe later, if Rivera and his men make a mistake, he thought. The cocky ones usually do.

Rivera waited to see how Morgan would react—perhaps shout or even spit at him. Something like that would be all Rivera needed to kill him right now. But he quickly saw that Morgan was too smart for that. He told himself not to underestimate this man, regardless of his battered appearance.

Rivera turned to Garcia. "See if anyone else is here. And close the blinds on those front windows."

Garcia gestured at Chavez, who left the room as Garcia began shutting the blinds. Morgan hoped Karen had hidden somewhere and then decided she must have, because Chavez came back in less than a minute and shook his head.

Rivera turned to the black-haired woman, who now looked pale beneath her tan. She seemed reluctant to look at him and kept her head turned away. Her profile reminded him of Ana's, as did her size and shape. In fact . . . .

"Hello, Ana," he said, still not quite certain.

Her head jerked toward him, and then he was sure.

"Well, well, it seems you've made a few changes." He studied her. "I think I liked you better before. But now we're together again, and that's the important thing, isn't it?"

She said nothing as he put his gun away.

"Where's the money?"

Still she said nothing.

"The money, Ana—*my* money."

He waited a couple of seconds, then whipped out his knife, flicked it open, and held it near her face. "Where's the money, whore? Tell me, or I'll change your face permanently."

She looked into his eyes for a moment, then glanced at the blade an inch from her nose. "In the guest bedroom," she said tonelessly.

Rivera jerked his head at Chavez, who headed for the bedrooms.

"Take the money and leave," Morgan said.

"You're hardly in a position to give orders, my friend." Rivera's face hardened. "In fact, later we'll see how well you can take a few."

"If you don't just leave, you'll wish you had." The way Morgan spoke, it wasn't a threat, just a statement of fact.

Rivera laughed. "I don't know what they taught you in military school, but one thing I learned on the streets: never talk back to someone who has a gun pointed at you."

"I promise you'll regret it."

Rivera studied Morgan. "Well, you're not a coward, I'll say that much for you. Neither was your friend Luis."

Luis. Morgan and Ana started at Rivera's use of the name.

"Yes," Rivera said, "we met him outside after we followed Bolaño here from the airport. Too bad Luis didn't live long enough for us to become better acquainted."

Morgan squeezed his eye shut and exhaled, hard, through his mouth, his body slumping. He remained that way for several seconds. Then he looked at Rivera as though he wanted to remember the man's face for a long time.

Chavez returned with the blue bag and tilted it to show Rivera what was inside.

Rivera smiled, not as coldly as usual. "Good. Very good." He looked back at Morgan. "All right. You—get up. Unless you want to die like your friend."

Morgan struggled to his feet. Garcia and Chavez didn't offer to help. He looked at Bolaño. The stain was still spreading but very slowly now.

Rivera stepped over to Ana. "You and I need to have a little chat about why you left with my money. That was embarrassing for me, you know." He reached down, put a palm under her chin, and moved her head from side to side. "And you know how I hate to be embarrassed."

She glared at him but didn't push his hand away. After a moment he dropped it and said, "I don't always know what others are thinking, but at this moment I certainly know what is on your mind."

His smile lingered a moment, then vanished. "Have you heard that old song? The one that says there's a thin line between love and hate?" Rivera thought the best thing about America—well, besides baseball—was its pop music.

"Don't forget the rest of it," Morgan said.

"What?" Rivera looked at him, surprised.

"You can make a sweet woman mean if you treat her that way."

Rivera thought for a moment, silently moving his lips as he worked through the lyrics. He nodded. "Yes, that's true. I'd forgotten that part." He looked at Ana, then back at Morgan. "But perhaps you know, eh? A little meanness in a woman can be a good thing—at the right time."

Morgan said nothing.

Rivera held out his hand to Ana. "I think we're ready to leave now."

She looked at his hand but didn't take it. She pushed herself up from the sofa and stood, a bit unsteadily.

Rivera's hand hung in the air, and for a moment he looked as though he might hit her the way he'd hit Morgan. But then he smiled again and said, "Yes, I think we'll have a little chat. Later, when we are alone."

Aware that there was a dead man in their car trunk and another man dead or dying six feet from them, Garcia said, "Chief, we need to get out of here."

Rivera gave El Segundo what his deputy thought of as "the look." "I know that. We have what we came for: the money and Ana—and this Morgan."

"What about him?" Garcia jerked his chin toward Bolaño.

Rivera looked at the man he'd thought of as his friend—or at least a friendly acquaintance. It was a shame he'd had to shoot Bolaño. It made him feel . . . not bad exactly but regretful. Yes, that was it: for once he regretted the necessity of killing a man.

"Well, what about him?" he said to Garcia. "These things happen when personal feelings interfere with business."

Standing there, watching his chief standing next to Ana, who'd started this whole thing by running away from Rivera, taking all that money with her, Garcia thought, yeah, right.

But he was too smart to say it. He didn't want to end up as Bolaño had. Or as Morgan was surely going to. Maybe Ana also unless she gave the chief the best fuck of his life, making him forget how angry he was with her.

That was her problem. His was to get Jaime past enjoying this scene, get him headed out the door.

"Sure, chief, but are we going to leave Bolaño here?"

"Yes. If the cops figure out who he is—was—they'll think he came on some secret mission for the Cuban government. Then the cops will bring the CIA into it, and those stupid Americanos will fuck things up so badly no one will ever be able to connect us with it."

It sounded reasonable to Garcia. He thought about giving Bolaño another bullet, just to make sure, but the man didn't appear to be breathing, and Garcia didn't want to risk the sound of another gunshot. He could suggest the knife, but he knew Jaime used his blade only when he was angry or wanted to threaten someone, never in cold blood.

Fuck it—the man was dead or soon would be. They should get the hell out of there.

"Okay." Garcia turned to Morgan. "You're coming with us."

"Yes," Rivera said, "but kill him if he tries anything foolish."

Garcia nodded and gave Morgan a hard look to make sure he understood. The reference to the CIA surprised Morgan, but he was careful not to let it show—easier now than when all his facial muscles worked. Morgan decided Ana hadn't told him the whole truth about her uncle, and considering what the truth was, her reticence didn't surprise him.

He glared back at Garcia, who found it unsettling to have a one-eyed man staring at him. "You heard the chief," Garcia said. "No tricks."

Morgan said nothing but didn't resist when Garcia took his arm and pushed him forward.

"Go on," Rivera said. "I'll bring Ana. And her present from her uncle." He'd recognized the booklet as a U.S. passport and opened it to see Ana's picture as she'd looked before. No need to leave the passport for the police, he thought. Even though it was counterfeit.

Chavez went first, carrying the bag and checking to make sure no one was on the sidewalk or the street near the house. Then Garcia prodded Morgan out with his gun, keeping close behind him.

Rivera gestured for Ana to go ahead. She swept past him, fury plain in her movements. He followed her out, pushed the door shut with his foot, and guided her to the car.

Rivera walked up to Morgan, standing between Garcia and Chavez. "I should make you ride in the trunk with your dead friend," Rivera said, "but I want you where I can see you."

He took the bag from Chavez. "Put him in the back seat with Ana between him and me. You drive. Benito, you keep your pistol on him the whole way."

"Right," Chavez said, opening the rear door on the driver's side. El Segundo said nothing but pushed Morgan into the seat while Ana and then Rivera got in on the other side. Then Garcia and Chavez climbed into the front.

Garcia turned to put his pistol on top of the seat and look at Morgan. "It's no time to be a hero, my friend. Understand?"

Morgan didn't reply.

Garcia sighed. "Seriously, I don't want to clean your blood off the seat."

"He won't do anything with his hands tied and your gun on him," Rivera said. "He's greedy enough to try to take my woman and my money, but he's not stupid."

Morgan knew Rivera was speaking to him as much as to Garcia. He still said nothing.

Garcia nodded. "You hear that?" He switched to English to make sure Morgan understood. "Eh, hombre? If you are not stupid, do not do something that is stupid."

"Drive," Rivera said, and the car pulled away.

Sitting down the street in the Nissan, the silent man had to make a quick decision. He'd watched Rivera kill that guy with the grocery bag, so it certainly seemed that Rivera was looking for the money—looking urgently.

The man thought the money was probably in that blue bag the short guy had carried—what was his name? Chavez?—but he didn't know for certain. Maybe the money was in the house. It could even be somewhere else, but he didn't think so. Rivera's woman—that Ana Bolaño, beautiful but with a steel edge to her—wouldn't let that money out of her sight if she could help it.

So the smart play was to follow her—and Rivera. He could always come back to this house if there was a reason to do so.

The man started the car and drove off after the Mercedes, which was just barely visible a few blocks down the street.

CHAPTER SEVENTEEN

The Mercedes wound through San Juan's narrow streets to a highway and then rolled along with the traffic for a while, almost everyone going as fast as possible and cutting in and out of the lanes as though a great prize awaited the driver who arrived first. Mindful of what they had in the trunk, Chavez drove like a tourist from the mainland—slowly, staying in the right-hand lane. Rivera started to tell him to speed up, then remembered the body. He also remembered he'd left men at the airport, and he made a quick call to say they could leave.

The day had been bright, with only a few fat, white clouds drifting above the emerald island and sapphire sea. But the sky had gone gray while they were in the house, and now it was growing darker, the wind rising and sending scraps of paper scudding down both sides of the road.

As they drove, big raindrops began spattering the windshield. Chavez turned on the wipers. Soon the rain was so heavy he slowed down even more. The water beating on the roof sounded as though a giant were pouring ball bearings over the car, and the cool, wet scent of the rain came in through the vents.

After only a few minutes of tropical downpour the rain stopped and the sun came out again. An enormous rainbow arched the city, and the cars and pavement steamed. A quarter-hour later there was little sign of the rain.

When they got close to the ocean, they left the highway and went down more narrow, winding streets until they came to a marina entrance. Recognizing the car and its driver, the bored guard waved them through.

They parked near a big power boat, a gleaming stack of fiberglass, chromium, and teak with *El Rey del Sol* and "San Juan, P.R." painted on the stern. Rivera kept the 61-foot cruiser to use on his frequent visits to the city. He and his men—and, of course, their women—could stay on the boat, where they could party as long and loudly as they liked, were not under hotel surveillance, and, if necessary, could make a quick getaway by water.

His tax advisor, a clever man sensitive to the special needs of a client such as Rivera, had figured out a way to write off the entire cost of the boat as a business expense. Rivera was careful about his taxes—he had watched Robert De Niro as Al Capone in *The Untouchables* too many times not to be.

Rivera led Ana up the gangway, the three men following in single file, Morgan in the middle. If Rivera had glanced back at the group, he might have noticed the gray Nissan parking next to a nearby boat. He might have even realized he'd seen that car earlier in the day. But he didn't glance back.

He unlocked the main hatch and waved Ana in ahead of him. She stepped down into the salon, a wood-paneled compartment laid out and decorated like a sea-going living room. Rivera followed her. The air-conditioning was on, and Ana felt almost chilly in her light clothing.

"Sit down, Ana. You're probably tired after your . . . adventures of the last two days."

Ana sat in a low chair across the compartment and pulled the skirt down to cover her thighs. She saw how Rivera looked at her in the thin camisole, and she crossed her arms across her chest.

Rivera smiled without warmth. "I like modesty in a woman as long as it's not overdone. Later you and I will have time to explore that. Yes, that and many other things. Lots of time."

Now she did feel cold. She forced herself to keep from shivering.

Garcia pushed Morgan through the hatch, making him stumble and almost fall down the steps. But Morgan managed to regain his balance and stand up straight as Garcia and Chavez came into the salon and Chavez locked the hatch.

"Search him," Rivera said.

Garcia patted Morgan down, finding nothing but his phone. "Just this, chief."

Rivera stepped over to take the phone, which he laid on the navigation table. Morgan was an inch or so taller than Rivera, and he stared down at the gangster. He wanted Rivera to know that although he might be a prisoner, he wasn't beaten—not yet.

Rivera liked the way Morgan looked at him. He was going to hurt Morgan anyway, but the man's disrespectful gaze would make it easier. And more agonizing for him, Rivera thought.

"Hold him," Rivera said. "Let's see if he's as tough as he looks."

Garcia and Chavez seized Morgan by his arms. Rivera stripped off his shirt, staring at Ana the whole time. He tossed it to her, saying, "You probably won't enjoy what's about to happen, but some things can't be helped."

Then he stood squarely in front of Morgan, the muscles in his lithe frame standing out like whipcord. He flexed his fingers a few times before making them into fists, and Morgan knew what was coming.

Rivera imagined himself back in the Santo Domingo slum he'd managed to escape but only after fighting—and beating—every boy who'd had the balls to challenge him. He crouched and shot his right fist once, twice into Morgan's hard abdomen. He heard Ana gasp behind him.

Morgan fought the urge to double over even though he couldn't have with Rivera's men holding him upright. He was sucking some air back into his lungs when Rivera starting hooking in from right and left to batter his kidneys.

"How does that feel, asshole?" Rivera asked between punches, his breath coming faster now as he warmed up and got into the rhythm.

It hurt like hell, but Morgan wasn't going to give Rivera the satisfaction of telling him so. Morgan had been beaten by professionals in SERE training—Survival, Evasion, Resistance, and Escape—and knew that soon he'd be numb and the blows wouldn't hurt as much. To distract himself, he thought about what he was going to do to Rivera if he got the chance. The things he had in mind would hurt a lot more than this.

When Morgan said nothing, Rivera wasn't surprised. He'd already learned that the big man kept silent unless he had something to say and that when he did speak, he sounded as though he meant what he said. Too bad he was on the other side in this thing. Rivera might have been able to use him. This Morgan would scare the hell out of anybody Rivera sent him to scare.

Hitting the man in the body and visibly making him hurt was fine, but Rivera wanted to see Morgan's blood. After all, the Americano had been helping Ana steal the money, which was the same thing as stealing it himself. And maybe he'd been trying to steal Ana too, even though he was so very ugly. He looked as if he'd already burned in the hell to which Rivera planned to send him.

Rivera used uppercuts on Morgan's face, hitting him hard enough to draw blood but not so hard as to break his own fingers or wrists. As he punched he made sure to dig in with the ring on each hand.

Hitting Morgan's jaw was like pounding stone, and for a moment he wished he'd wrapped his hands. But then he thought that would've taken too long and perhaps made him look weak. He switched back to body blows, feeling his fists sink deeper now that Morgan didn't have the strength to keep his muscles tight.

Morgan's face was bleeding, and there were smears of blood on his polo shirt where Rivera had punched him after hitting him in the face. His face was bruised too, and Rivera knew the bruises would be worse under the shirt. Despite the air-conditioning, Rivera was sweating now, and it felt good, like being back in the gym.

Rivera thought back to the boxing lessons he'd started taking when he was eighteen and beginning to make real money, the other hustlers blowing all their cash on girls and liquor. Rivera had wanted to be sure he could win any fistfight. He hadn't had to get into many since then, not after word of his skill with a knife spread around, but he'd been in a few and had won them all.

A big reason was that he'd remembered the lessons his coach had taught him. Pepe, that brown, wizened man who'd been the Republic's bantamweight champion almost thirty years before. Teaching him how to move, how to hit with power instead of just punching, and, most important, how to take a punch. Pepe, who'd seen—and felt—so much pain that nothing could frighten him, telling Rivera he was a good pupil. Laughing as he said that if Rivera hadn't become a gangster, he might have had a career as a boxer.

Rivera wasn't sure how to take that and thought of killing Pepe for it—at the right time and place, of course. But then he saw the little man eyeing him, sizing him up, and he decided to laugh too.

Pepe nodded. "That's right. Don't take offense where none is given. Don't fight unless you have to, but then fight to win. Even to the death, if necessary."

With that admonition echoing in his head, Rivera gave Morgan another driving blow to the midsection, hitting as hard as he could. Morgan sagged between Garcia and Chavez, head lolling. Rivera finished the job with a brutal right-left combination to the head that knocked Morgan unconscious.

Impressed with how Morgan had taken the beating, Garcia and Chavez lowered him gently to the floor. Garcia was careful to put Morgan on his back so he wouldn't bleed on the carpet.

Rivera unclenched his fists and looked at his bloody hands. "Get me a towel."

While he waited for Chavez to bring him one, he glanced at Ana. She was flushed with rage, leaning forward, hands clenched white on the arms of the chair.

"So, you feel sorry for this—this pirate? Is that it?" Rivera asked. "Were you planning to run away with him?"

Ana gave him a contemptuous look. "No, not with him. I was only planning to run away from you."

Rivera took the two steps to her chair and backhanded her as hard as he could. She partially blocked it, but still he almost knocked her out of the chair and sent a flash of hot, blinding light through her skull. The blow left some of Morgan's blood on her hand and cheek.

The sight enraged him, and he hit her again, several times, leaving more blood on her and drawing some of her own. He stopped when he heard someone loudly clear his throat, and he turned to see Garcia and Chavez looking at him.

Chavez held out a towel. "Here you go, chief."

Rivera wondered if he'd heard something different in the way Chavez said "jefe," but he wasn't sure and decided not to press it.

He mopped the sweat from his chest and arms and the blood off his hands. He wadded up the towel and threw it at Ana. "Clean yourself up."

Ana gave him that look again. She waited a few seconds before picking up the towel and slowly wiping the blood from her hand and face.

Rivera turned to his men. "Put him in the empty room." As they picked up Morgan's inert body, Rivera looked at Ana. "You go with him—you seem to enjoy his company. Clean him up if you like. Not that it will do him any good once we're at sea."

Rivera's blows had made her face hot, but now Ana felt the chill again. She knew at least part of what he planned to do once the boat was out of sight of land.

She followed Garcia and Chavez to a small stateroom, where they slid Morgan onto the berth. "May I have some water, please?" she asked Garcia. "Or is that too much to ask now?"

Chavez looked at Garcia, who thought for a moment before saying, "Sure, we'll get you some." He nodded at Chavez, who left the compartment.

Garcia started to speak, then changed his mind. He'd always liked Ana and didn't think Rivera should've started mistreating her. The chief's growing lack of self-control set a bad example for the men, making it harder for Garcia to keep them in line. He didn't blame Ana for running away, but taking the money was another thing. She'd crossed the line there and would just have to face whatever Rivera decided to do about it.

So Garcia and Ana stood in uncomfortable silence for the few seconds it took Chavez to bring a bottle of water from the galley. Then the two men left, and Ana heard them lock the door. She remembered that all three staterooms had originally locked from the inside but that Rivera, always looking for any extra advantage, had modified the two smaller ones to lock only from the outside.

They found Rivera sitting in the salon chair Ana had vacated. He'd put on his shirt and poured a drink. "That was warm work," he said, wiping his brow. He waved toward the bar. "Help yourselves."

Neither of his men said anything. They went to the bar and fixed their drinks.

"We'll leave tonight," Rivera said. "We'll bring that body in the trunk with us and feed it and Morgan to the sharks."

Garcia sipped thoughtfully. "Don't you think we ought to leave now? I mean, just get the body and go? The cops may be looking for us."

"No, there's no hurry. Morgan's friend Herrera is dead, Bolaño is dead, and Morgan is going to be dead. With two of the bodies gone, no one will connect the murders to us."

"But what if someone finds Bolaño's body? We don't know who else might go to that house."

"I told you: if the police figure out who he is, they'll just think it was some business between the Cubans and the Americanos. No one saw us enter or leave, and there's no way to trace Bolaño to us."

Garcia thought some more. "Maybe his Cuban friends knew where he was, who he was looking for."

"I doubt it. Bolaño kept quiet about his niece and me. He didn't like to share credit, so he didn't want anyone to know I was helping him."

Garcia took another sip. "Well, I don't like it."

That was too much of a challenge. Rivera put down his glass and took a long look at his deputy, so long that first Chavez, then Garcia, looked away. "You don't have to like it. You just have to follow orders. I have business in San Juan this evening, and we're not leaving until I'm finished. Understand?"

Garcia had seen, several times, how easily Rivera could kill a man, even one of his own men. He forced himself to look Rivera in the eye again. "Yes, chief, I understand."

"Good. I'm going to clean up. While I'm doing that, bring Herrera's body on board. Wipe down the inside of the trunk if you need to. I'll take the other car." He drained his glass and stood. "Then have some food delivered for yourselves but don't give any to Morgan or Ana. There's no need for him to eat, and I want to make her a bit more . . . cooperative."

He waited. Garcia said, "Got it. But if we're not going to leave until tonight, shouldn't we wait until it's dark before getting that body?"

Rivera smiled. "Good point. That's why you're El Segundo. Sure, have a couple of drinks and do the job later." He left for the main stateroom, which had its own head.

Garcia waited until he heard the door close, then said quietly, "I have a bad feeling about this. Killing two men we didn't have to, one of them a Cuban spy, bringing Morgan along." He looked at Chavez. "I know he wanted the money back and Ana too, but this is getting out of hand."

"Sure," Chavez said in an equally low voice. "But what the fuck can we do about it? He's the boss." He rattled the ice in his glass and headed back to the bar.

Garcia sipped thoughtfully again. "Yes, he is. At least for now."

CHAPTER EIGHTEEN

After she heard the front door slam shut, Karen forced herself to wait a minute or two before leaving her hiding place near the patio. When she came back inside, she could smell the gun smoke all the way out in the kitchen.

In the living room she found the man Ana had called "Tío Paco" slumped in his chair, a large bloodstain on the front of his shirt. Reaching back to her Girl Scout training, Karen put two fingers against his neck. His skin was cool but not cold, and she could feel his pulse.

She'd been alarmed when he'd come in carrying a gun, but Ana's explanation had driven away most of her fear. Ana had said he was her uncle and would help her get away from Rivera. The man had smiled at Karen and put away his gun, so things seemed all right.

Still, the fear hadn't left her entirely. She didn't like someone bringing a gun into her house. She thought Morgan probably had one and maybe Ana did too, but at least neither had pointed a gun at her the way this man had.

And she'd been worried about Luis. Where was he? He shouldn't have been gone so long. When, out in the kitchen, she'd heard someone come in, Karen had thought it was Luis, and she'd leaned her head into the doorway to see.

Instead it was those three men, all armed. Knowing she couldn't do anything to help Morgan and Ana, not against three armed men, she'd tiptoed across the kitchen, eased the back door open, and hidden in the shrubbery. If she hadn't, the three men probably would've shot her just like they shot Ana's uncle. And she was terrified that they might've done something to Luis.

But she couldn't think about that right now. She wouldn't let herself. She had to try to save this man's life if she could.

At her touch the man opened his eyes. It took him a few seconds to focus, but then she could see he recognized her.

"What—what happened?" he asked in a strained voice. He spoke in English with a slight accent.

Karen tried to reply in Spanish but the right words wouldn't come, so she switched to English. "Some men came in with guns. I don't know who they were. I was in the kitchen and just caught a glimpse of them. They shot you, and I thought they would search the house, so I hid outside in the bushes."

"That was smart." He took a deep breath, winced. "If they had found you, they would have killed you."

"You're badly hurt. I'll call 911."

"No!" He put a hand on her arm. "No, please do not do that. I will be okay—for a while—if I can stop the bleeding."

For a moment she thought of overruling him, but his commanding tone stopped her. "All right, I'll try to do that. But first you need to lie down."

She took a towel from the linen closet and spread it over the cushions. Then she helped him get out of the chair and turn to stretch out on the sofa. Remembering something about avoiding shock, she pulled his feet up onto the armrest.

"I'll be right back."

From her hairdresser's kit she pulled scissors and a clean pair of the rubber gloves she used when dyeing hair. Then she took disinfectant, gauze, and tape from the medicine cabinet.

She cut off his shirt as gently as she could, but still he groaned. The bullet had gone in about two inches above his left nipple. The wound was small and dark and had almost stopped bleeding.

A little lower and he'd be dead, Karen thought. It might not be as bad as it looked from all the blood. She pushed her hand under his back but didn't feel an exit wound, and when she pulled her hand back, there was no blood on the glove.

"It did not go through, did it?" he asked.

"No, but I don't know how to get it out. I'd be afraid—"

"Do not worry. The bullet did not hit bone—at least I do not think it did—so we can leave it in for now. The main thing is to bandage the wound."

"All right, I can do that."

She was able to clean the blood off his chest, disinfect the wound, and bandage it reasonably well. Bolaño kept her from using as much tape as she thought necessary.

"I need to be able to move that arm."

She stared at him. "Why? Aren't you going to the hospital, get the bullet taken out?"

"No, not right away."

"You're in no condition to do anything but see a doctor."

He smiled, making the lines around his eyes crinkle. He looked as though he'd spent a lot of time outdoors under a hot sun. "Thank you for your concern, and thanks, too, for the first aid. But I know what I need to do."

He stood, and she could tell the movement hurt him. She put out her arm to steady him, but he gently pushed it away.

"I will be fine, really. I am stronger than I look. But I would be grateful if you could lend me a shirt." Even though he was standing there half-naked with a big bandage on his chest, his manner was genteel.

"I'll get one of Luis's." Saying the name of her lover, who was now so long overdue she knew something must've happened to him, made her eyes well, and she hurried from the room.

When she came back the stranger was sitting on the sofa and holding his phone. She handed him one of Luis's guayaberas. He had the look of a man who'd wear one, and the loose, short-sleeve shirt would be fairly easy to put on over the bandage.

He smiled again. "Thank you, but this shirt is much too nice. I am likely to get some blood on it. A T-shirt will do just as well."

"No, please take it. You can't pull a shirt over your head right now—or at least you shouldn't."

He paused. "That is true. All right, but you must allow me to replace it with a new one."

"Don't worry about it. Luis has several of them."

"Luis is your man?"

"Yes. He went out for a little while but hasn't come back. I think those men . . . found him."

Bolaño frowned. "Perhaps not. And he may be all right even if they did pick him up."

Karen wasn't sure whether to believe him, but she certainly wanted to. "Do you really think so?"

In her eyes Bolaño saw how much she loved this Luis and how concerned she was for him. "Yes," he said, telling himself the lie was justified. Karen rewarded his reassurance with an attempt at a smile and a light touch on his good arm.

He stood and slowly and gingerly put on the shirt, Karen helping him. Sweat beaded on his forehead.

"Do you have anything to drink—any rum, perhaps?"

As she left the room again he sat and thumbed the phone, calling Havana. Bolaño cut short the usual pleasantries and told his colleague to determine the location of Rivera's boat.

"A power boat named *El Rey del Sol*. He usually keeps it in San Juan. And no, I don't know the registration number."

"Is everything okay?" his coworker asked.

Bolaño gritted his teeth at a twinge that sawed through his chest. "No, everything is most definitely not okay."

"Do you need help?"

"I just need for you to find that boat. I can handle things after that."

"All right, I'll call you back in a few minutes."

Karen returned with a short glass of rum. She'd fixed it the Caribbean way: a wedge of lemon and no ice.

Gratefully, Bolaño took a long sip. "Ah, that tastes good. Thank you, my dear." He tried to remember how she'd introduced herself after Ana had explained who he was. "Your name is Karen, yes?"

"That's right. Karen Ginsberg. I'm sorry my Spanish is so poor."

"No need to be—I am sure it is better than my English." It wasn't, but he wanted to put her at ease. Especially considering the favors he had to ask. He took another long drink and felt the warmth start to spread.

She sat next to him and held out her hand. "I thought you might want these."

He glanced down and saw four plain, white capsules. Although he badly wanted some pills, his training made him hesitate. "What are they?"

Karen seemed surprised. "Pain reliever, of course. They'll also help your fever."

Bolaño gazed at her for a moment, then reached for the capsules. He looked them over, trying to be subtle about it, before swallowing all four with the last of the rum.

"Thank you. I appreciate your kindness."

"It's nothing." She took his glass. "I'll get you some more."

"Only a little, please. I need to be clear-headed for what I have to do."

She stood and looked at him. "What's that?"

"Go after them, of course." He spoke as though telling her the time.

Her eyes widened. "In your condition? And against three of them? That's crazy. Shouldn't you call the police?"

"No. With Rivera's political connections they might not even arrest him. And with his money for lawyers he could beat any charge." He made a slight dismissive gesture. "I know how your justice system works."

"But what can you do?"

"Get my niece away from them, for one thing. Morgan too, if I am lucky."

As he mentioned Morgan, he wondered whether Ana might've told the man about his connection with DGI. If she had, he'd have to kill Morgan to be assured of remaining covert when he traveled in the United States, even though he always used a different name when doing so. He hoped things wouldn't come to that, but . . . .

Karen said nothing, and he could tell she was trying to decide whether he was brave or crazy. He needed her help, so he played the ace.

"And perhaps I can find Luis." Or at least his body, he thought.

Her face brightened. "Do you really think so?"

"I can try."

"Oh, that would be wonderful! Thank you!" She clasped both hands around the glass, which seemed to make her remember it. "I'm sorry— I'll get your drink."

As she left the room his phone chirped.

"Yes?"

"I think we found that boat."

"Aren't you sure?"

"Pretty sure. Our man in San Juan phoned the most likely marinas. At the third one a woman said, yes, the boat is here, then a man came on the line and said the boat wasn't there and asked who wanted to know about it."

"That might be the place—it's certainly worth checking out. What's the address and phone number? And what's it near on the waterfront?"

Bolaño memorized the information as his colleague gave it to him. "Thanks. I'll let you know if I need anything else."

He was sitting there thinking, the phone in his hand, when Karen returned. "Thank you," he said, taking the glass with its two fingers of rum. "I think I have located Rivera—at least where he is staying. Ana and Morgan are probably there."

"And Luis?"

"Maybe." He shifted uncomfortably.

"How did you find him?"

"A . . . friend asked around, then called me with the information."

Her eyes narrowed. "You're a pretty mysterious man, Mr. Bolaño. What do you do when you're not being Ana's uncle?"

He smiled. "I do not mean to be mysterious, my dear. I am a Cuban businessman. I have dealings with Rivera from time to time, which is how he met Ana."

"If you're Cuban, how did you get into Puerto Rico? Isn't it hard for Cubans to travel to U.S. territory?"

"Yes it is—with a Cuban passport. Let us say I am using a passport that is something like the driver's license Morgan told me Luis was getting for Ana."

"*Was* getting?"

"I am sorry—I misspoke. I meant 'left here to get.'" He sipped the rum, giving her a moment to calm down. "And I need your help to find him."

"My help? How?"

"Is there a gun in the house? They took mine."

"See, this is why you should call the police. More guns won't help anything."

He set the glass down sharply on the coffee table. "One more might help Luis. And Ana and Morgan—if it is in my hand. I know where the boat is and time is running out."

Karen didn't speak for several seconds. Then she said, slowly and quietly, "All right. I'm not sure what kind of businessman you are—maybe the same kind Rivera is. But you obviously love your niece and want to help her. Maybe you can help Luis and Morgan too. You seem like a good person, so I'm going to trust you."

She left the room again, and he finished the rum while he waited. She was back soon, carrying a pistol in a concealable belt holster.

"Here. It's Luis's gun for his job at the casino. Be careful—it's loaded and there's no safety."

An expert with firearms and many other lethal tools of his trade, he wanted, especially because of how he ached, to make a sharp retort to her unnecessary caution. But he resisted the temptation and merely smiled at her as he took the pistol. It was a Heckler & Koch USP, a semiautomatic commonly used by security personnel. He extracted the 9mm magazine and checked it—for some reason there were only seven cartridges and none in the chamber, but maybe that would be enough. Then he looked over the rest of the weapon, pleased to see that the H&K was clean and lightly oiled.

He handed the holster back to her, then balanced the pistol in his hand, getting used to its weight and feel. "Thank you. I hope I will not need to use the gun, but I am glad to have it just in case."

"I hope you don't have to use it either."

Bolaño stood, wincing again but pleased he'd gotten up without Karen's help. He stuck the pistol in his waistband and draped the shirt over it.

"I regret that I must ask you for one more thing."

She gave him a skeptical look. "You want some money, right?"

"No, not money. I have enough of that. Do you have a car?"

"Yes. You want me to drive you somewhere?"

"It might not be safe for you to come along. But I do need to borrow your car."

She sighed. "Okay. I guess if I can give you Luis's gun, I can let you use our car. But you're in no shape to drive. Please let me do it."

"I appreciate your concern. I think your Luis is a lucky man. And I know he would want you to stay here where it is safe."

"Safe? You were shot, and they took Ana and Morgan away."

"It is safe now. They have what they want."

She looked into his eyes a moment, then looked away. "Luis isn't—he isn't coming back, is he?" Her voice sounded distant, hollow. "Rivera has killed him . . . or will kill him."

Bolaño put his hand on her shoulder. "We do not know that. He may be okay. If he is, I will bring him back to you."

She put her hand on his and squeezed it. "Thank you. Please do whatever you can."

She took a set of keys from a hook by the front door and worked one key off the ring. "Here. I'll walk you to the car."

"No," he said, taking the key. "Rivera may have someone watching the house. Just tell me where the car is."

"It's the red Honda down the street, to the right as you walk out. There's an 'I Love New York' sticker on the rear bumper and a Fort Buchanan base sticker on the front windshield."

When she mentioned the Army post in San Juan, Bolaño smiled at the thought of a Cuban spy driving around in a car with a U.S. military decal. "I will find it. Thank you again. You have been very kind."

She tried to smile as well but couldn't quite do it. He gave her a quick hug with his good arm and kissed her lightly on the cheek. She hugged him and stepped back, brushing at her eyes.

"Good luck," she said.

He looked at her for a moment, then nodded. He eased the door open and glanced up and down the street and sidewalk. He didn't see anyone, so he stepped outside.

He spotted the car and walked quickly to it, using his peripheral vision to see if anyone was coming toward him. No one was, and in a few seconds he was headed for the marina.

CHAPTER NINETEEN

As Ana gently wiped the blood off his face, Morgan regained consciousness. His eyelids fluttered for a moment. Then he blinked hard a few times and looked at her.

He opened his mouth slightly but made no sound. She saw his tongue moving over his teeth, the white stained with red. He motioned for the towel, and she held a corner to his mouth.

He raised himself on an elbow and spat blood onto the towel. She used a clean part to wipe his lips.

He lay back in the berth. "Thanks," he said. His voice was hoarse from Rivera's blows to his throat. "Who—who won the fight?"

She smiled. "The judges did not all agree," she said, keeping her own voice low. "I voted for you."

He did his best to smile back, but it was more like a grimace. "Split decision, huh? Good girl. Is there any water?"

She held up the bottle, and he raised himself again. He drank, spilling some onto the berth. He waited a moment, then drank more. This time a few drops dribbled down his chin, and she wiped them off.

"Thanks again." His voice was clearer now. "I didn't mean for you to have to nurse me."

She held the bottle in both hands. "I do not mind. I am just sorry for what he did to you."

"So am I. But I'll pay him back if I get a chance."

She didn't know whether he'd said that to keep her spirits up, but she knew there was little chance of either of them getting back at Rivera. She looked at him.

"Take off your shirt, and I will wipe away the rest of the blood."

"I'm not sure I can get it off."

"Here, I will help you."

She undid the one closed button and pulled the shirt over his head as gently as she could. Still, he moaned softly. She gasped as she looked at the purple bruises on his chest and abdomen. "¡Que barbaridad!"

"A little black and blue, huh? You probably should've voted the other way."

"No," she said, wetting the towel. "I think what Jaime did was much harder for you to take than for him to do."

"Well, I would've been happy to trade places with him."

She began wiping off the blood. She focused on the task, careful to hurt him as little as possible. After a minute she looked up and saw him watching her.

"You are kind," he said, and she heard more than simple politeness in his tone.

"It is nothing." She switched to one of the last clean parts of the towel. "Nothing compared to what you have done for me."

"And for the money—don't forget the money."

She looked at him and was pleased to see that his crooked grin was back. "Oh, yes, I know how much the money means to you."

"Does it mean less to you now?"

She thought about that as she finished working. Now that the blood was gone, she could see his scars. The ones on his chest were not as bad as those on his leg, but they were bad enough. She didn't find them repellent, but she was sorry he'd had to suffer the pain that had come with them.

"Perhaps. If you are asking me would I trade the money for my life, of course I would."

"Too bad Rivera has us *and* the money."

"Yes." She folded the towel to cover most of the blood and tossed it on the deck. "Do you feel a little better now?"

"Much better, thanks. Is there any more water?"

She handed him the bottle and perched on the edge of the berth as he drank, not spilling any this time. "What do you think he will do to us?"

"As Stonewall Jackson said, 'Never take counsel of your fears.'"

She looked puzzled. "A stone wall said what?"

He touched her hair. "A Civil War general said don't think about things like what the ememy might do to us—let's think about what we're going to do to him. He's got to let us out of here eventually, no matter what his plans for us are. When he does, I'll try to create a distraction so you can dive over the side and swim away."

"What if we are far out at sea?"

"Then take a life preserver. You can swim a long way with one, several miles. But maybe he'll get careless—he's so sure of himself—and then I can grab his gun."

"Maybe," she said without conviction.

"Or get a gun from one of his men. I doubt the guy built like a fireplug moves very fast."

"That's Chavez. But if you try, they might shoot you."

He wanted to tell her that if he didn't try, Rivera or his men would kill him and probably her too, but he didn't want her more scared than she already was. "Okay, I won't try anything unless I think I can do it."

"I am not sure I believe you." She paused. "Listen, I do not want you to—oh, I do not know how to say it. Like when they kill a sheep in the Bible?"

"Uh, I think you mean 'sacrifice'."

"Yes, I do not want you to sacrifice yourself for me."

"Oh, so now I'm a sheep, am I?"

She leaned toward him. "No, you are more like a bull that is mad at the bullfighter."

He touched her hair again. "That sounds better."

She put her hand on his arm and looked at him, holding his gaze. He hesitated but only for a moment before pulling her down to him.

She came willingly, and her lips were full and soft and warm on his. She lingered there a few seconds, then leaned back to look at him again.

"That was nice," she said.

"I think so."

"I have been wondering if you would ever try to kiss me."

"You have? For how long?"

"For a while—since the boat, when Chavez pointed the rifle at you, and you were so brave."

"Or stupid." He softened it with a smile.

"No, do not make a joke of it. I am glad you are so brave. It helps me to be brave too. And I think—" She looked away.

He raised himself, put his hand beneath her chin, and gently turned her face back toward his. "What?"

"I think both of us will need to be brave now."

"Hey, Ana, don't give up. The game isn't over yet—we still have a turn at bat."

"Are you sure?"

"Sure I'm sure. Rivera's too cocky not to lord it over us some more, and that'll give us a chance."

"'Lord it over us'?"

"Remind us he's in charge, the boss. The man with the gun."

"I see. Yes, I think you are right. So perhaps he will make a mistake, no?"

"Perhaps *yes*."

"Good. But now I do not want to think about it anymore."

"That's fine. I think both of us could use some rest."

"You need to sleep. Here, I will help you be more comfortable."

She reached for his belt buckle, but he blocked her hand. "No, Rivera could come for us any time."

"He has gone ashore for the evening. I overheard him talking to Benito—that's Garcia, his number two—as he stepped off the boat. Benito did not sound happy about it."

"I'm sure he's not. The smart thing would be to leave while they can, take this boat to the D.R. or somewhere else the cops won't be looking for them."

"Well, Jaime thinks he is smarter than everyone."

"As I said, all the better for us."

"Yes," she said with an enigmatic smile. "We have some time now—hours, perhaps."

She reached for him and again he stopped her. "No, I can do it."

"Do not be foolish. You are hurt, and I can help you. Lie down."

She said it in a commanding tone, and he found himself obeying. She unbuckled his belt and zipped down his fly. The she removed his boat shoes and eased off his trousers.

She had seen some of his wounded leg before but never so much of it. The burn marks didn't bother her now as much as they had at first. Now they just seemed part of who Hal Morgan was, as much a part of him as his silence and strength, his skill with boats and guns, his gentleness with her. She eyed his briefs but didn't move to take them off.

"Get under the covers," she said, and he complied, moving stiffly but less painfully than earlier.

He closed his eyes even though he didn't feel especially sleepy. Then he heard cloth rustling and opened his eyes. Ana was getting undressed herself, sliding the skirt down over her hips.

"What are you doing?"

She paused, looking at him with a faint smile. "Oh, I think you are smart enough to figure it out."

He was, so he didn't say anything, just watched, as she gracefully slid her feet from the sandals and stepped out of her skirt. Then she crossed her arms to pull the camisole straps off her shoulders.

The camisole slid down, revealing the tops of her breasts. She crossed her arms again and grasped the bottom of the shirt. She saw him looking and paused, holding the pose for a moment. Then she pulled the camisole over her head in one smooth motion.

Naked except for the string bikini panties she'd borrowed from Karen, she put her hands on her hips and looked at him. "Do you like this?"

He shifted uncomfortably. "You know I do—very much. But this isn't the right time."

"Oh?" She came over to him. "Is now not the right time?" She leaned down to kiss him. It lasted a while, and he put his arms around her.

When their lips parted, he said, "No, it's not the right time. We need to think about how to get out of here. Besides, even if Rivera is gone, those other two could walk in any minute."

She stood. "We can think better once we have rested. And I do not care what they might see or what they might think. We may be dead soon, and I am past caring about little things like that."

She slid her thumbs beneath the strings of the panties. She smiled again, a dreamy, far-away smile, and he wondered what she was thinking. Perhaps she was remembering how making love felt when she was young and innocent. Before she learned how cruel the world can be.

She slid the panties down and stepped out of them. She stood before him, beautifully nude, enjoying the hungry way he looked at her.

Despite his desire, he forced himself to say, "I appreciate the offer, but that beating took a lot out of me. I tried not to let on, but it did. I'm not sure I can . . . ."

"It will not matter. I just want to be close to you. And if I am on top, you will not have to move much."

She leaned down again as though to kiss him, but he turned his face away. She frowned. "What is wrong? Do you not want me?"

He didn't speak for a few seconds. Then he said in a husky voice, "Yes, of course, I want you. Any man would. You're one of the most beautiful and desirable women I've ever known."

"What is it then?"

He didn't reply, and she tried to think of what might be wrong. Then it came to her.

"Is it—your wounds—you cannot . . . ." She spoke as gently as possible. "You cannot make love?"

"No, thank God, the war didn't take that away from me. A lot of things, but not that."

"Then what? It might be our only chance."

He turned back to look at her. "I know. It's because . . . ." He swallowed hard and forced himself to continue. "It's because it's been a long time since I was with a woman I cared about."

She reached out to stroke the side of his face, the left side.

"The others . . . well, that was just sex. And I hated the way they wouldn't look at me, wouldn't touch . . . ."

"The burned places."

"Yes, that's right."

"I do not mind about that."

"I know. But it's hard for me to believe when you're so beautiful and I—oh, hell, I know how I look."

She put a finger on his lips. "Hush. First you never talk, and now you say such foolish things. Move over."

He pushed himself closer to the bulkhead and made room for her on the narrow bunk. She crawled underneath the covers and lay on her side, putting an arm on his chest and a leg over his legs.

He could feel her naked body along almost the whole length of his. He could feel the warmth of her skin and the rise and fall of her breathing. But he couldn't feel her heartbeat—his own was too strong and fast.

He put an arm around her and drew her closer to him. She raised her head and smiled before kissing him again, and this time the kiss lasted even longer than before.

While they were kissing she stroked his arm and chest, then moved her hand slowly down his flat stomach to the barrier of his briefs. She playfully pulled at the waistband and then eased her hand inside.

She broke off the kiss and said, "Oh!" She stroked him once, twice, and gave him another smile. "No, I do not think you have any problem making love."

□ □ □

Afterward they pulled just the sheet back over their sweating bodies and lay there, feeling the boat rock slowly under them.

"The tide must be coming in," he said, stroking her hair.

"Is that what is making the boat move?" She chuckled. "I thought we did that."

"I think we did our part—or at least you did. You were right about being on top. The whole thing was . . . wonderful."

"Yes? You think so?"

He could hear the pleasure in her voice. "Yes, I think so."

"Good. I enjoyed it as well. I see that you know about things other than guns and boats."

"Thanks, but you're the skillful one. I just tried to keep up."

She raised herself to look at him. "But you do not think I am too skillful?"

"What do you mean?"

"You do not think I have had . . . too much practice?"

He laughed. "Of course not. Besides, your past is your past. All I care about is the future."

"If we have one."

"Don't talk that way. We'll get out of this somehow."

"You don't know Jaime. But I will try to be as brave as you."

"And I'll try to be as brave as you think I am."

She answered him with a kiss and lay back beside him. Neither of them spoke for two or three minutes, and then she said, "You have never told me anything about your family."

"Well, I'm not married, if that's what you mean."

"I thought you were not—a woman can usually tell—and I asked Karen to be sure. But I mean your parents, your brothers and sisters."

"Why do you want to know?"

"Because I want to know everything about you. Or everything you will tell me."

He stroked her hair again. "All right. My mother died eight years ago. Hit by a drunk as she was driving home late from work one night. Killed both of them instantly and crippled the woman riding in his car. A stupid, senseless thing."

He was silent a moment before continuing. "My father left us when I was little. I don't know if he's alive or dead, and at this point I don't care."

"No brothers or sisters?"

"No, just me."

"Ah, then we are alike. I have no one except Tío Paco." She paused. "I mean, I had no one but him."

"We don't know—he may still be alive."

"Do you really think so?"

"Well, they only shot him once, and that was in the chest. It's hard to kill a person with just one shot there unless you hit the heart."

"But could he not bleed to death?"

"Karen was there somewhere, hiding. She's a good person. She wouldn't let your uncle die if she could help it. She probably called an ambulance."

"Oh, I hope so. But your friend Luis . . . ?"

"Rivera said they killed him. If that's true—and if I get a chance— I'll make Rivera pay for it."

CHAPTER TWENTY

Bolaño took back streets to the marina. He didn't have a map, but he'd been to San Juan several times, and his colleague had given him pretty good directions. He got turned around twice but eventually found the place.

On the way he put his hand underneath his shirt and touched the bandage. His fingertips came out pink, so he knew he was still bleeding but not too badly.

His story about having to deliver a part for Rivera's boat didn't seem to convince the gate guard, but his $100 bill did and the man waved him through. Bolaño drove slowly past the pier where *El Rey del Sol* was berthed.

Garcia and Chavez were sitting on the aft deck, an awning shading them from the late-afternoon sun. Bolaño saw one of the men glance at the car as he went by, but he didn't seem to attract much attention.

He went five boats down and parked. He hadn't been in much pain driving, but climbing out of the car brought it all back to him. He touched the bandage again, and this time his fingers came out more red than pink. Soon the blood would soak through the white guayabera.

Bolaño walked back up the dock, staying close to the water and keeping as much cover as he could between himself and Rivera's boat. Halfway back he saw a small wooden workboat bobbing at the end of a finger pier between two of the huge yachts.

He went down to the pier and pulled the boat to him by her frayed bow line. A canvas tool bag sat in the middle of the boat, surrounded by paint cans and brushes. A paint-stained T-shirt was wadded up on top of a roller tray.

Grimacing, he eased himself down into the little boat. He took off his shirt, the movement stabbing knives into his shoulder.

He checked the bandage. It had a red spot as large as a rose. And he knew that what he was about to do would only make the bleeding faster.

He pulled on the T-shirt, gasping this time. He smeared dirt and grease from a rag onto his face and hands. He took most of the tools out of the canvas bag and flopped the bag onto the pier. Then he climbed up after it.

The agony of the climb made his eyes water, and he lay there for a few minutes until some of the pain went away. Then he picked up the tool bag and shuffled down the dock toward Rivera's boat.

Bolaño didn't have to put on an act to look like an old man who worked at the marina—he *felt* old. Old and tired. He knew he'd be more tired later and for a moment wondered if he'd live to get any older. But then he thought of his niece and pushed the other ideas out of his mind.

He felt guilty that Ana was in this grim situation. He'd never wanted her to fall in love with Rivera, never imagined she would. And he'd certainly never thought Rivera would mistreat her—he knew Rivera was a gangster, but he'd mistakenly assumed Rivera would respect Ana if only because she was his niece.

In fact, if he'd thought that Ana's being with Rivera might lead to this day, he would have stopped her from going to the Dominican Republic to live with the man. Maybe he should have stopped her anyway.

But maybe there were a lot of things he should have done. Gone with his cousins to Miami, for instance, instead of staying to see Havana, once a scenic, cosmopolitan city, rot in the tropical sun. Become an American instead of spying on foreigners and his fellow Cubans to help the Bearded One preserve "the Revolution." An endless, fruitless revolution he no longer believed in, no matter what Fidel thought about the cause or those who did not embrace it.

Now it was too late. Far too late. His life was what it was, and he felt he had no choice except to play the cards he'd been dealt. He didn't like the hand, but it was all he had.

He remembered an American movie he'd seen when visiting Rivera and Ana in Santo Domingo, a violent Western called *The Wild Bunch*. It had so much shooting that Ana had left the room.

But Rivera had sat spellbound, drinking his scotch and staring at the big TV screen, following every move the outlaws made. Later he'd said that the big shoot-out at the end was almost like watching ballet—those hardened professionals moving gracefully even as they died.

Bolaño hadn't thought so. He'd seen enough death in Africa and Central America to know how horrible it really was. The bare ground soaked with blood, and the dead African or Latino guerillas and Cuban soldiers all reeking from their piss and shit.

No, Bolaño hadn't liked that part of the movie much. What he had liked was when the four men decided to go get their friend, to take him back from the Mexican general holding him prisoner. He was pretty sure the men knew they were all going to die in the attempt.

He had also liked the way they came swinging down the unpaved street of that dusty Mexican town, walking, almost marching, in a line, holding their weapons in the different ways each of them preferred, but all of them looking determined. And deadly.

He knew he didn't look very deadly now, but he wanted to be determined. He was single with few close ties to anyone, and he felt he had little to lose. Just a job, an existence, that he'd been tired of for a long time.

There was only Ana, whom he thought of as his daughter. His, yes, since her father, who had hated the Bearded One's brutal regime and had spoken out against it, died in one of Castro's grim prisons when Ana was only four.

Bolaño, just a young case officer then, had warned his brother-in-law not to be so vocal, but the man wouldn't listen. He continued his anti-Castro activities, which Bolaño thought brave but foolish. Less brave but also less foolish, Bolaño had swallowed his anger and continued to work for the Cuban government.

The guards reported that their prisoner had committed suicide, but Bolaño knew better, even then and certainly now. As a DGI agent he'd seen a few of those "suicides" and heard about many others.

Ana had become his daughter even more after his young sister, devastated by her husband's death, tried to escape to America by risking her life on a leaky boat Bolaño wouldn't have trusted out of the harbor. She'd left him a note saying that if she got to the United States, she would send for Ana.

Bolaño didn't know whether Castro's government would have let Ana go. Probably not. But it didn't matter because he never heard from his sister again. Through his job he was finally able to learn that the U.S. Coast Guard found some scraps of a boat about where hers would have been—or could have been. The rest was silence.

That's why he was doing this. Maybe he hadn't protected Ana enough. No, to be honest, he certainly had not. He'd raised her as well as he was able, relying heavily on a succession of nannies and housekeepers. But as Ana grew into a young woman—and as he became jaded, cynical about the world and its people, even himself—he'd failed to look after her as a father should.

Well, that was all done, all in the past. He would try to make up for it now.

He kept moving down the dock toward Rivera's boat.

□ □ □

Morgan and Ana lay in the bunk. He'd thought the narrow bed was barely big enough for him, so he was surprised at how comfortable it seemed for the two of them.

More comfortable than with Susan in that bigger bed, he thought. He tried to conjure Susan's face, but for some reason her features remained indistinct. After a moment he gave up the effort, and the ghostly image vanished.

"I think it was nicer the second time," Ana said, snuggling into him.

He kissed her temple. The fresh scent of her hair made him think of the sun and the sea. "Just nice?"

She smiled, not so faintly this time. "Okay, great. I am only sorry we may not have another chance to make love."

"Well, maybe we'll be lucky and get out of this yet. Just be ready for anything when the time comes."

"All right, Hal." She chuckled. "'Hal.' Such a silly name, but I like saying it."

He smiled and kissed her again.

She moved her hand down under the covers, reaching for him. "Perhaps we have just enough time to—"

"No." He stopped her hand with his. "I'd love to, but we need to get dressed. Rivera will be back soon, and we've got to be prepared."

The mention of Rivera made her somber. "Regardless of what happens, thank you for what you have already done for me."

"No, thank *you*. It's . . . been a while."

"I was not referring to this. But you do not seem—what is the word?—to have rust."

He grinned. "Rusty. Maybe it's like riding a bicycle. Sort of."

She turned her head to look up at him. "What?"

"Skip it. What I wanted to say was that not many women . . . well, this face . . . ."

"I think you are like a stone carved by the weather."

"So I've gone from fierce to rugged, have I? Okay, I'll take that."

"My thanks are for protecting me from Jaime."

"I haven't done a very good job of it."

"Yes, you have. You stood up to them on the boat, fighting the helicopter and then Jaime and his men." She brushed his arm lightly with her fingertips. "And now I know you did it for me, not for the money."

"Are you still glad you left him?"

"Yes, but I wish I had gotten away. Perhaps if I had not taken the money he would not have tried so hard to find me."

"Perhaps, but I don't think he's doing it for the money either."
She looked away. "No, I do not think it is just the money."

□ □ □

Bolaño stopped at the boat next to *El Rey del Sol* and put down the tool bag. He was careful not to look over at Rivera's boat. Walking up the dock, he had seen that the two men were still sitting on the aft deck, talking and drinking.

He looked down at the boat in front of him as though gauging the work he was supposed to do. The boat was a power cruiser, not quite as big as Rivera's but still large. All the hatches were shut and the curtains closed. He didn't think anyone was aboard.

He walked down the finger pier on the side opposite *El Rey del Sol*. Trying to ignore how much he hurt, he swung the bag onto the boat and then climbed over after it.

He turned his back to Rivera's boat and sat on a cockpit seat. When the wound no longer felt on fire, he dug in the tool bag until he found a scrap of sandpaper. Then he began sanding a discolored patch on the boat's fiberglass.

Using even his good arm and shoulder hurt, and he knew the movement would make him bleed faster. But appearing to work was the only way to avoid suspicion.

He sensed more than heard someone softly walking over to the side of *El Rey del Sol* to peer at him. Bolaño kept sanding, pausing every few seconds to run his hand over the fiberglass.

After a minute he heard the person go back. Then he heard a man say, "Who is it?" The speaker must not have realized how far his voice would carry over boat hulls and calm water in the quiet afternoon.

Another man—presumably whoever had come to look at him—said, "Just some old guy. He's working in the cockpit."

After a pause the first man said, "You're sure?"

"Yeah. You should see him—got enough paint on his shirt to cover a boat."

After another pause the first man said, "Okay. He'll probably knock off soon anyway—it's almost sunset."

"Yeah. Want another drink? It's happy hour, after all."

"Sure. You know Jaime's knocking them back wherever he is."

So Rivera is not here, Bolaño thought. But he left these two men to guard the boat. Ana must be on board . . . and that Morgan.

He heard faint sounds of someone doing something with a bottle and cups and then for a while nothing else but the lapping of water. Then he heard the second man say, more softly, "Should I check on them?"

"No, leave them alone. He's too beat up to go anywhere, and she's too scared. Besides, they're locked in."

"All right. Say, do you think he's too beat up to do something else? I mean, stuck in there with that hot little bitch?"

"Probably. But I don't care if they do get it on—it'll be his last time. Let the poor fucker get laid on his last day on earth. Plus we've got to get that guy out of the trunk."

Bolaño was seething over the man's insult of Ana, but he was too experienced to miss the reference to someone in a trunk. They almost certainly meant Luis. He felt badly for Karen, but he couldn't worry about that right now.

He kept sanding, moving as little as possible so he wouldn't bleed too much. In addition to disguising his identity, the T-shirt, with its multi-hued paint stains, hid the blood that was now seeping through the bandage.

Twilight came and soon faded into night. A few overhead lights winked on in the marina, but the place was much darker now.

Bolaño put the bag on the cockpit floor, being careful not to let the tools clink. Then he lay on the floor on the side next to Rivera's cruiser.

Before long he heard one of Rivera's men say, "Well, I guess it's dark enough now."

"Yeah, I guess so. Is that old guy still there?"

There was a pause, then, "No, I don't see him."

"He must've finished for the day."

"Okay, let's do it. I'll get a blanket."

After a minute or two he heard the men walk across the deck, down the gangway, and up the pier to the dock. He raised his head over the side and saw them headed for a nearby car.

El Callao saw them too. Since arriving at the marina he'd been sitting in his car, trying to think of a way to find out if Rivera did have the money. He could simply go on board and see for himself. But Rivera and his men were probably jumpy now and might shoot him—certainly they would if they thought El Viejo had sent him to kill them. And where was that other guy, the man Rivera had followed from the airport? Maybe he was coming here. If so, he might walk right into the middle of a confrontation and become an inconvenient witness.

So the best thing had been to do what the silent man had done: watch and wait.

He'd seen Rivera leave empty-handed, so he hadn't followed him. That old workman with his bag of tools couldn't have anything to do with the situation. And these two guys weren't carrying anything, so if they left, he'd search the boat. Ana and that banged-up gringo wouldn't be able to give him much trouble.

He thought about calling El Viejo, but he had little to report and, more important, he didn't have the money, so he'd just be giving the Old Man a chance to chew him out for not having it. He knew the others called him El Callao behind his back, and he knew something else—something that many of them didn't: the value of silence. He forced himself to relax in his seat and keep on watching. And waiting.

Sitting on the boat next to Rivera's, Bolaño knew he had to move quickly. He allowed himself a flash of regret at not having brought his lock picks on this trip. Then he pulled a screwdriver from the bag and crawled to the main hatch, trying to ignore the sharp pain the movement sent stabbing through him.

Boat locks are usually weak, even on expensive boats, and this lock was no exception. He jimmied it in a few seconds and opened the hatch.

He ducked inside, bringing the tool bag with him, and closed the hatch. The interior of the boat was completely dark. The air was stale and warm but not hot, as the window curtains had kept out the day's sun.

He stood still for a few seconds, catching his breath and letting his eyes adjust. As the adrenaline rush faded, the grinding ache took over, gripping him like a vise, and he felt his way to a seat, banging his knee sharply on something.

A couple of minutes later he heard Rivera's men coming down the finger pier between the two boats. Their steps sounded heavy, and he could hear their harsh breathing.

He lifted the corner of a curtain and peeked out the window. The two men, one walking backward, were carrying what was obviously a body wrapped in a blanket. He was sure it was Luis.

He watched them struggle to get the body aboard *El Rey del Sol*. They managed it but not without a good deal of grunting and cursing.

Holding his breath, he silently slid the window open half an inch. The breeze, which felt good on his face, brought the men's words to him.

"Have you ever noticed how guys always seems to weigh more dead than alive?" one man asked.

"Girls too."

"I guess so. I've never had to carry a dead girl."

"It's a lot less fun than if they're alive."

"Yeah, unless maybe that's your thing."

"What?"

"Dead girls. I hear some guys like it better that way."

"Carlos, you're one sick motherfucker, you know that?"

"Hey, I didn't say I was into it—just some guys."

"Right. Shut up while we get this thing below. Put it down so I can open the hatch."

Listening to them, Bolaño wondered how many more dead bodies there would be before the night was over. And whether his would be one of them.

CHAPTER TWENTY-ONE

Morgan and Ana heard Rivera's men leave. Dressed again, Morgan stood and shuffled to the door. Soreness was setting in, and he moved more stiffly than he'd have imagined. He swallowed hard and used the mental tricks he'd been taught in SERE training to block what his body was telling him. It worked—sort of.

He rattled the knob even though he knew the door was locked. He looked around for something to pick or jimmy the lock but didn't see anything.

The only way was brute force. At one time kicking open a light door like this would've been easy for him. But this wasn't that time. Rivera's beating had taken a lot out of his already abused body. Still, he had to try.

"If I can get this door open, I want you to run. Get off the boat as fast as you can and keep going. Understand?"

Ana looked at him. "But what about you?"

"Don't worry about me. Just keep going."

She shook her head. "No, I will not leave—they will kill you."

He forced himself to smile at her. "They'll try. We'll see who's left standing."

"Do not talk that way. I hate it when you do."

"Sorry. But you must run. Call the police and send them here."

"To find you dead."

"To find whatever they find. Are you ready?"

"No." She paused, looking at him. Then she sighed. "All right. Yes, I am ready."

He turned his back to the door. He raised his good leg and kicked backward toward the door.

Once, twice, like a mule kicking. The door shuddered but didn't give. He braced himself on the bunk rails and kicked again. Then again. At the fourth kick the door flew open. He pushed Ana out into the dark passageway and stumbled after her.

They were heading for the aft deck and open air when they heard the men coming back on board. Morgan frantically looked around for a gun or knife. All he saw was the small knife the men had used to slice lemons in the galley.

He snatched the knife and held it at his side, not in front the way amateurs do. He looked at Ana. "Get to one side and stay still. I'll try to bring them all the way in, and maybe you can slip past them." She nodded and crept over to the bulkhead.

They heard someone scrabbling at the main hatch. After a moment it opened, and Morgan saw a man silhouetted against the lights of the marina.

Seeing Morgan, Garcia whipped out his pistol and pointed it at Morgan's chest. "Don't move!"

Morgan understood Garcia's clipped Spanish, but he took a step backward, holding his breath and hoping Garcia would come down into the salon where Morgan might be able to grab his shirt and use the knife. Garcia could still shoot him, but maybe the wound wouldn't be fatal.

Garcia was too smart to take the bait. "I said don't move! You won't get another chance. And drop that knife."

Morgan could tell Garcia meant what he said. He let the knife slip from his hand to bounce on the carpeted deck.

"Now turn around."

Morgan complied.

"Carlos," Garcia said, speaking over his shoulder, "it's Morgan—he got out."

"How?"

"I don't know."

"And where's Ana?"

"I don't fucking know!"

"Jesus, I hope she's still here. Rivera will kill us if she's gone."

"Shut up and cover me."

Holding his gun in front of him, Garcia slowly came down the steps. He kept his eyes on Morgan.

"Sit down—hands underneath your thighs," he said, and again Morgan complied.

Garcia went over to Morgan. "Where is she?"

Morgan said nothing. Quick as a cobra, Garcia struck him across with the face with the gun barrel.

Moving almost as fast, Morgan grabbed for the gun, but Garcia jerked it out of his reach. He kicked Morgan's bad knee, making him cry out.

Morgan's face began to bleed again, this time where the gun sight had cut him. Without looking away, Garcia said, "Tie his hands, Carlos, so he can't cause any more trouble."

Chavez came down into the salon. As he passed the place where Ana was hiding, huddled against the wall, back in the shadows, she darted for the hatch.

The sudden movement startled Chavez, and, he froze, half-turned, watching Ana flash through the narrow opening.

"Go get her, you idiot!" Without thinking, Garcia used the gun to gesture toward Ana, and that brought Morgan up from the seat.

As Chavez scrambled up the steps and out the hatch, Morgan chopped Garcia's gun hand hard on the wrist, knocking the pistol to the floor. Garcia made the mistake of looking for his gun instead of watching Morgan, and Morgan clipped him on the jaw.

Garcia's head jerked to one side, and Morgan took aim again. But Garcia struck first, hammering a hard right into Morgan's face.

Morgan counterpunched, and the two men traded blows for several seconds. Battered by Rivera's beating, Morgan felt his wind going. He feinted desperately with his right, got the opening he needed, and hooked his left into Garcia's belly.

Garcia doubled over, and Morgan slammed him with a fist to the side of the neck. Garcia fell, grabbing for Morgan's feet, but Morgan stepped back and kicked him in the head. Garcia went limp.

Morgan knelt and reached for the gun. His fingers were about to close on it when he heard, "No you don't! Hands in the air!"

Morgan looked up and saw Chavez standing at the top of the steps and aiming a gun at him. Morgan paused, calculating the odds.

"No, don't try it," Chavez said, breathing hard. "I've had just about enough of you, orders or no orders. I'm ready to blow you to hell if you so much as twitch."

After a moment Morgan slowly put his hands in the air. "That's better," Chavez said, coming carefully down the steps. "Now move away from the gun and sit down, just like you were before."

Morgan stepped back and sat, watching Chavez as he scooped up Garcia's gun and stuck it in his waistband. Keeping his own gun pointed toward Morgan, Chavez went to the galley and got a bottle of water. He twisted off the cap with his teeth and splashed some water on Garcia's head.

Garcia groaned and rolled onto his back. He lay there for several seconds, then pushed himself to a sitting position.

"Where's Ana?" Garcia asked as Chavez bent to give him back his pistol.

"Gone." Chavez avoided El Segundo's eyes. "She was too fast—I couldn't catch her."

"Goddamn it! Jaime may kill us for this." He shook his head. "Here, help me up."

Chavez helped him stand and was rewarded with a sharp slap across the face. "That's for letting the girl get away," Garcia said.

Chavez glared at Garcia but said nothing. He touched his cheek, filing the insult away in the special place he reserved in his mind for all the shit he had to take from Rivera and Garcia.

Seeing Chavez's expression, Garcia said, "He'll do a lot worse to me—to both of us—if she's gone when he gets back. You stay here and guard Morgan. I'll go after Ana."

Garcia stood above Morgan. "That wasn't smart, amigo," he said in English. "He was going to kill you, yes, but he might have done it quickly. Now you will suffer—and Jaime Rivera is a man who knows how to make another man suffer. I have seen it."

Morgan said nothing.

"I know you think you are a hard man—and maybe you are, compared to most. But you will cry like a little girl before he is done. You will beg for death."

Still Morgan said nothing.

Garcia hit him with the gun again. This time Morgan didn't try to grab it. A fresh line of blood appeared on his face.

"Now you are even uglier than before," Garcia said, "and that was ugly enough for three men."

Morgan looked at him, memorizing every line on his face. He wanted a chance to kill this man, and if he got it, he wanted to be able to remember what Garcia had looked like alive.

Annoyed that he hadn't been able to provoke Morgan into doing something that would justify shooting him, Garcia said, switching back to Spanish, "Okay, Carlos, I'm going. Keep your gun on him. If he moves more than a centimeter, shoot him."

"Got it."

"If Jaime comes back, tell him what happened. Tell him I've gone after Ana. She can't have gotten far on foot."

"What if someone picked her up, gave her a ride?"

"Then I'll deal with it!" Garcia made an angry gesture with his pistol. "You should start thinking about how you're going to deal with Jaime."

"Is that why you're going—so you won't have to deal with him first?"

"No, I'm going because losing Ana is my responsibility even if it's your fault. Jaime will blame me, so I've got to find her."

"It's not my fault! She was too fast—"

"Shut up! It doesn't matter now. We're wasting time. I'll be back as soon as I've found her." Garcia turned and trotted up the steps.

Chavez sat down, angry at Garcia and angry with himself. He drank from the water bottle. He saw Morgan look at it but didn't offer him any. They sat in silence.

The silence didn't last long. After two or three minutes Garcia came back.

"What—" Chavez said, then closed his mouth as he saw Rivera and Ana in the cockpit.

Rivera had his gun on Ana, and he used it to nudge her forward. When she moved, Chavez saw another woman standing behind them, a bleached blonde in a low-cut blouse and a short, tight skirt.

Ana came down the steps into the cabin. Rivera followed her, and the new woman brought up the rear.

"Well, well," Rivera said in Spanish, looking at Morgan and then at Garcia and Chavez. "It looks like we're all back together again. Not without a little difficulty, however."

"Chief, I—" Garcia began, but Rivera silenced him with a wave of the gun.

"No, we'll discuss it later. I must say I was surprised to see Ana running toward the gate as I drove in. Fortunately I was able to persuade her to return." Rivera's smile was icy.

"But I'm forgetting my manners," he said, gesturing toward the blonde. "Boys, this is Emilia. She works at the casino. I told her about my boat, and she said she'd like to see it. Right, Emilia?"

Morgan saw how thin the woman was—everywhere but her ridiculously large breasts. Her tiny pupils made her large, dark eyes look enormous. Cocaine, he guessed, and she confirmed it by sniffing and absently rubbing her nose before nodding her answer.

"So now that everyone is here, I think we'll have a little party," Rivera said.

"Chief, I thought we were going to leave—"

Rivera cut Garcia short. "We are, later tonight, but that doesn't mean we can't have some fun first. You want to party, don't you, Emilia?"

She nodded again. "Yes, if you've got more blow."

Rivera pulled a small glass vial from his pocket. "Sure, I've got it right here." The woman's eyes glittered, and she reached out.

"No, not yet," Rivera said, putting it back in his pocket. "I want to eat first. I know you're not hungry, but I am. You and Ana fix us dinner. And make me a drink—you know what I like."

He turned to Garcia. "Didn't you leave something up on deck?"

"Yeah. Morgan sort of interrupted that job."

"No excuses—you were supposed to keep him locked up."

Garcia glowered but knew better than to argue with Rivera. Still, he thought, the boss couldn't control what was in his mind. One day Rivera would push him a bit too far, and then . . . .

Rivera said, "You two get that body down here and put it in the same stateroom as Morgan. That'll give him something to think about."

The two men looked at each other and trudged back up to the deck. Rivera sat, keeping his gun pointed at Morgan. Emilia handed him a glass of scotch with three ice cubes. He tasted it and smacked his lips.

"Ah, that is good," Rivera said in English. "There is nothing like a drink at the end of a long day. But we have a lot more to do before this day is over." He smiled at Morgan, showing his teeth. "Do we not, my friend?"

Morgan didn't answer. He could hear Ana and Emilia moving in the galley and the clinks of metal and glass as they prepared dinner. He wondered if there were any chance Emilia would help Ana and him to escape. Only if we had some cocaine, he thought, and then only if we had more than Rivera.

The gangster had another sip of his drink. "I would let you have one, but I want your mind sharp. I do not want your senses dulled so that you cannot feel . . . everything."

Morgan knew Rivera was trying to frighten him, so he remained silent. Rivera frowned.

"You must be stupid, the way you never say anything. You know I can kill you anytime I like. Why do you not beg me to spare your life?"

Morgan gave him a contemptuous look. "Because I know it wouldn't do me any good."

Rivera smiled again, pleased at having gotten Morgan to speak. He drank more scotch. "Perhaps you are right about that. But you will beg me before this is over—I guarantee you will."

CHAPTER TWENTY-TWO

Leaving the blanket on deck, Garcia and Chavez hauled Luis's body into the salon. When he saw his friend's bloody body, Morgan's fists clenched. He blamed himself for Luis's death. Rivera or one of his men had done the killing, but Morgan had put Luis in front of the killer. Luis would still be alive if Morgan hadn't dragged him into this mess.

Morgan wondered how he could ever face Karen again but then realized he probably wouldn't have to. He regretted that she'd never know for certain what had happened to Luis. She'd never know what had happened to him, either—Rivera must be planning to dump his body at sea along with Luis's. Ana's too, if Rivera decided to kill her, which he might do now that he had another woman to amuse him and take care of his needs.

Garcia and Chavez squeezed past Rivera and took Luis's body to a stateroom. Morgan heard them swing the body onto a bunk. Then they returned, obviously relieved to have that job behind them.

"Tie his hands and lock him in there with his dead friend," Rivera said in Spanish, gesturing at Morgan. "They can say goodbye to each other." He laughed at his own joke and finished the scotch. "Then get me another drink. You can have one yourselves."

Rivera saw Garcia's jaw tighten at the peremptory way he was ordering them around, but El Segundo said nothing. Rivera imagined Garcia was thinking he was lucky to be alive after letting Morgan and Ana break out of the stateroom and Ana escape from the boat.

He's right—he is lucky, Rivera thought. So was Chavez. Rivera needed the two of them until he took care of Morgan. After that . . . well, not so much. Maybe not enough to keep them around. He could always find men to replace them. There were plenty of young, ambitious criminals in the slums of the Dominican Republic who were eager to move up by working for a boss like Rivera.

"Come on," Garcia told Morgan. "Don't give us any more trouble. We're all tired and hungry. Cooperate and maybe we'll give you something to eat."

Morgan stood and looked Garcia in the eye until El Segundo turned away.

"Get some line to tie his hands," Garcia said to Chavez.

They started to tie his hands in back, but Rivera stopped them with a gesture. "No, in front. I've planned something special for him, and

I want him comfortable enough to . . . enjoy it."

Garcia and Chavez locked him in the stateroom with Luis's body. Morgan stared down at it for several seconds. Then he began looking for a way to cut his hands free.

In the galley Ana was putting chicken, rice, and salad onto plastic plates. Emilia had found two bottles of white wine in the little refrigerator and was struggling with an old-fashioned corkscrew.

It slipped off the top of the first bottle. "Shit! This damn thing is impossible." She slurred her words, sniffing loudly after she spoke. "Is Jaime your man?"

"Not anymore."

"Oh, I see. That's why you were trying to get away."

The unintended irony of the comment almost made Ana smile. "Unfortunately, I didn't quite make it."

"Is he angry with you?"

"Yes, I took something of his."

Emilia had finally gotten the screw to bite and was twisting it down into the cork. "What was that?"

"Money—a lot of it."

"Oh. What happened to it?"

"He got it back."

"And he got you back too."

"Yes. Now we'll see what he wants to do with me."

Emilia thought about that, grunting a little as she struggled to pull the cork from the neck of the bottle. The cork suddenly popped out, causing Emilia to spill some wine on the deck.

"Goddamn it!" Emilia blinked at the splattered wine and rubbed her nose. "I'm sorry."

Ana shrugged. "No need to be—it's not my floor."

As Ana mopped up the spill with a paper towel, Emilia said, "Say, do you have any coke?"

"No, you'll have to ask Jaime for that."

"Okay. Will he want me to fuck him for it?"

"Probably—or be with one of his men while Jaime watches. Maybe both of them."

Emilia thought some more. Ana could tell she wasn't used to the effort.

"That might be okay," Emilia said, starting on the other bottle. "I've done two guys before. Three once. That Garcia is kind of cute. The shorter one, not so much. And I don't mind if someone watches—

that can be kind of hot, actually."

"Well, Jaime will expect you to do whatever he tells you to—and to do it quickly with no argument."

"Fine. Just as long as I get some blow first." She looked at Ana. "Have you ever tried it? It's so good. It's like—"

"I know. I tried it a couple of times. I decided to leave it alone."

"You did? That must've been hard. Especially with Jaime just handing it to you."

"It wasn't that hard. Giving up other things has been harder."

"Like what?" She had the screw down in the cork now, and she pulled on it, straining.

Ana watched her for a moment. "The parties. The clothes and jewelry. The life."

"Yeah, there's all that too." Emilia yanked at the cork, but it didn't move." She cursed again and banged the bottle down on the small counter. "Why is *this* so hard?"

"Here, let me help." Ana tucked the bottle under one arm and twisted the screw until she could ease out the cork.

Emilia was pouring wine from the other bottle into the glasses they'd found in a drawer. The plates were plastic, which made sense on a boat, so Ana was surprised Jaime had real wine glasses. Then she remembered that, probably because of his childhood poverty, he liked to add a touch of elegance to things. She flicked a fingernail on a glass, making it ring softly, and bit her lip, thinking.

"So why did you give it up?"

Ana frowned. "I'm not sure I did. It looks like he's got me back now. If he lets me live."

"You don't think he'd—'

"Yes, I do. I know he's done it, lots of times. You saw them bring that body in." She paused. "And I know he's going to do it to Hal."

"Hal?"

"The big man with the eye patch. The one who doesn't say much."

"Were you running away with him?"

She considered the question for a moment. "He found me out at sea, in a little boat that was sinking. Then he helped me for a while. Finally we—well, I'd begun to think we might end up together. But I know Jaime's going to kill him, and there doesn't seem to be anything I can do about it."

"Is he your lover?"

Ana glared at her. "What business is that of yours?"

Emilia looked away. "I'm sorry. I didn't mean to pry. The coke makes me talk too much."

They had the dinner ready then, and they carried the plates and glasses into the salon. They put everything on the table that, although small, had six chairs around it. The men were still drinking, and none offered to help.

The women served the men and went back for their own plates. When they returned the men were seated at the table, and Rivera was lighting the polished brass oil lamp that hung above it. He had turned down the rest of the lights in the salon, and the lamp cast a warm yellow glow over the compartment. Emilia sat next to Rivera and snuggled in close to him, obviously angling for more cocaine.

Two seats were empty. Ana started for the one farther from Rivera, but he stopped her.

"No, come sit by me. I always enjoy my meal more if I'm next to a pretty woman. This time I'll have one on each side. Here, Benito, scoot over and let Ana sit down."

El Segundo stopped chewing and looked at Rivera a couple of seconds, then picked up his plate and shifted. Ana sat, saying nothing. She looked at the plate in front of her but knew she was too tense to eat.

"Yes, this is nice." Rivera smiled expansively. "Good food and wine with my good friends. And Ana is back with us now. Aren't you, my dear?"

To avoid answering, she forced herself to pick up her glass and take a sip. She looked at Rivera over the rim. Her hand would have trembled, but she held the glass tightly so it couldn't. She thought it would break if she squeezed any harder.

Rivera waited. When she didn't answer, a dark look flickered across his face, but he laughed. His men joined in, their laughter sounding even more forced than his.

Locked in the stateroom, Morgan wondered why they were laughing and figured it was probably at Ana's expense. He flexed his wrists, feeling the line bite into his skin but also feeling it give a bit. He flexed harder, and the line loosened slightly.

Ignoring how much it hurt, he began working his hands free.

Over on the other boat, Bolaño also heard the laughter. He liked the sound because it meant Rivera and his men were relaxed, not expecting any trouble.

He rooted around in the galley until he found a knife sharp enough for his purpose and small enough for his pocket. Then he looked for a boat hook, finally finding one in a locker that held smelly swabs and extra dock lines.

Now that he had darkness, Bolaño slipped off his shoes and socks and went back on deck. Moving slowly and quietly—and trying hard not to pass out—he worked his way forward to where the boat was broadest in the beam and hence closest to Rivera's boat.

He twisted the boat hook to unlock it, extended it about halfway, and locked it again. He knew that sticking the hook out over Rivera's boat would hurt too much, so he knelt, angled the long handle on the deck, and slowly pushed the hook across the gap between the boats. When he had the far end of the hook on Rivera's boat, he nudged the hook around a cleat.

Holding his breath, partly from anxiety and partly to avoid crying out from the pain, he slowly pulled on the hook. Because of the size and weight of the two boats, nothing happened for several seconds. Then his boat began to inch toward Rivera's bigger vessel.

Bolaño didn't think of himself as religious, but now he prayed to the Virgin that Rivera and his men wouldn't notice the subtle change in the boat's slight movement on the swells. He'd had enough bad luck for one day.

When the boats were about three feet apart, Bolaño let go of the hook. He stepped to the edge of the deck and gauged the distance. It looked like a very big step, especially for a man with a bullet in him, but he had no choice—he couldn't risk the thud of the boats' bumping into each other. He had no time either, as he knew that within seconds the boats would begin drifting apart.

He swallowed hard and took the step, stretching his legs as far as he could. He'd been on boats enough to know that the secret to stepping on or off them is to take the step without hesitation and let your body's momentum carry you across.

He just made it, gasping from pain and then almost falling back over the side before grabbing a lifeline stanchion and finding his balance. He felt the boat shift slightly beneath his weight and sent up another prayer that he wouldn't be noticed.

Bolaño waited, making no sound. He thought he heard the conversation inside stop for a moment, then resume, but it could've been his imagination or simply a natural lull. The main thing was that no one came up on deck to investigate.

The Virgin must be in a good mood tonight, he thought and smiled to himself at the mild sacrilege remembered from childhood.

Moving slowly again, in part because he wanted to keep the boat from shifting but mostly because the throbbing wound wouldn't let him move any faster, he worked his way forward. He hoped to find a deck hatch propped open or at least unlocked so he could get inside the boat.

He found two closed hatches and tugged lightly on each. Both were locked, and he knew he couldn't open them without tools. Even with them, the noise from using them would've brought Rivera and his men out with guns in their hands.

He sank to the deck, dispirited, almost angry. So close . . . but not close enough. Still, he had the gun. Maybe a chance would come to use it.

As he sat there he could hear small waves occasionally slapping the hull, the slight breeze tinkling the rigging of the sailboats in the marina, and the low muttering of the conversation going on inside.

Then he heard something else—a tapping on the underside of one of the hatches.

Bolaño leaned close and heard the tapping more distinctly. Three quick taps, three slow ones, then three quick ones again. After a couple of seconds the pattern repeated. He recognized the Morse code. SOS.

Ana probably doesn't know that signal, he thought. It had to be Morgan.

He tapped the signal back and waited. The tapping inside stopped, and he heard someone fumbling at the catches. Then the hatch swung up and away from him.

He looked down into the boat and saw Morgan, standing with his hands loosely tied. He also saw Morgan's cuts and bruises and could guess how they got there.

Although his burned and now battered face made reading his expression difficult, Morgan looked surprised. He probably thought I was dead, Bolaño thought. He wasn't far wrong.

Morgan motioned him inside. Bolaño put his feet through the hatch, and with some difficulty Morgan helped him lower himself to the deck. Morgan saw the agony etched on Bolaño's face.

Morgan guided him to the only chair in the stateroom and held his arm while he collapsed into it, wheezing. Morgan looked at the blood spreading on the front of his shirt.

"Wait a bit before you try to talk." Morgan spoke in English, his voice so soft Bolaño could barely hear him a foot away.

Bolaño nodded and tried to control his breathing. After a few seconds he looked around and saw the body on the bunk.

"Is that your friend?" He matched Morgan's whisper. "If so, I am sorry."

"Yes, it's Luis. Rivera or one of his men got him with a knife."

"It was probably Rivera himself. He likes to use the blade—I have seen him do it."

"If I get a chance, I'll make sure he never does it again." Morgan's voice was flat, and Bolaño didn't think he was bragging.

Morgan gestured toward Bolaño's shoulder. "Here, let me take a look at that." He gently raised Bolaño's shirt and looked at the blood-soaked bandage. "Karen?"

"Yes. The bullet is still in there."

"I can probably get it out but not right now."

Bolaño nodded. "I understand. It will wait. We have more important things to do."

"You're in no shape to—"

"Please." Bolaño raised a hand. "Do not argue with me. I must do this. It is my fault that Ana is with Jaime Rivera."

Morgan said nothing.

"Plus I have a gun." Bolaño showed his pistol. "Do you have a weapon?"

Morgan shook his head.

"Then take this." Bolaño reached in his pocket for the galley knife. "Here, I will cut that rope off your hands."

"No, leave it on. I've got it pretty loose now, and I should still be tied up if they come for me."

"But if they come, should we not attack them?"

"No, not at first. You hide here in the stateroom. They won't lock it when they take me out, and then we'll have them between us."

Bolaño paused. "Good idea. I should have thought of it." He looked closely at Morgan. "You were U.S. military, no?"

"Yes, a SEAL officer. Mostly recently in Iraq."

"I see." Bolaño instantly regretted his remark, but apologizing would only have called attention to his unintended double meaning. "Did Ana tell you about me?"

"Just that you work for the Cuban government."

"That is true." So apparently Ana hadn't mentioned the DGI, Bolaño thought. Good—right now he and Morgan needed to be on the same side.

"And that you've seen some fighting."

"Yes, in Angola and other places."

"But probably not wearing a uniform, right?"

Bolaño was surprised at this yanqui's intuition.

"No, not usually."

"Got it. I worked with guys like you from time to time. You remind me of some of them—the quiet, competent ones."

Bolaño started to say something but was interrupted by the sound of the engines starting.

Neither man spoke for a moment. Then, over the low rumble, Morgan said, "Sounds like we're getting underway. Well, no matter what happens, it's going to be an interesting ride."

CHAPTER TWENTY-THREE

Morgan and Bolaño heard someone moving up on deck. Whoever it was stopped near the porthole in their cabin. Bolaño looked at Morgan and raised an eyebrow.

"Probably casting off the dock lines," Morgan whispered.

Bolaño nodded. The person on deck grunted, and a dock line slapped down on the pier. A pair of feet shuffled by the porthole, and the sounds repeated a few feet aft.

A man called, "All clear!"

Then Morgan and Bolaño felt the boat begin to move, heading out into the harbor. She went slowly at first, surging up and down on the swells.

◻ ◻ ◻

The man watched the boat leave. Now he was certain that the money was on board—Rivera wouldn't have taken the boat out to sea otherwise. Now that he had something to report, he picked up the phone and called El Viejo.

"Where do you think he's going?" the Old Man asked.

"Probably back to Cabo Rojo. With your cut of the money."

"Or maybe to Santo Domingo—with all of it."

"Maybe. But is he that stupid?"

"Greed makes men stupid," the Old Man said. "In my life I have seen it many times."

He was sure El Viejo had, so he didn't reply. Instead he asked, "Want me to come back?"

"Do you know where that other man is—the one Rivera followed from the airport?"

"No."

"Then stake out that house you mentioned. If he comes back, find out who he is and what he's doing with Rivera. Maybe they're up to something I should know about. I will have other people find out where the boat went."

The man didn't like the idea of watching the house, maybe all night, but he knew better than to argue. In person he would have just nodded, but on the phone he said, "Yes, sir."

His boss clicked off, and he dropped the phone on the passenger seat. Mentally replaying the conversation, he frowned. Why didn't El Viejo simply ask Rivera who this other man was and what, if anything, the two of them were doing together? If it seemed Rivera was lying—or simply seemed he might be—he could use his pliers and find out for certain. Hell, Rivera had that coming just for losing the money . . . .

□ □ □

The harbor lights Morgan could see through the porthole seemed to be moving backward. Soon there were fewer lights, and those were dimmer than before.

After a few minutes the engine noise grew louder and higher in pitch, indicating they had reached the channel. The boat settled into the trough, down slightly at the stern, and her surging motion evened out into a smooth ride.

Morgan looked at Bolaño. "Once we're well out of the harbor, they'll probably come to get me. I figure they intend to kill me and dump Luis's body and mine in the ocean."

"I think you are right. You must know the layout of this boat—do you have a plan?"

"Give me the knife. You keep the gun. Try to surprise them, and then I can make a move."

"There are three of them," Bolaño said. He put the knife in Morgan's hands, and Morgan awkwardly slipped it into a pocket of his trousers.

"I know. Maybe four, if that other woman throws in with them."

"One man will be at the helm, so we should deal with the other two first."

"Right. You better hide in case we don't hear them coming."

Bolaño nodded and moved to the other side of the door so he'd be behind it when it opened. Morgan sat in the chair, taking long, slow breaths and trying to keep his face blank.

He didn't have long to wait.

Chavez unlocked the door and moved into the opening. He looked at Morgan and motioned with the gun. "Come on," he said. "He wants you."

Morgan stood and stepped close to Chavez to make him back out the door without looking around the cabin. Morgan twisted his wrists to tighten their bindings and held up his hands.

"Here, cut off this line. Give me an even chance."

Chavez shook his head. "No way, man. He would kill me for that."

"He *is* going to kill me. At least let me take a swing at him."

"That's up to him. Ask him and he might free your hands. He's not a coward."

"No?" Morgan glanced at the body on the bunk. "We could ask my friend Luis about that."

Chavez gave a short laugh. "We could ask, but I don't think we'd get an answer. Now come on. He's waiting." Chavez gestured for Morgan to walk ahead of him down the short passageway into the salon.

Rivera was sitting on the built-in sofa that ran along a side bulkhead. He held a glass of wine and a cigar and looked quite content. Ana and the other woman were clearing away the last of the dishes. Morgan did-n't see Garcia, so he knew the man had to be piloting the boat from her bridge, which was above and forward of the salon.

"Sit down," Rivera said in English. "I am sorry we were not able to offer you any dinner, but you would have had a hard time eating it with your hands tied."

Out of the corner of his eye Morgan saw Ana glancing at him as she and the other woman carried plates toward the galley. He looked at Rivera and forced himself to smile. "That's okay. I'm really not hungry."

"That is too bad. A condemned man should have an appetite for a last meal." Rivera smiled too and puffed on his cigar.

Morgan knew Rivera was trying to see whether he was scared, so he said nothing. He chose a seat not too close to Rivera but not too far away either. He was careful to keep his hands close together.

"But if we have no last meal for you, at least we can have some entertainment. Ana! Emilia! Come out here!"

The two women emerged from the galley, Ana drying her hands on a dishtowel. She looked at Rivera but said nothing. Emilia said, "What do you want, Jaime? Is it time to party?"

"Oh, yes. Definitely party time. Are you ready?"

"Sí," she said, switching to Spanish from anticipation. "I'm always ready to party." She hurried over to him. "Especially if you have more blow."

"I thought so," Rivera said, also in Spanish. "You like that stuff more than you do me."

"Oh, no, honey." She leaned down to kiss his cheek. "I like it because it helps me to like you—like you more. I mean—"

Rivera frowned. "I know what you mean. Here." He pulled the vial from his pocket. "Go ahead. Then we'll party."

The four of them watched as Emilia eagerly opened the vial and used one of her long fingernails to scoop out some white powder. She lifted the nail to her nose and snorted into one nostril, then the other. Almost immediately her eyes brightened and she smiled, showing slightly crooked teeth.

"Thanks, Jaime. That's just what I needed." She sniffed, rubbed her nose, and looked at the vial.

"No, no more. That's enough for now."

Although clearly disappointed, Emilia said nothing. She screwed the cap on the vial and handed it back to Rivera, offering none to the others.

"All right," Rivera said, "now I think we're ready. Carlos, turn on some music. Some dance music."

"You're in the mood for dancing?" Ana asked, looking puzzled.

"No," Rivera said, smiling. "I'm in the mood for watching *you* dance." He glanced at Emilia. "Both of you. Together."

"You must be kidding," Ana said, turning back toward the galley as salsa music began thumping from the speakers.

"Stop!" Rivera wasn't smiling now. "I'm not kidding. You'll do as I say or I'll cut Morgan right in front of you and make you watch him bleed to death."

He looked at Morgan to make sure he understood. Morgan kept his face blank, but he didn't doubt that Rivera meant what he said. Morgan glanced at Ana, who'd frozen where she stood, glaring at Rivera.

Rivera turned to Emilia. "You don't mind dancing for me, do you, Emilia?"

"No," she said, apparently relieved that dancing was all she'd have to do to earn more cocaine. "I like to dance."

"Good," he said. "Go ahead. But strip first. Or if you prefer, strip to the music."

"What?"

"I said get naked. I want to see you dance in the nude."

Emilia waited to see whether he might be kidding. When she decided he wasn't, she said, "Well, okay. It won't be my first time."

"No," Rivera said, "it certainly won't." He turned to Ana. "You too. And I think this will be *your* first time."

"Wait!" Morgan said, scooting forward in his chair so he could stand with his hands tied.

Rivera looked at Chavez and motioned with his head. Chavez stepped over to Morgan and put the muzzle of his pistol an inch away from Morgan's ear.

Morgan looked at Rivera with an expression much like Ana's. He let his hands drop in his lap and stopped moving.

"That's right," Rivera said, still in Spanish. "You just sit there like a good boy while your new girlfriend and Emilia entertain us. I've been looking forward to this—and to sharing it with you." He turned to Emilia. "Go ahead, sweetheart. Show us what you've got."

Emilia smiled uncertainly and began to dance in the small open space in the center of the salon, her movements jerky and not coordinated with the music. After half a minute she kicked off her shoes. After a few more seconds she pulled off her top, revealing silicone-filled breasts with no tan lines. Her breasts looked rock-hard and didn't move when she did.

"Nice," Rivera said, "very nice." He looked at Ana. "Come on, Ana. Dance with her."

"No!" Ana said, "I won't."

"Oh, I think you will. Carlos."

Chavez cocked the pistol. The others could hear it over the music, and Morgan thought it was the loudest sound he'd ever heard.

Rivera looked at Ana again. "Now will you dance? Or would you rather mop up his brains?"

Ana said nothing, still giving Rivera that look.

"If you think I'm joking, Ana, I'll prove I'm not." Rivera glanced at Morgan. "I'll be more than happy to."

Ana threw the dishtowel to the deck and stepped toward Emilia, who'd stopped moving.

Emilia hugged Ana and whispered in her ear. "It's okay, honey. It won't be that bad. Just pretend you're somewhere else, dancing for yourself."

Ana hesitated, then began moving to the music. Emilia started dancing again, but having a partner didn't make her more graceful.

Rivera gave them half a minute before saying, "Ana," in a low voice.

She glanced at him and then looked back at Emilia, who said, "Here, I'll help you." Emilia reached down to grasp the hem of Ana's camisole. She pulled it halfway up, exposing Ana's toned midriff, but couldn't lift it any farther because Ana didn't raise her arms.

"In five, Carlos. Four, three." Rivera paused, cocking an eyebrow at Ana.

She raised her arms, not looking at him, and Emilia was able to pull the camisole over Ana's head. Her breasts were natural, smaller than Emilia's but equally tanned.

Two of the three men in the salon had previously seen her naked, but nevertheless Ana felt ashamed. She saw Chavez staring at her and imagined he'd fantasized about seeing her this way. She was glad her uncle wasn't there to see it. To hide at least some of her humiliation, she turned her back on Rivera and resumed dancing.

Emilia playfully tossed the camisole to Rivera, who caught it and chuckled. "Good—very good. I'm certainly glad we brought you along on this little cruise. Now the rest of it."

Growing more certain of herself, Emilia smiled at him and unfastened her skirt. With an inelegant move, she stepped out of it, leaving her in only a black thong. She started to slip that off too, but Rivera said, "No, don't get too far ahead of Ana."

Angry but now resigned, Ana smoothly took off her skirt. Her tiny panties were pale peach.

"You two sure look good together. I'm glad I thought of this. Aren't you, Carlos?"

Chavez licked his lips. The salon wasn't hot, but he could feel sweat popping out on his forehead. "Sure thing, chief."

"Too bad Benito is missing all the fun." He cupped a hand to his mouth to be heard on the bridge above the noise of the music and the engines. "Hey, Benito, put her on autopilot for a moment and come take a look at this."

After a few seconds Garcia came down and saw the two women dancing almost nude. He turned toward Rivera, trying to keep his expression neutral. "Quite a party. You sure this is the right time for it?"

"Yes, I am." Rivera held Garcia's gaze, noting that his deputy didn't look away. "Want Carlos to spell you at the helm so you can watch for a while?"

Chavez didn't appear happy about the suggestion.

"No, thanks. Navigating can be tricky at night. We're still going where you said?"

"Yes, that place we've used before. Quiet and out of the way." He looked at Morgan. "The fish seem to like it. We'll be there in less than an hour."

Ana stopped dancing, which caught Rivera's eye. "Ana," he said. After a moment she started again, but her movements had lost all gracefulness and become jerky.

Morgan caught the flicker of disgust on Garcia's face. El Segundo said, "I better get back to the bridge," and returned up the steps.

Rivera sipped his wine as he watched the women dance. A fast song wound down, and a slower one came on. "Ah, that sounds good. Now, girls, let's see you dance with each other. You know what I mean."

Emilia giggled and moved toward Ana, who took a step back. "No, don't be frightened. This'll be fun."

She took another step toward Ana, who didn't move this time, and embraced her. Ana kept her arms at her sides. Then Emilia began swaying to the music.

The two women were only an inch or so apart. Their breasts touched, and Emilia murmured, "Relax—I won't bite. Haven't you been with another girl before?"

Ana, her eyes closed so that she could keep from crying, shook her head. She felt furious, affronted, scared. And she blamed herself not only for being in this fix but also for Morgan's being there with her. She was the one who'd taken the money and run away. He'd merely tried to help her, and now he was going to die for it.

"I remember my first time," Emilia said softly. "Of course, we didn't have an audience like this. But it's nice. Here, I'll show you." She pulled Ana closer and began to kiss her.

Ana pulled back and looked at Rivera, who shook his head. "No, no, Ana, I don't think you're quite into the spirit of things. Maybe this will help."

He put down his glass and stepped over to Morgan, opening his knife. With Chavez's gun at his ear, Morgan didn't dare move. Rivera put the point of the knife into Morgan's nose.

"I saw this in a movie," Rivera said, switching to English. "Some little guy slit Jack Nicholson's nose. But I'm going to improve on that by cutting Morgan's nose completely off. Unless you do what I want, Ana. Right now."

She stared at the tableau. She had no doubt Jaime would do exactly what he'd said. She turned to face Emilia, who despite her high, seemed surprised at how far Rivera was taking things.

"Looks like you have no choice," Emilia said. "Don't worry—I'll take the lead."

Ana didn't know what to do. She felt Emilia's tongue snaking between her teeth. It was a soft, warm kiss, something like the way Morgan had kissed her, and not at all like Rivera's brisk, almost brutal approach.

"That's it," Rivera said. "Nice. Very, very nice."

Emilia cupped one of Ana's breasts and kissed the other. Morgan was enraged but could barely breathe much less move.

"Wonderful," Rivera said. "It'll be even better once both of you are fully undressed."

Emilia pulled back and smiled at Ana. She slipped her fingers beneath the waistband of the thong, eased the filmy black garment down over her hips, and stepped out of it. She pirouetted to show Rivera her shave and her tan, then moved closer to Ana.

Ana made no move to take off her own panties. Emilia said, "Let me help. You know he's going to make you do it."

Ana did know it, so she didn't resist as Emilia reached for the panties and then knelt to pull them down Ana's legs. But she was surprised when Emilia, instead of standing to resume the dance, remained kneeling.

Ana glanced down to see Emilia looking up at her. "Here's what they want," Emilia said, a note of desire in her voice. "Just relax—I think you'll like it."

Emilia put her hands on Ana's hips and pulled Ana toward her as she tilted her head, guided by the narrow strip of pubic hair that was like a sign pointing the way. As her lips came close enough to kiss Ana's skin, her tongue flicked like a snake's.

Rivera gave Morgan a triumphant smile and pulled the knife out of his nose, pricking him just enough to draw blood. Morgan could smell it—the sharp scent of metal—and breathed through his mouth so he wouldn't inhale any blood. Rivera stepped back toward his chair but didn't sit and didn't close the knife.

Bolaño had heard the music start and wondered what was happening. Cautiously, he'd waited until the slow song came on before easing out of the stateroom, gun in hand. He'd shuffled down the passageway, the pain so familiar it felt as much a part of his body as his sense of touch. He knew he wouldn't last much longer.

At the end of the passageway he peeked around the corner to see a woman he didn't know taking off his niece's panties. Then the woman began to have oral sex with Ana in front of Morgan and two leering men, one of whom was Rivera.

Ana seemed completely passive, so Bolaño assumed Rivera had forced her to participate in this show. The other woman was probably doing it for money or drugs or both.

Bolaño saw the blood on Morgan's upper lip and the red tip of Rivera's knife blade. He also saw that Morgan was looking harder at Rivera than at the women.

As Emilia began to lick Ana, moving a hand up between Ana's legs, Morgan couldn't contain himself any longer. "Stop this!" he shouted to Rivera. "They're not circus animals! Leave them alone, you bastard."

CHAPTER TWENTY-FOUR

Rivera started as though struck with a whip. Chavez clicked off the stereo, and except for the muffled rumble of the engines, the compartment became quiet.

Emilia pulled back from Ana and stood, looking puzzled. Ana and Chavez held their breath. Back in the entrance to the passageway, so did Bolaño.

After a moment Rivera smiled, a cold, scary smile. "What was that you called me?" The words dripped like oil.

"You heard me—bastard. For once why don't you act like a man, not a spoiled boy?"

"What do you know about how a man acts?" Rivera looked him up and down. "You, with that melted face and scarred body. Hairless as an egg and missing an eye. Why, you're a scarecrow, not a man."

Morgan roared like some wild beast. He surged to his feet, trying to ignore the agony it cost him. The quick movement surprised Chavez, knocking him back.

Morgan twisted his hands, trying to free them. Chavez got his gun aimed again, but Ana stepped in front of him, blocking the shot. Rivera set his feet to lunge at Morgan.

Bolaño stepped into the compartment and pointed his gun at Chavez. Ana saw him first and gave a little cry of surprise. Then Chavez and Rivera saw him as well.

With his bloody shirt, pale face, and burning eyes, Bolaño looked like the angel of death. He held the gun as though it weighed a thousand pounds.

"Buenas noches," he said. Then he shot Chavez in the chest, twice, the two shots so close together that they sounded like one.

Chavez slammed back against the bulkhead, eyes wide open as blood flowed from the wound. He raised his pistol and fired at Bolaño. The bullet caught the Cuban in the side and spun him. Bolaño let go of his gun, which bounced on the carpet a few feet away from him. He collapsed on the deck and lay still.

Morgan yanked his hands free of the line. He pulled the knife from his pocket and lurched toward Rivera.

Rivera brought up his own knife, and the two men began circling each other. Chavez slid down the bulkhead and collapsed like a bloody bag of clothing.

Up on the bridge Garcia heard the commotion and cursed out loud. He'd known something bad would happen, and clearly it had. But maybe in dealing with whatever it was, he'd also have a chance to deal with Rivera . . . .

He gave himself a few seconds to think, considering options and figuring odds. Then he switched on the autopilot, grabbed his pistol, and began clattering down the steps to the salon. Ana heard him coming and snatched up Rivera's glass, slopping wine over the rim.

As Garcia reached the bottom step, Ana threw the wine in his face. That stopped him cold and made him lower the pistol while he rubbed his eyes with his free hand. Ana broke the bulb of the glass on the table and rammed the jagged edge into his throat.

A bright red geyser spurted from Garcia's jugular vein. He cursed again and fired the gun blindly. As Ana ducked, she heard Emilia scream.

Ana thought Garcia's bullet must have hit Emilia, and she looked over at her. Emilia had closed her eyes, clamped her hands over her ears, and was screaming as loudly as she could. Ana saw no sign of a wound.

She's hysterical, Ana thought.

Garcia staggered, dropped the gun, and put his hands to his neck. He sank to his knees, his ragged breath making a ghastly bubbling sound as blood dripped from his clenched hands.

Ana stepped over to Emilia and slapped her, hard. The screaming stopped as suddenly as it'd started although the sound rang in the air for a moment. Emilia's pupils had shrunk to pinpricks, and her skin was as white as paper.

The silence made Rivera edge away from Morgan and glance across the salon. He saw the two naked women standing next to each other and Chavez and Garcia lying on the deck. Chavez was obviously dead, and Garcia was bleeding so badly he couldn't live long. Rivera realized that somehow he'd lost his three-to-one advantage in a matter of seconds.

Then Rivera looked back at Morgan, who'd noticed his opponent's momentary distraction and come a step closer. Rivera knew that if he didn't kill Morgan, he'd soon be dead too. Furious at how the situation had changed, he slashed at Morgan but cut only air.

Morgan made an awkward return thrust, also missing. "Get on the bridge and steer!" he said to Ana as he and Rivera continued to circle each other.

Ana watched, frozen, as their knives flickered in the lamp light.

"Go!" Morgan said. "Or the boat will head to the beach and run aground."

His tone snapped her out of her fog, and she dashed up the steps.

Rivera took advantage of Morgan's own distraction to slash at him again. Morgan tried to dodge the blade, but the tip scored his abdomen, drawing blood.

Rivera's smile was reptilian. "It won't be long now. No one has ever beaten me in a knife fight."

Morgan, saving his breath, didn't bother to reply. He kept moving, both to make it harder for Rivera to strike and to give himself an opportunity to attack.

When Rivera seemed to stumble over something on the deck, Morgan thought his chance had come. He lunged, but Rivera deftly sidestepped the knife and cut Morgan again, deeper this time and drawing more blood.

He was only pretending, Morgan thought. If Rivera fooled him like that again, he'd be dead.

He heard something behind him, a sound like something heavy being dragged across the deck, but he refused to be distracted again and didn't turn to look. Rivera felt confident enough to glance in that direction, and whatever he saw made his eyes widen.

Morgan saw the opening and took it, lunging at Rivera, who moved fast enough to deflect most of the thrust—but not all of it. The blade licked along Rivera's forearm, leaving a long gash, and his blood began flowing freely.

Rivera stepped back, looked at the wound, and grinned. "Well, Morgan, perhaps you'll give me a good fight after all. It's no fun to win too easily."

"You haven't won yet."

"No, but I will." He turned his head slightly. "Emilia, the Cuban isn't dead—get a gun and shoot him!"

Morgan glanced behind him. Bolaño was crawling in agony toward his gun. His outstretched hand was only inches from it.

Emilia had picked up the two pistols lying by Chavez and Garcia. She weaved toward Rivera, holding one in each hand. Morgan thought she looked like a nude, coked-up cowgirl headed for a showdown.

"Shoot him!" Rivera said. "He's going to get his gun!"

"What?" Emilia glanced around blankly, then saw Bolaño crawling crab-like on the deck. She gave Rivera a puzzled look. "Shoot that guy?"

"Yes! Quickly!"

She sniffed and pointed one of the pistols at Bolaño, whose fingers were closing on his gun. "If I do, will you give me more blow?"

"Yes, yes, but do it! Now!"

"Well, all right," Emilia said, no emotion in her tone. She squinted down the barrel and squeezed the trigger. Morgan tried to move into her shot, but he was too late.

The report boomed in the salon, and the unexpected recoil snapped Emilia's hand up and back, making her drop that pistol.

"What is it?" Ana shouted from the bridge. No one answered.

Bolaño felt the fire start in his gut and knew he was finished even though his fingers now rested on his pistol. He looked over toward Morgan and was surprised at how dark the salon was growing. He hoped Morgan would find a way to save Ana even though his new ally appeared done for too.

Bolaño wondered how he, a man with his training and experience, had ended up being killed by a Dominican gangster and his drug-addled girlfriend. As the world slipped away from him, Bolaño smiled, as he had many times before, at the irony of life. Then he died.

"Okay, give it to me." Emilia thrust out one hand, palm up, and raised the other, the one that still held a pistol.

"In a minute. We have to take care of Morgan first."

"No, now! You promised. I need it!"

Emilia stepped between the two men, facing Rivera. From the table Morgan seized a rum bottle, the only solid thing within reach, and hit her on the back of the head. As she fell to the deck, he tossed the open bottle back on the table. He and Rivera stared at each other for a moment before they dove for the two guns remaining on the deck.

Rivera came up with one first—Bolaño's—and snapped off a shot at Morgan, missing him by inches. Morgan grabbed the other gun, but before he could aim it, Rivera fired again, ripping a bullet all the way through the outside of Morgan's right thigh. Morgan gasped from the hot pain that flashed through him, pain almost as bad as he'd felt in the desert, and knew that he had only one chance left.

As Rivera was taking aim again, Morgan shot him, hitting his gun arm in the shoulder and making him let go of his pistol. Morgan kicked Rivera's feet out from under him and threw himself on top of Rivera as the man crashed to the floor.

Morgan dropped his gun and the galley knife on the deck and clamped his hands around Rivera's throat. Snarling like a wounded animal, he took out two days of anger, fear, and frustration by squeezing until Rivera's face turned blue, then almost black. He remembered his vow to make Rivera pay for what he'd done, and he squeezed even harder.

"Do not kill him unless you have to!" Ana was standing at the top of the steps to the bridge. She'd found a squall jacket and put it on, so she was bright yellow from mid-thigh up and golden skin from there down.

"Why not?" Morgan kept his hands clenched around Rivera's throat.

"We are in enough trouble without that."

What she said made sense, but Morgan didn't want to listen to sense. He wanted to kill this man who had threatened, beaten, and tried to kill him, who had caused the deaths of his best friend and Ana's uncle, and degraded Ana simply for amusement. He very much wanted to kill this man.

But after a few seconds more of choking Rivera, he realized he wouldn't do it. He knew Ana was right. Despite all that Rivera had done to Ana, to him and Bolaño, even to Luis, Morgan couldn't justify killing the man now that he was no longer a threat. Even with his burning hatred of Rivera, he couldn't bring himself to do it.

But he could bring himself to reach up, pull the rum bottle off the table, and break it over Rivera's head. Almost all the rum had run out, soaking the tablecloth and dripping onto the deck. The empty bottle shattered on Rivera's skull more easily than Morgan would've liked, but it was enough to knock the man out.

Morgan staggered to his feet and looked at the carnage all around. He walked unsteadily to the steps as Ana came down. They embraced. Neither spoke for several seconds.

With her slim fingers Ana gently wiped the blood from Morgan's lip. Then she said, her voice almost a whisper, "Tío Paco . . . ?"

Morgan looked into her eyes. "Yes. The girl shot him—Rivera told her to."

Tears filled Ana's eyes and she buried her head in his shoulder. "He was tough," Morgan said. "It took three rounds to kill him. He was trying hard to save you."

"I know." Ana cried for a while, her sobs muffled against his shirt. After a couple of minutes she lifted her head and brushed her eyes with the back of her hand. "I feel I am responsible for getting him into this— this awful thing."

"Well, I think he felt he got you into it by introducing you to Rivera. But things don't always work out the way we plan."

"No." She looked at the three dead bodies and two unconscious ones on the deck and wiped her eyes again. "None of us planned this. Now what do we do?"

"Take the boat back. Talk to the cops. I think I can leave you out of it. Pitch it as a drug deal gone bad."

"No!" She shook her head. "I do not want to be left out of it. I am part of it now. As much as you are."

"Ana, think. You're a Cuban citizen who's been using a Dominican passport. If they don't put you in jail here—for taking Rivera's money if not for killing Garcia—the Puerto Rican authorities will either send you back to Cuba or the Dominican Republic. In Cuba you'll go to jail for betraying the Revolution, and in the D.R. you'll be killed because of the missing money—Rivera's associates will see to that."

She started to speak but stopped. She looked at him for several seconds, then said, "But what about you? I mean, what about us?"

"Us?" As soon as the word left his lips, he knew he'd said the wrong thing.

"Yes, 'us,' damn it! Did we not make love today? I think that means we are now 'us,' not just you and me. Unless I am nothing but an easy fuck for you."

He leaned down and kissed her on the cheek. "No, chica, you are certainly not that. If . . . if things were different, I'd—"

"You would what?"

"I'd take you with me, away from here, wherever I was going, but . . . . ."

"But what?"

"I may have to go to jail. It's going to be hard to sell what happened here as entirely self-defense."

"Then I will go with you."

"Don't be foolish. You couldn't go with me—you'd be somewhere else, and we'd never see each other."

His words stung, but she knew he spoke the truth. She pulled herself away and looked at the crumpled body of her uncle. Walking as though she were half-dead herself, she went over and knelt beside him.

Morgan watched her, knowing there was nothing he could say to ease her suffering. He also knew he had to get busy if he were going to bring the boat safely back to harbor.

He grabbed the boat's medical kit from its bulkhead mounting and found some adhesive dressings. He peeled the backing off two and slapped them on the worst of his wounds, making the bleeding slow if not stop. Then he checked Rivera, who was still out cold. He snatched the line they'd used to tie his hands and began tying Rivera's behind his back. He used sailor's knots to tie Rivera more tightly than he'd been tied himself and, just to be safe, also tied his feet.

As he worked, both legs throbbing and his hands sticky with blood, he glanced at Ana. She was on her knees, holding her uncle's broken body in her arms and crying softly. Her tears fell freely onto the dead man's face.

Although he'd barely known Bolaño, Morgan felt as though he'd lost another of his Navy shipmates. Bolaño had been strong and determined. He'd died bravely. Seeing him shot made Morgan remember that night in the desert. The muzzle flashes like stabs of lightning in the darkness. The spreading pools of blood looking black in the starlight. And then the fire . . . .

He shook his head, but the images lingered.

When he'd finished tying Rivera's hands, he looked over at Emilia. Like Rivera, she was still unconscious. He thought that without a weapon she was probably harmless, but he decided to tie her hands anyway. He didn't have another piece of line, so he cut a short length from the tail of Rivera's bindings and did the best he could with that, tying her hands in front so it wouldn't hurt as much. The knot wasn't perfect, but he thought it would hold her.

Morgan picked up Rivera's switchblade, wiped the blood off on the carpet, and then closed the knife and put it in his hip pocket. Next he picked up the pistol Rivera had dropped and checked the magazine. It held only three cartridges, but he didn't see a need for any more shooting, so he simply put the gun in a front pocket. Last he retrieved his phone from where Rivera had put it on the navigation table.

Leaving Ana to grieve over her uncle, he climbed to the bridge to figure out where they were and how to get back to the marina. The moon was up, shining brightly and leaving a long streak of gold across the water, which was ink-black except for the starry reflections twinkling from the mild waves.

For some reason the golden color made him think of Ana's money. Ana's or Rivera's? Or anyone's—who knew where it had come from or what had been done to get it? All this killing . . . over a bag of money. He was tempted to bring the blue bag topside and throw it overboard. But he knew that Ana wanted the money as at least partial compensation for all she'd endured, and he might need some of it to convince the police about what had happened.

He checked the compass heading: west-northwest. There was a chart on the bridge, but Garcia hadn't bothered to maintain a course plot. Fortunately, the boat had GPS, and Morgan marked their position and the time on the chart. Garcia obviously hadn't been enough of a sailor to know how many things can go wrong on a boat and require a manual backup.

Morgan checked the distance back to the marina. The boat had plenty of fuel, so he figured that at a higher speed, they could be back in a couple of hours even with the detour he was planning. He studied the chart closely, tracing the shoreline with his finger.

There. There it was, exactly what he was looking for. He got the parallel rulers and laid the course.

He had just turned the boat to her new heading when Ana came on the bridge. She was wearing khakis, a long-sleeve white shirt under the jacket, and low-heeled shoes. Part of his brain recognized that she must have kept some clothes on Rivera's boat, but most of it wondered how she could look so good at a time like this.

Ana pulled his face down to hers and kissed him. The kiss was soft and warm and long. When it was over, he said, "I don't know what that was for, but thanks."

"That was for saving me—again. And for trying to save Tío Paco."

"You're welcome, but I was saving myself too. I'm sorry about your uncle."

"Thanks. I know you are." She looked out across the water for a few moments, then back at him. "I remember he told me once he was in a dangerous profession and did not expect to die in bed."

"He must've been quite a guy. I wish I'd had the chance to know him better."

"In a way you did know him—the two of you are much alike."

"Both of us care about you. Or he cared . . . well, you know what I mean."

"Yes, I know." She put her hand to his cheek and held it there for a few seconds before saying, "Now, what is your plan?"

"What makes you think I have one?"

She lightly tapped his face. "Oh, I already understand you well enough to know that you always have a plan. What are we going to do?"

"I'm going to put you off in the dinghy. Right here." He pointed to the spot on the chart. "You can go ashore, and in the morning you can catch a taxi someplace."

"A taxi to where?"

"To one of the big hotels in The Condado. Just go inside for a few minutes, long enough for that taxi to leave, and then take another to Karen's. She can give you the driver's license Luis ordered, and you can fly to Miami and disappear. Take the money bag, but leave me ten thousand in case I need it to persuade the police to believe my story and not go looking for you."

"But you will go to prison."

"Maybe not. I think the police are more likely to believe me than a gangster and a cokehead. I'm going to leave you out of it, and by the time the cops figure out that another woman was involved, they won't be able to find you."

"But—"

"Shhh." He put a finger on her lips. "I've thought it through, and this is the only way. You have to trust me."

After a long pause she said, "All right. I do. I will."

"Good." He gestured toward the compass. "Keep her on this course while I get the dinghy ready. I'm going to drop you off in about half an hour when we pass close to that point of land."

He throttled back until the boat was leaving little wake and turned the controls over to Ana. Then he went outside and back to the stern, climbed the ladder to the top of the deckhouse, and stepped over to the dinghy. This one was large enough to have a motor mount, but the motor was missing. More amateur boating, Morgan thought, shaking his head. Well, at least a couple of paddles were aboard. Plus a plastic bottle of water, three signal flares in a transparent plastic pouch, and a small, black flashlight, also in a waterproof pouch. There was even a compact first-aid kit. He lowered the dinghy to the aft deck, climbed down, and cinched its bow line on a cleat.

He slipped the dinghy over the side and let out the line. Empty, the dinghy rode high behind *El Rey del Sol*, bobbing along in the turbulence made by her big engines.

Morgan returned to the bridge and took the helm. "She's ready. Here's my phone—you may need it. My key ring too—I put the car key on it. And take this pistol, just in case."

Ana's eyes widened when he handed her the gun, but she put it and the phone in the pockets of her jacket.

"Now go below and get the money. When we're there I'll come to all-stop and help you climb down."

Ana seemed about to say something but then merely nodded and went below. A minute or two later he heard her yell for help.

CHAPTER TWENTY-FIVE

Morgan dropped down the steps into the salon. Across the compartment he saw Ana struggling with Emilia, who was kneeling, still nude, by Rivera. The gangster hadn't regained consciousness, but Emilia had and somehow had managed to work her hands free.

The blue bag was by Ana's side. She turned her head at the sound of Morgan's feet hitting the deck and in excited Spanish said over her shoulder, "When I came back from the stateroom, she was trying to untie him!"

Looking like a madwoman, Emilia slapped Ana with the back of her hand. The *craaack* sounded like a rifle shot, and Ana fell back, visibly shaken.

"No, you stupid bitch," Emilia said, digging into Rivera's pocket. "I want this!" Triumphantly she held up the vial.

Emilia surged to her feet, and Ana followed. She grabbed for Emilia's arm, but Emilia shoved her hard against the table.

Ana flung out a hand to stop herself from falling. She hit the oil lamp, knocking it off its hook. The lamp fell onto the table and the glass chimney broke, letting the fumes from the rum-soaked tablecloth get to the flame.

The tablecloth caught fire, and within a couple of seconds flames covered it entirely. Still dazed, Ana watched in horror as her shirt sleeve also ignited.

Morgan plunged forward and caught her by the shoulders. He pushed her to the deck and rolled her beneath him on the carpet. Putting out the fire on her shirt took only a moment, but he could smell the smoking cloth and even her seared skin.

Again, that eternal night in the desert flickered before him, a terrible movie that refused to end. Trying to ignore the flashbacks, he called Ana's name but she didn't answer. Her eyelids fluttered but she couldn't seem to focus. Apparently the combination of falling to the deck and being rolled had stunned her.

He glanced up at the table. The fire was still spreading, and now it had leaped from the table to the bulkhead and chairs. He saw that the whole salon would soon be ablaze.

He looked at Emilia. She was so high she hadn't noticed the fire—but she did when he shouted at her. She lowered her hands and looked around blankly, the flames throwing patterns of red and orange light on her pale skin.

Then, despite her drug haze, Emilia panicked.

Clutching the little glass vial to her chest, she screamed and began running. But she ran the wrong way—forward toward the staterooms, where the fire hadn't gone but certainly would go, drawn by the draft from the overhead hatch Morgan had left open.

He looked around for a fire extinguisher but didn't see one. He thought of Rivera's speedboat, which hadn't had a visible extinguisher either. These guys who went out on boats without knowing much about them . . . .

Ana moved her head and moaned, and he knew he had to get her out, fast. He stood, picked her up—gasping from the pain—and managed to heave her onto his good shoulder. Then he picked up the bag and staggered across the burning compartment to the main hatch.

He had to fumble one-handed to open it. Those few seconds seemed like forever, and he felt the heat from the fire spreading all around him.

Finally he got the hatch open and began to maneuver through it, trying not to bump Ana on the frame. Just as he crossed the threshold, Rivera began to scream.

Morgan knew that no matter how long he lived, he would never forget that awful sound. It was loud and high-pitched and went on and on. It carried all the horror of knowing you were about to be burned alive—helpless, with your hands and feet tied.

Trying desperately not to stumble and fall, he carried Ana and the money to the stern. Rivera's screaming followed them all the way, almost as loud as inside. He lowered Ana to the deck and patted her cheeks and wrists for a few seconds until she regained her senses.

"Hurry!" he said. "Get in the dinghy, and I'll pass you the bag."

She looked up at him. "And then you will come with me?"

"Not right now." He looked away, not sure why he was about to say what he was about to say. "I'm going to try to get them out."

"No, you cannot! See, the whole boat is on fire!"

She pointed, and his gaze followed. Harsh yellow light glared from every porthole, flame licked out of the main hatch, and dense black smoke poured from the topside hatch. He could hear the snapping of the fire over the rumble of the engines. The situation seemed hopeless.

Still, he knew he had to try. "Get in! There's no time to argue." He pulled on the line until the dinghy was riding at the bottom of the swim ladder and motioned for Ana to climb down to it.

She said nothing further. She reached out and he took her hand, squeezing for luck. She stepped over the side and clambered down the ladder, keeping her hand in his as long as she could. Then she let go and took the last two steps.

Morgan leaned over with the bag. "Here." He dropped it into her waiting hands and she set it between her legs.

"Come with me! Please!" she said, looking up at him.

"Soon. But if fire gets back here to the engines, cast off."

"What about you?"

"I can jump off and swim to you." He didn't know whether he could do either of those things, but he spoke with conviction, willing her to believe he could. He looked into her eyes a moment, then dropped the line and limped forward.

Between the lurid light of the fire and Rivera's unending screams, returning was like going to meet the devil. Or walking back into the desert. Morgan felt the heat as he approached the hatch. He tottered to the opening and looked inside.

The salon was almost completely engulfed in flames. Only the sofa where Rivera lay remained untouched, but the fire was very close to it.

Rivera saw Morgan and stopped screaming. He held up his hands as though praying. "Here! Get me out! Please!"

Morgan said nothing. He was trying to decide whether he could get to Rivera, cut him loose, and carry him out before the fire killed them both. The fire made it hard to decide, but so did remembering Luis and Bolaño.

"Please! I will give you the girl and the money! Just get me out of here!"

Morgan was about to go to Rivera when the fire overruled him. Flames licked at the sofa, igniting the fabric as if with a blowtorch.

Rivera began screaming again, even more loudly. Morgan watched in horror as the man's clothes caught fire. He knew he couldn't save Rivera now and would only die if he tried.

The screaming went on for a few seconds, growing even higher in pitch as Rivera's clothes burned. Then it began coming in short little bursts as he writhed in agony, and Morgan closed his eyes. Finally it stopped, and he opened them.

The interior of the cabin was now a solid mass of flame, and the heat was intense. Morgan thought about trying to get up on the bridge to shut off the engines—with their fuel pumps—before the fire got to the fuel lines, but he realized the fire would trap him up there.

He backed away from the heat and the stench of burning plastic, rubber, and, now, flesh. He knew that if he lived he'd have nightmares about this night just as he did about that night in Iraq.

The only thing he could do now was try to save Emilia. The fire was spreading to the staterooms, but if she'd gone into one with a closed overhead hatch and shut the door behind her, she might still be alive. He worked his way forward, soreness and fatigue making him slow and clumsy, with the glare through the portholes lighting his way.

In what was just over a minute but seemed much longer, he reached the outside of one of the two smaller staterooms and bent to look through the porthole mounted a couple of feet above the deck. The compartment was dark except for a crack of flickering light beneath the door. The light, growing stronger by the second, showed him that she wasn't there. On the opposite side of the boat the twin stateroom, the one with the open hatch, was full of fire, and if she'd picked that compartment, she was already dead.

In a few more seconds he reached the bow section and looked through a large porthole into the lighted main stateroom. There she was—bent over the tiny desk and insanely snorting up a rapidly dwindling pile of white powder. Along with the light, some dark smoke was beginning to come under the closed door.

Morgan rapped on the glass, and Emilia turned toward the porthole. Her eyes were even larger than before and crazed with fear. He could tell she either didn't see him or didn't recognize him. She made no movement toward the porthole. Instead she bent back over the desk.

He rapped harder on the glass. "Unlock the overhead hatch!"

Again she looked at him but otherwise didn't move except to snort the last of the white powder and tap the mouth of the vial against the desk. No more cocaine came out. She started knocking the bottle against the desktop.

He shouted again with even less result than the first time. Flames licked under the door, and black smoke poured through the crack. She banged the bottle on the desk.

The vial broke and cut her hand. She stared at the blood, then looked at him again, her mouth opening. If she made any sound he couldn't hear it over the combined noise of the engines and the fire.

Emilia was so skinny Morgan thought he might be able to pull her through the porthole. He raised his foot, sucking in his breath from agony, and brought his heel down on the glass, which didn't break. Either he was too weak or the glass was too strong. He kicked at the porthole again. Again it didn't break.

But the noise from his kicking jolted her into movement. She came toward the window, holding out her cut hand, and dripping blood on the deck.

Smoke was filling the stateroom now, and the fire was beginning to come through the bulkhead. He kicked one more time. The glass cracked but still didn't break out of the frame.

Now she was screaming, her face grotesquely flattened against the fractured window as the flames approached her. Muffled by the glass, her screams weren't as loud as Rivera's, but they too went on and on and on, and he knew he must be in hell.

Morgan looked back at the stern. The fire was there now, so it also must've reached the engine compartment below.

In the dinghy behind the boat Ana was on her knees, watching as the fire spread throughout the entire boat and sent sparks soaring toward the stars. He could barely see her through the flames but hoped she could hear him. He cupped his hands and shouted as loudly as he could. "Cast off! Cast off!"

She shouted back something he couldn't understand, then threw off the dinghy's bow line. As the cruiser continued to power forward, the dinghy dropped back, bobbing in the wake from the flaming engines.

He looked back at the window. Emilia's face had vanished and he could no longer hear her, so she must have passed out from the heat and smoke. But she might still be alive.

As he raised his foot for one more try at the window, the fuel tank exploded with a blast that blotted out everything else in the world. Something large, hard, and sharp stabbed him in the side, burying itself there and forcing a scream out of him. The impact knocked him off the boat and into the ocean.

The water was warm, but the sudden immersion was a shock and the salt burned in his cuts. Stunned and disoriented, he fought for the surface, SEAL training making him stroke hard for several seconds. Then he felt the pressure increase and knew he was headed the wrong way. He changed direction and began stroking again, but now he was growing short of oxygen. He knew that if he didn't come up soon, he'd drown.

Just as his chest felt as though it would burst, he broke through the surface. He gulped the cool night air and gagged as saltwater came in with it.

He coughed, spat, coughed again, and then settled down, kicking slowly with his legs and sculling the surface with his arms. He'd been taught how to tread water for hours, but he knew that in his condition he probably wouldn't last more than half an hour.

He considered reaching down to pull the . . . whatever it was out of his side, but he knew that would cause more bleeding than he was already doing and might attract sharks. So he left it alone.

He could try swimming to shore, but it was miles away. He knew he'd never make it, not without some sort of flotation device. Maybe, if he wasn't hurt too badly, he could improvise a life jacket from his trousers by tying the legs behind his neck and trapping air with the waistband—more survival training—but then he wouldn't be able to swim.

He'd heard drowning wasn't a bad way to die—that you suffered for only a minute or so. He didn't know how anyone could be sure of that, but now it looked as though he'd find out for himself.

With a couple of weak strokes he turned to look back at *El Rey del Sol*. The boat, now about 200 yards from him, was dead in the water and engulfed in flames, the fire feasting on the diesel fuel. As he watched, bobbing in the water, the fire got to the emergency-gear locker and ignited the flares. They began going off inside the boat and must have blown or burned the locker door open, because a few came shooting out, bright red, over the black water.

With the flames reflecting in the water and the flares arcing into the sky, the scene would've been striking if it weren't so tragic.

Six people dead, he thought. Over what? A bag of money and a runaway. Now the money wouldn't do Rivera or his men any good, and they should've let Ana go in the first place.

Luis, Bolaño, and that crazy Emilia—just people who got caught up in this thing. But it had killed them, and he knew it was probably going to kill him too. Very soon.

He kept treading water as well as he could. Maybe there'd be some floating debris left from the boat, something he could lie across while he tried—assuming he didn't bleed to death first—to kick his way to shore.

Or maybe there wouldn't.

He sensed movement behind him that was something other than the motion of the waves. He turned to look.

It was the dinghy. The light from the burning boat was just bright enough for him to see Ana anxiously peering across the water. He heard a paddle splashing—faint at this distance.

"Here! Over here!" He waved his good arm.

She didn't see him. He kept trying. After two or three minutes she raised herself in the dinghy and shouted, "Hal!"

He raised himself as far out of the water as he could and called to her again. She shouted back, "I see you! I see you!" Then she turned in his direction and dug hard with the paddle.

He swam slowly toward her, and eventually they met. He was winded and hung on the side of the dinghy to catch his breath. She put both her hands on his. He saw the muscles in her throat working, but she didn't speak.

After a minute or two Morgan had recovered enough to give her a grin. "Nice night for a swim."

He took her wrists, and working together, he and she were able to pull him halfway over the side. Then he rolled himself into the boat. The movement took almost all of his remaining strength, and he felt himself growing dizzy.

"Oh, Hal! I saw you blown off the boat, and then I could not see you anymore. I did not know whether you were alive or . . . ."

For several seconds he lay in the bottom of the dinghy, looking up at Ana's face framed by the stars. He thought he had never seen a sight so beautiful.

"I almost was. I would've been if you hadn't come along. You saved my life."

She smiled and touched his face. "I am glad I had a chance to pay you back for saving mine."

He raised his head to look at *El Rey del Sol*. She'd burned almost to the waterline, and the flames were beginning to die. What was left of her would probably sink in the next half hour or so.

As the thought crossed his mind, a wave of nausea hit him. The small part of his brain still clear realized that the beatings, loss of blood, lack of sleep, and hunger were all catching up with him. He fell back to the bottom of the boat.

Ana saw something glitter in the moonlight and reached down to touch it. Feeling the warm wetness, she drew her hand back and wiped it on her jacket.

"Hal! You're hurt! What is that?"

"I don't know," he said through gritted teeth, "but see if you can pull it out."

"It may hurt."

"It hurts already."

"Okay." She reached down again and gingerly tugged at the object, cutting her hand in the process. She tugged harder, making him cry out, and then gently withdraw a six-inch shard of metal, which she held up for him to see.

"Shrapnel off the boat," he said, breath rasping in his throat. "Toss it as far as you can, so it won't cut a hole in the dinghy. Then try to can stop the bleeding."

She turned and threw the piece of metal as hard as she could toward the burning boat. She hissed a curse in Spanish that Morgan didn't catch. He felt the blood pumping out of his side and knew it was enough to kill him if it continued.

"Get the first-aid kit. Back there, in that pocket sewn into the side."

She found the kit and pulled it out. She took the largest bandage in it, ripped off the backing, and pressed it to Morgan's side, forcing a groan from him.

"This is bad, Hal. And you were already hurt. We need to get you to a doctor."

"I'll live," he said, trying to sound more optimistic than he felt. "Let's head for shore ."

"All right, but I cannot see it. I am not sure which way to go."

He tried to answer, tried hard, but nausea choked off the words. He vomited seawater onto the bottom of the dinghy.

Darkness closed in on him, and the world went as black as the ocean that stretched away from them on every side.

CHAPTER TWENTY-SIX

Ana's arms burned with fatigue. She had paddled and paddled and then paddled some more, going at it for hours. She hoped she was headed in the right direction.

In the dinghy she sat so low she could see little above the waves. But when she'd gotten about a mile away and turned to take a last look at what was left of the burning boat, she'd noticed another boat, much smaller, moving slowly toward *El Rey del Sol*. Maybe some people had been night-fishing, seen the flames, and come to investigate. Or maybe Garcia, when the fire started, had made a call for help, and it was more of Rivera's men.

Regardless, she wasn't going to stick around to find out. She'd kept paddling

That glow of lights off to the left had to be San Juan. She imagined herself back at the helm of *Sun Chaser* with the binnacle in front of her and the boat headed two or three compass points to the right of the city. That should put her on shore fifteen or twenty kilometers west of San Juan.

Unless the glow was Arecibo, which would put her far west of where she wanted to be. Or maybe it was just a couple of freighters close together, and she was headed out to sea. That last possibility was something she didn't want to think about.

Even if it distracted her from the fire in her hands. The incessant paddling had left them raw and blistered, and now they were beginning to bleed. She dipped them in the sea every few minutes to cool them and wash the blood away. The salt sting was minor by comparison.

She was exhausted. All she wanted to do was lie down, rest her head on Hal, and sleep. Sleep until they drifted to land, were picked up at sea, or had to face whatever else fate had waiting for them.

But she knew she couldn't, not until they were on shore and safe. Or safer, anyway.

She glanced down at the blue bag. If she hadn't earned the money before, she certainly was now.

The only thing in their favor was the relative calmness of the sea. The light breeze was too slight to raise whitecaps but felt cool on her laboring body, drying the sweat on her face and arms.

Ana kept peering into the darkness in front of them, hoping to see some sign of land. She thought she could smell it—that warm, wet fragrance of plants growing in the earth—but the scent of the sea was stronger, so she couldn't be sure.

At last she saw lights ahead that didn't look like stars low on the horizon. She paddled on, trying to ignore her bloody hands. After a few minutes the lights seemed brighter and closer, and she knew she was headed for shore.

But now there was another glow, a reddish light smoldering beneath the clouds on the horizon to her left. The sun was about to rise, and she didn't want to be out on the ocean in daylight. She didn't want anyone to find her again, especially after the horror of the fire only hours—or was it days?—ago.

She paddled harder, faster. As the sky lightened from black to gray, she could see the land rising from the ocean, and now she was sure she could smell land too.

The scent reminded her of Cuba, of home, and she felt a pang of homesickness that lasted until she remembered what the government would probably do to her if she returned. Then she tried to think of other things.

She glanced down at Hal, still unconscious and lying on his back in the half-inch of bloody water sloshing in the dinghy. His skin looked ghostly pale. He needed medical attention—quickly. But he was strong, and that would help. She thought of their love-making, and despite the danger and discomfort she was in, she smiled.

In another half hour she was studying the beach, looking for a good place to land. She didn't have much choice—the dinghy was so slow and hard to maneuver that she could do little more than let the waves direct her. She got lucky, and the sea pushed them toward a flat, sandy beach with relatively few rocks.

As soon as the little boat touched bottom, she climbed over the side, stepping into water up to her knees, and pulled the dinghy up onto the beach. Then she lay beside it, intending to rest for only five minutes. The sound of the waves was soothing, and the early-morning sunlight felt good on her wet skin and clothes. She closed her eyes.

When she awoke, the sun was well above the horizon, and the sky was a deep blue with a few cottony clouds drifting in the east. She sat up and looked in the dinghy. Morgan's eyes were closed, but he was breathing slowly, the black stubble of his beard contrasting sharply with his paper-white face.

She dug his phone out of her jacket pocket. The phone was damp but still worked. She scrolled through the stored numbers until she found one marked "Luis and Karen."

Karen answered, breathlessly, after two rings. "Yes?"

"It is Ana."

"Oh, thank God! Where are you?"

"On a beach west of San Juan—at least I think so. We were on Jaime's boat."

"What happened?"

Ana paused. "I believe you say, 'It is a long story.' I will tell you when I see you."

"Is Hal there?"

"Yes, but he is hurt."

"Badly?"

"Yes, he was cut with a knife and shot. Then a piece of the boat flew . . . no, what is the word? For apuñala? In his side."

"Stabbed him in the side?"

"Sí. When fire tore the boat apart—ay! like a big bomb. He has lost much blood. But if we can get him to a doctor, he may live."

Now Karen paused. "And Luis?"

Ana tried to think of a gentle way to put it, but there wasn't one. "He is dead, Karen. Jaime and his men killed him."

Karen make a sharp, wordless cry and then began to sob. Ana could feel the woman's heart-wrenching sorrow coming through the phone.

"I am sorry, Karen, very, very sorry."

The woman continued to sob for a full minute. Then she sniffed once, twice, and said in a hard, brittle voice, "That won't bring him back. You killed him."

"*I* killed him?"

"Yes, you, you little . . . . . Oh, if only you and Hal hadn't gotten Luis mixed up in this! He'd still be alive."

Ana had nothing to say to that. She knew that Karen was right even though Rivera was directly responsible for Luis's death. But Ana and Hal had certainly led Rivera to him.

Karen sobbed again, louder this time, and Ana waited, knowing that any comfort she might try to offer would only make things worse.

After several more minutes Karen exhausted her tears, at least for the time being. There was silence, and then Karen sniffed again and blew her nose. After a long pause she said, "So, what are you going to do now?"

"Get off the island if we can."

"'We'? You mean you and Hal?"

Ana hesitated. "Yes."

"So, it's like that with you two now?"

"I—I think so."

"Well, perhaps it is. I saw the way he looks at you."

"His face is hard to read, but I hope that you are right."

After another long pause Karen sighed and said, "I suppose you need me to come pick you up. Where?"

"On the highway along the coast west of San Juan." She closed her eyes and imagined the chart. "Maybe sixteen or seventeen kilometers beyond the city center, perhaps a little more."

"Okay. I'll look for you on the right side—the beach side—of the road."

"No, I think that would be too dangerous. The police may be looking for us."

"Then how will I find you?"

Ana stared at the boat, thinking. "I know. I will tie a paddle to a tree by the road so it looks like a cross. You pull off the road there, and I will come out to meet you."

"That should work. Can Hal walk?"

"I hope he can by then. I think he is too heavy for us to carry."

"All right. I should be there in about an hour, maybe less."

Ana struggled to untie the mooring line from the dinghy, cursing under her breath at the stubborn knot and at the fact that she didn't have a knife. Finally she worked the knot loose. She took the line and the paddle out to the road.

She walked up and down until she found a tree that was by itself and close to the road. She tied the paddle crosswise to the tree and facing drivers coming from San Juan.

She knew an experienced sailor like Hal wouldn't think much of her knot, but it would have to do. She stepped back and looked at her handiwork. The signal wasn't as visible as she'd hoped. She whispered a quick prayer that Karen would see the cross.

Back on the beach she sat by Hal. The sea was still calm, green near the shore, turquoise farther out, and royal blue toward the horizon. The sun was bright, but the breeze kept the temperature comfortable. She thought how lovely the scene would be if only she didn't keep seeing gruesome images from the previous night.

She looked down at Hal. The sun on his face was pushing him toward consciousness, and he was beginning to move his head slightly. She put her hand on his, and he curled his fingers around hers.

After a few minutes he blinked some and then kept his eye open. When his sight focused on her, he smiled. "Hi."

Somehow his expression didn't seem as crooked to Ana as it had before. "Hi. How do you feel?"

"Awful. But glad to be alive." He turned his face toward the sun. "That feels good—it's warming me up inside. I feel like I was frozen for a long time and now I'm thawing out."

"You must have been cold from being in the water so long."

"Maybe, or cold from . . . other things. But it doesn't matter—I'm warm now."

She replied by gently interlacing her fingers with his.

He glanced over the edge of the dinghy and saw treetops. "Thanks for getting us ashore."

"I was not sure I could. It was a long way, and I got very tired."

"Well, you don't know what you can really do until you have to do it." He tried to sit up, groaned, and lay back down. "I guess I'm more banged up than I thought. Where are we?"

"Not very far from San Juan. I called Karen. She is going to pick us up." Ana told him about the marker.

"Good." He squeezed her hand. "Thanks again. For saving my life, I mean."

"I should say the same to you. Two or three times."

"You've already said it, and no one's keeping score."

"But—"

He put a finger to his lips and held it there for a couple of seconds. Then she leaned down to kiss him, her lips parting his and saying everything there was to say.

□ □ □

El Callao watched the woman, wearing shorts and a T-shirt, hurry from her house and get into a car parked nearby. Where is she going? he wondered. Maybe to that man?

He waited until the woman had pulled out and was half a block away. Then he started the car and pulled out after her. He picked up his phone, checked the time, and mentally debated whether he should call El Viejo.

Too early in the morning, he thought, especially if he didn't know where she was going. Maybe she was headed to a gym class or something like that.

He put down the phone and pulled out his pistol. Steering with his left forearm, he used both hands to check the weapon. He knew it was ready, but whenever he thought he might have to use it, he checked, both to be sure it was and to prepare himself to do whatever he had to do.

CHAPTER TWENTY-SEVEN

About three-quarters of an hour after Ana's phone call Karen saw the paddle-and-tree cross. She braked, pulled her car off the road, and looked toward the ocean glinting to the right. The foliage was too thick for her to see much of the beach.

She got out of the car and pushed her way through the weeds, bushes, and tree limbs until she came out onto the sand. Then she saw the orange dinghy down near the water, the waves almost reaching it as they slid up the slope of the beach, stopped, and rolled back into the sea.

She saw Ana kneeling by the dinghy and a figure that must be Hal lying in it. She scudded her way toward them through the fine sand.

Ana heard or sensed her coming and turned to look. She stood but said nothing as Karen walked up to the dinghy. Karen looked Ana up and down, taking some slight satisfaction in how bedraggled she was, and then leaned over to look at Morgan.

"Well, how is he?"

"Still alive."

"Good."

Morgan, who had been drifting in and out of consciousness, heard them talking and turned his head to look up at Karen. He tried to speak but had a fit of coughing and then spat blood into the bottom of the dinghy.

Finally he was able to say hoarsely, "Thanks for coming."

Not trusting herself to speak at that moment, Karen merely nodded.

"I guess Ana told you about Luis."

Karen swallowed and nodded again.

"I'm sorry, Karen, so very sorry. You know Luis was like a brother to me."

Then she couldn't help herself. "Yes, but he was my husband! He was everything to me! Why did you have to get him mixed up in this shit? Why?"

Morgan had been asking himself the same thing but didn't have a good answer. There wasn't one except that he hadn't known things would turn out this way, and he realized that saying so would be useless. So he simply repeated, "I'm sorry."

Karen curled her slim fingers into fists so tight her hands shook. After several seconds she uncurled them and stood rock-still. She stood that way for what seemed to Morgan like a long time before finally saying, "I know. I know you are."

There was silence again, and Morgan could hear the waves rolling in toward the shore and the light wind sighing in the trees overhead. Then he heard something else, something coming from the direction of the road: the faint hum of an engine and the slightly more audible sound of a car crunching over gravel.

"Karen—" Ana began, but Morgan gestured for her to stop.

"Hush. Listen."

The humming and crunching stopped in a few seconds, and then came the louder sound of a car door closing. Morgan looked up toward the road but couldn't see anything through the thick greenery.

Then Morgan looked at the two women, both frozen in place. He didn't know who'd been in that car, but he wasn't going to take any chances.

"Ana," he whispered, "give me the gun."

She turned her head to look at him but otherwise didn't move.

"Give me the gun—now!" His voice was still low but commanding.

Ana reached into her jacket and pulled out the pistol. She looked scared, and he didn't blame her—he was scared himself. Her fear made her fumble, and she dropped the pistol in the sand. She snatched it up and handed it to him.

As he tried to brush and blow all the sand off the pistol, he heard someone moving through the foliage. "Take the bag, Ana. Run down the beach, both of you, and get up among the trees."

"No, I will stay with you."

"Damn it, this is no time to argue. Take the bag and go. Now! Do it!"

Ana hesitated a moment, then grabbed the bag in one hand and Karen's wrist in the other. "Come on," she said, pulling Karen toward her. "Let's go."

The touch of Ana's hand jolted Karen into motion, and she followed as Ana dropped her wrist and began to run, awkwardly because of the bag but surprisingly fast, even on the sandy beach. Still partially numb with grief, Karen was slower but didn't lag more than a few yards behind.

Morgan rolled over in the dinghy, gasping and almost passing out. Then he pulled himself to the end closest to the road and raised his head just over the side, keeping his gun hand low and out of sight. That movement was agonizing too, but he forced himself to do it because he had a good idea what would come next. And what he would have to do then.

Whoever had been in that car might be a police officer, but he didn't think so.

He remembered Ana's telling him about the party at Cabo Rojo. Telling him that Rivera and some of his men had been there but also "the one they call El Viejo." The Old Man who was like the Godfather.

A gangster didn't live that long by being stupid. Rivera had gone after Ana and the money, sure, but the Old Man might have sent someone too—at least for the money.

And maybe he had, because here someone was. A man in a lightweight suit, no tie, emerging from the green wall, taking a few steps down the beach, and stopping to study the dinghy. He held a pistol in one hand, not pointed at anything in particular but out where he could use it quickly if he needed to.

No, he wasn't a cop, not dressed like that and with his weapon already drawn. Coming here alone, not bringing a backup man, he must be good with a gun.

So the Old Man had sent him, or perhaps another of Rivera's associates had. It didn't matter now. All that mattered was keeping this man away from Ana and Karen because if he found them, he'd kill them. Partly for the money—even though he could probably get it without firing a shot, shooting would be quicker—but mostly to leave no witnesses behind.

Of course to do that he'd have to get past Morgan. That might not be difficult now, Morgan thought, with him wounded and having only three cartridges in his pistol. He remembered thinking on the burning boat that there wouldn't be a need for any more shooting.

Well, he'd been wrong.

As the gangster continued to look his way, Morgan remembered that night in the desert. The situation had been a bit different then—two men, not one, coming after him, but still he'd been the attacker. Now, wounded as he was, he had no choice but to wait.

Wait for what he knew was about to happen . . . something deadly he couldn't prevent. His only option was to deal with it as best he could.

The night in the desert hadn't ended well—one man killed and two wounded. And it had been his fault for not doing a better job of looking out for those under his command. Just as he hadn't prevented Luis from being killed yesterday.

Morgan tried to think of what he might have done differently before Rivera and his men closed in on them. He couldn't think of anything, but surely there was something. There always was—always something you could have done better.

Morgan was sure that Ana's uncle, if he were still around, would agree. The man had clearly been a seasoned professional, and Ana and Morgan might not be alive if he hadn't been and hadn't chosen to deal himself into the game.

But here Morgan was with another chance. A chance to make up for Luis and for what had happened in the desert. If he could kill this man before the man killed him, Ana and Karen could get away.

He made sure the gun's safety was off and its hammer cocked. As he did that, the gangster started toward him, now carrying his pistol a little higher and pointed toward the dinghy.

For a moment Morgan thought he'd get lucky and the man would come straight down without pausing along the way. But this guy wasn't an amateur—after a few steps he stopped and studied the dinghy again.

As he did, Morgan studied him. He was fit, of medium height, and with a medium build. Nothing about him was unusual, but his stolid, almost grim expression, implied he'd seen and done some hard things. Well, Morgan thought, resisting the temptation to adjust his eyepatch, he's not the only one.

Morgan knew the man could see him lying in the boat, but he also knew there was no way to tell from that distance whether Morgan was alive or dead. Obviously, though, the man wasn't taking any chances. Definitely a professional, with what looked it might be another gun sagging in a pocket.

Morgan considered playing dead until the gangster got to the dinghy, but that would negate whatever advantage he might have from being a SEAL-trained marksman. Lying there hurt with only three rounds, he hoped it was a hell of an advantage.

No, he'd have to try to take this guy when he got close enough that Morgan wouldn't miss but the gangster might. Another twenty yards or so might do it.

The man resumed walking forward but stopped again after a few seconds, just out of range for anything but a desperation shot. He turned sideways to present a smaller target and studied the dinghy some more. Morgan lay still, taking shallow breaths and even trying not to blink.

When the man started forward again, Morgan waited until he thought he had a reasonably good chance of hitting him and then fired, aiming for his chest. With a gun he'd shot before and knew better, Morgan probably would have hit the moving target, but with this unfamiliar pistol the shot went slightly wide.

The gangster moved as fast as Morgan had ever seen, sprinting forward, dropping to the sand, and rolling behind a low bush. Morgan could see part of one leg stretched out behind him, and it made an invitingly still, if small, target. Wounding the man in the leg wouldn't be enough to stop him, however, and would leave Morgan with only one round. And what if he missed with his last one?

"Who are you?" the man shouted in Spanish, his voice so rough and angry that Morgan could hardly understand him.

When Morgan didn't answer, the man snapped off a shot, sending a bullet whizzing an inch over Morgan's head. He might not have been SEAL-trained, but he knew how to shoot.

"If you have the money, give it to me," the man called out. "I'll leave."

Morgan knew the statement was true as far as it went—the gangster would leave, but he'd kill Morgan first. And then the women, even after he had the money. Their tracks were too obvious to ignore.

Talking was pointless, so Morgan kept quiet, thinking. He had to draw the man into the open, but his adversary seemed too smart or at least too experienced to leave cover unless he thought it was worth the risk.

Morgan wished he had another pistol, even an empty one, to use as a decoy. But of course he didn't. He glanced around the dinghy. Nothing but the paddles, the first-aid kit, and the bloody water in which he was lying. Oh, and the water bottle, floating now that it was almost empty.

And there, still in their clear pouches, the flares and the flashlight. The small flashlight, black and cylindrical. Just like . . . .

"Come on," the hard-looking man said in a more normal tone. "Just give me the money, and I'll go. Or tell me where it is." He paused. "You can't get away without doing one or the other."

To make his move more convincing, Morgan waited another minute. Then in Spanish he said, weakly—which he didn't have to fake—but loud enough for the man to hear, "Okay. I have the money, but I'm injured. Badly. I'll give you a third for a ride to the nearest hospital."

"Half," the man said.

Although he could feel his life slipping away, Morgan smiled. This guy was good. He wasn't taking Morgan anywhere except perhaps to a shallow grave dug here on the beach, but he knew how to play the game.

Morgan waited again but not as long. "Okay, half. But you have to take me there right now."

"Sure, sure. First throw out your gun."

This was the tricky part. Morgan had to throw the flashlight so that it looked, at this distance, as if it had the shape and weight of a pistol, But he couldn't let the man see the lens.

Morgan rolled onto his side and was surprised to find that it hurt less than he'd imagined it would. I must be getting numb, he thought. There was little time left. Not much, no, but enough.

He put the pistol in his left hand and gripped the flashlight with his right, holding it so that the butt faced outward. He raised himself slightly in the boat so that he was visible to the man without presenting too tempting a target.

"Here," he said in the weak voice that sounded strange to him. He side-armed the flashlight forward, trying to throw it so that it flew in a straight line and didn't tumble. The flashlight fell a few feet forward of the dinghy, its lens facing Morgan. To distract the man from studying the object too much, he added, "Now come and get me. And your money."

CHAPTER TWENTY-EIGHT

After a few seconds the gangster stood, still behind the bush in case he had to take cover again. He waited a few seconds, and then, when no shot came, began walking slowly toward the dinghy, holding his pistol in front of him in shooting position.

Morgan waited too, letting the man close in on him. He had his gun back in his right hand with his finger on the trigger. He moved that hand toward the front of the dinghy, careful to keep the motion down where the man couldn't see it.

When the man was about thirty feet away, he said, "Throw out the money."

"I can't. The bag is too heavy for me to lift now." Morgan coughed wetly, making it loud enough for the man to hear him. "It's next to me here in the boat."

The hard-looking man hesitated. Maybe something didn't seem quite right. Then Morgan saw him look down at the flashlight. Morgan saw his eyes widen.

The man looked back at Morgan and started to say something, but Morgan shot him before he could get it out. The bullet slammed into the right side of his abdomen and ripped all the way through, making him jerk his arm and drop the pistol. Morgan tried to fire again, but the gun jammed.

The gangster watched as Morgan, cursing, tried to work the slide against the friction of the sand that had worked its way into the mechanism. Then the gangster reached into his jacket pocket and pulled out a pair of needle-nose pliers. Snarling wordlessly, he lurched toward Morgan, holding the pliers out in front of him.

Morgan had a good idea what the man planned to do with the pliers. He jerked at the slide again, but his pistol was hopelessly jammed. As the gangster closed in, Morgan threw the pistol at him, missing him by inches.

The gangster, the right side of his midsection covered with blood, reached the dinghy and bent down, thrusting the pliers at Morgan with his left hand. Morgan put up his own hand to block the thrust, and the man caught two of Morgan's fingers in the jaws.

The man squeezed, harder than seemed possible, and Morgan screamed. He had never felt anything so unbearable, not even when burning in the desert.

Morgan's scream seemed to give the hard-looking man even more strength, and he squeezed harder, cutting through Morgan's flesh into bone. His hand and the pliers and the gangster's hand were all covered in Morgan's blood. Morgan screamed again but not as loudly—he felt himself tottering near to a great black pool where he knew he would drown.

"The money!" The gangster glanced around the boat. "Where is it?"

"Burned up." Morgan managed to get that out through gritted teeth. "Just like Rivera's boat."

That made the gangster pause. As he did, something stirred in the back of Morgan's brain, something he ought to remember. He tried to pull the thought to the surface, but his brain wasn't working well. Too many injuries. Too much loss of blood.

What was it? Something that would help him now, he was sure. He tried harder and then he had it.

He groaned and moved his other hand down his side as though he were reacting to the pain from the pliers. He didn't have to fake it—the pain was excruciating as though any second the pliers might cut through his fingers.

"All of it?" the man, squeezing the pliers again.

"Yes . . . all." Morgan moved his hand another couple of inches and found his hip pocket. Despite his having been blown off the boat, lost in the water, and then pulled into the dinghy, the knife was still there—Rivera's switchblade.

He groaned again to distract the gangster and, with his last bit of strength, pulled out the knife and opened it. The faint "snick" made the gangster look at Morgan's other hand to see what he was doing.

The man let go of the pliers and reached for his own knife, but he was too late. Morgan thrust the switchblade into the man's chest and held it there as the man stopped scrabbling in his pocket and closed his hand around Morgan's, trying to withdraw the knife.

He managed to pull it back half an inch, then a full inch, but there it stopped as his blood flowed freely around the blade. After a few seconds he slumped forward onto the side of the dinghy, almost falling onto Morgan.

Morgan watched the gangster for a several seconds, and when the man didn't move again, Morgan sank back into the little boat. He tucked his injured hand into his side, curled up slightly, and let himself fall toward that black pool.

Some time later—he didn't know how long—he felt Ana's hand on his stubbled jaw. She was crying, and her tears ran down her cheeks and fell onto his.

He tried to speak, couldn't, and feebly cleared his throat. Then finally he was able to say it. "Now . . . now you're free."

That made her cry harder. He wanted to embrace her but couldn't move his arms. He looked up, and the sky, although almost cloudless, seemed darker than it had been.

Karen moved into his line of sight. She had the blue bag in her hand, the bag that had caused all the trouble. He knew what he had to tell her.

"Those guys followed you." He had to pause to take a breath. "Rivera's gang may know where you live. Or maybe that old man does . . . the one Ana told me about." He paused again. "You've got to get away . . . go to the mainland. Disappear."

"What the hell with?" she said. "You know I don't have that kind of money."

Ana wiped her eyes, then lifted her head to look at Karen. "With this." She touched the bag. "Take it—I do not want it. Not anymore."

"Too bad you didn't feel that way earlier."

The sarcasm in Karen's tone stung, but Ana knew there was truth in what she said. Ana struggled to find something to say, could not, and turned toward the ocean without seeing it.

In the same mocking voice Karen said, "And you think this money will make up for losing Luis—the man I loved?"

"No!" Ana paused. Then she said, "No, I do not. I know that nothing can replace him. But take the money, please. It is all I have to give you, and you can use it to get away."

"But what if someone is still looking for it? There must be more men who worked with Rivera or that other one and know about the money."

"Probably, but they may think it burned up." Ana told Karen about the small boat she'd spotted after Rivera's boat exploded.

"If that was not more of Jaime's men, whoever it was would have reported the fire," Ana said. "If it was Jaime's men, they saw the fire themselves. Either way, they must know about it. And they may think that if there is nothing left of Jaime, the money is also gone."

"And you too?" Karen said.

"Yes, if I am lucky."

Karen looked at Morgan. He said, "Yes, take it. Go the airport . . . today . . . fly to some city. Lose yourself."

Karen didn't speak for a moment. Then she said, "I would not want to stay here without Luis. And I have cousins in New Orleans."

"Good. Go. Don't . . . don't tell anyone . . . about the money. Safer that way."

She nodded. "Okay. But first we'll take you to the hospital."

"No use. Too much blood. I know . . . seen it before."

That made Ana start crying again.

"Ana, go with Karen. Brush out . . . your footprints . . . cops will figure . . . shootout. No one . . . else here . . . no money."

"I will not leave you."

"Please do . . . last thing . . . for me."

"No."

"You must."

"No, I cannot leave you."

"You . . . ."

She would never know what he wanted to say—his voice trailed off and he slumped down, all his muscles slack. He lay motionless in the dinghy, staring sightlessly at the sky.

Ana made a harsh cry like some wounded thing. She hugged Hal as though that might bring him back and held him for a long moment. Then she put her hand on the side of his face again and imagined she could already feel his skin beginning to grow cold. Despite the warmth of the sun, now well up over the horizon, she felt a coldness herself, a dark, empty place inside her where no light or heat could reach.

Karen gave her some time, shifting the bag from one hand to the other. Then she asked softly, "Do you want to say anything? A prayer maybe?"

"No." Ana paused. "He is with God now. He is praying for us."

"I hope so. We can use it."

When Ana looked at her, Karen said, "I wasn't trying to be funny."

"I know. And you are right—we can use it."

Karen waited a few more seconds, but when Ana didn't move, she touched her shoulder and said, "We've got to get out of here."

Ana still didn't move. Karen said, "Come on! We've got to go—now!"

That brought Ana around. She forced herself to pull back from Hal and get to her feet. "Wait a minute—let me think."

She tried to put herself in Jaime's position, tried to think about what he would do in this situation. He'd had a talent for survival, and now she had to develop one—fast. She knew El Viejo didn't care about her, but he wouldn't stop looking for the money, *his* money, unless . . . .

Unless he thought it was gone. Maybe he would think it was lost with Jaime's boat. But maybe not. That was a deadly chance she didn't want to take.

She looked at Karen. "I have an idea. But you have to help me. It will take both of us."

"Both of us to do what?"

"You will see. First we must drag the boat to this man's car."

"For God's sake, why?"

"There is no time to explain. We must do it quickly."

Ana pulled the knife from the gangster's chest and wiped the blade on his shirt, leaving a dark red smear. She closed the switchblade and slid it into her khakis. Then she searched the man's body until she found his car key. Last she wiped off the needle-nose pliers, leaving more blood on the gangster's shirt smeared whatever fingerprints she might have left, and put the pliers back in his pocket.

She bent to grasp the gangster's shoes and, grunting with effort, drag him off the dinghy and a few feet away. She picked up the flashlight and Hal's gun and stowed them in her jacket.

She bent again to take hold of the forward edge of the dinghy. Turning her head to look at Karen, she said, "Help me. Please. I cannot do it alone."

Karen made an angry gesture with her free hand. "No! Someone might see us—the police or more killers like that dead man. Even just some people going to the beach. It's too risky."

"No, it is too risky not to do it."

Karen was silent for a moment, studying Ana's face. Seeing the determination there, she sighed and said, "All right." She stepped to the opposite end of the dinghy and put the bag inside the boat. Then she squatted next to Ana and grasped the dinghy. She cocked her head to look at Ana. "Okay, I'm ready."

"Pull," Ana said, and the two women backed slowly toward the road that paralleled the beach. Despite the boat's flat bottom, the weight of the dinghy with a man in it made pulling the boat over the sand grueling work.

They had to stop three times to rest, but finally they got the dinghy up next to foliage between the beach and the road.

"We have to get him to that man's car," Ana said, stripping off the squall jacket and wiping her damp face with the bottom of her shirt.

Karen flicked sweat from her forehead and looked at the green wall ahead of them. "That won't be easy."

"No, but we can do it."

And they did do it, tugging Morgan by his arms and dragging the dead weight of his body through the thick brush. All the while Ana had to keep reminding herself that the man she'd loved was past all pain.

As they emerged from the foliage, Karen stopped abruptly. "Wait," she said and went to check the road in both directions.

She returned in a few seconds. "All clear. We're lucky there's not much traffic on this road at this time of day."

They moved Morgan's body to the car, which the gangster had left unlocked—perhaps in case he needed to get into it in a hurry. Ana opened the rear passenger door.

"We must put him inside."

Karen gave her another look, but she was tired and just wanted this . . . whatever hell it was . . . to be over. She helped Ana slide Morgan's torso onto the seat. When they couldn't push any farther, Ana went from the opposite side, climbed into the car and began pulling on Hal's collar while Karen continued to push. Slowly they slid the entire body into the car.

"Now the boat." Ana went back through the brush, Karen trailing. Ana took out the knife, opened it, and stabbed the blade into the dinghy's sides, over and over, deflating it.

As the sides collapsed, Karen pulled the bag out and put it on the ground. Ana grabbed the pouch of flares and shoved them into her pocket. Seeing what Ana was doing, Karen began to suspect what she had in mind.

When the dinghy was completely deflated, Ana used the knife to cut off the bow line and then cut it into two pieces. Kneeling next to the flattened dinghy, Ana said, "Help me roll it up."

Karen did, and Ana used the line to cinch the dinghy into a cylinder, tying the pieces a third of the way from its ends. Then they dragged the cigar shape through the brush, which was easier than moving Morgan's body had been.

Ana used the key to open the trunk. "I can guess this part," Karen said, as the two women picked up opposite ends of the dinghy and bent the rolled-up boat into the trunk.

Ana slammed the trunk shut. "Now the other one."

She picked up the gangster's dropped gun as they walked down the beach to his body. They dragged him to the car, walking backwards in the dinghy's track, Ana feeling herself almost exhausted by the effort and seeing that Karen felt the same way. But they got him there and into the vehicle, waiting in the bushes while a solitary car passed, and then putting the body, as Ana instructed, behind the wheel.

Panting, Ana pointed at the beach. "Please get some palm branches and brush out our footprints and the . . . pista—"

"Track."

"Sí, the track of the boat. I will finish here."

Karen, also winded, nodded and edged back into the foliage.

Ana put the gangster's gun into his right hand and forced his fingers around the butt. Next she inserted the key in the ignition switch, and lowered all four windows. She closed the door and went to look for a long, straight tree branch. A wire coat hanger was the usual tool for this particular job, but she didn't have one.

When she found a branch she thought would work, she used the knife to cut a narrow strip from the bottom of her shirt and tied it to the branch. She opened the car's gas cap and pushed the branch down as far as she could. She withdrew the branch and used it to rub gasoline on the car's dashboard.

She repeated the process two more times. Then she dropped the stick on the front passenger seat and shut the door on that side.

By that time Karen had returned, wearing Ana's jacket and carrying the bag in one hand and dragging some large palm fronds behind her with the other. "It's done—no more tracks."

"Bueno. Put the branches in the back seat. That way no one will wonder about them lying here."

Karen hadn't thought of that. She put the bag down, took off the jacket and laid it by the bag, and went to shove the palm fronds through the rear window on the passenger side. As she was wrestling with the branches, Ana stepped over to the bag and opened it. She took out several stacks of banded bills and carried them to the car.

Karen had meant what she said about the money's not making up for losing Luis, but she needed money to get away and so didn't like what she saw. "Wait—what are you doing?"

Standing by the front passenger door, Ana turned to look at her. "Would you rather live with most of the money or die with all of it?"

Karen knew the answer to that one. She pushed the last piece of palm through the window and said nothing further as Ana broke the bands, threw handfuls of bills through the other window, and scattered a few bills on the ground.

When she had done that, Ana pulled the pouch of flares from her pocket. She shook them out of the pouch, let the light piece of plastic fall to the ground near where the bills were stirring in the breeze, and dropped two of the flares into the car beside Hal's body, now lying under a canopy of green.

Holding the remaining flare, she studied the setup for a few moments. Then she said, almost as if speaking to herself, "What would you do if you were badly wounded and this man found you? Maybe on the beach somewhere after you had come ashore. If he took the money and hurt you worse, so much that he thought you were dead?"

Ana turned to look at Karen. "Then he put you in his car and brought you here to dump your body in these thick bushes so that it would not be found for some time—if at all. And you were lying on the back seat, almost dead, with no gun, and only these for a weapon." She held up the flare. "What would you do?"

Karen looked back at Ana with a new-found respect. How had this young woman—this gangster's mistress, who had just lost the man she loved—been able to think so clearly and quickly? Karen doubted that, under the circumstances, she could have done so well.

Karen was still angry about Luis's death and knew she would be for a long time, but she had to admit that when Ana needed to move, she *moved*.

"I'd be desperate," Karen said, "and shoot one off inside the car. Maybe I wouldn't get away, but he wouldn't either."

"Sí. I would do the same. And that is what El Viejo will think happened. With no little boat or even any marks on the beach, he cannot know for certain that anyone came ashore here."

She paused, thinking it all the way through. "He cannot know for certain that we are still alive and that you still have most of the money. There is no . . . prueba—"

"Proof."

"Right, no proof of that. So he may wonder, he may even suspect, but he cannot *know*. I hope that will be enough to make him stop."

Karen hoped so too. "Maybe it will. The police here are so swamped that they won't have time to do a thorough investigation." Her mouth twisted. "When I lived in New York I learned how cops like to close a case as quickly and easily as they can—even when they're wrong about what happened."

Ana wondered what Karen meant by that, but there wasn't time to find out. She checked the road in one direction, then the other. "It is still clear. Please get your car. We will need to leave very soon."

"Okay." Karen picked up the bag and jacket and started to go but then turned back toward Ana. "How did you know to do all this?"

Ana thought about how to answer that. "I learned many things from listening to Jaime Rivera and his men. Many things . . . and I would like to forget most of them."

Karen continued to look at her. After a long moment she nodded and headed for her car.

Ana waited until she hear Karen's car start. Then she took a last, long look at Hal, feeling that empty place inside her. That made her glance at the gangster, the man who'd killed him. Thinking of what he had done to Hal—and thereby to her—made it easier to step back a few feet, light the flare, and throw it through the front window toward the dashboard.

The flare hit the gasoline, and almost instantly the dash was ablaze. In less than a minute the whole interior of the car was burning fiercely, sending a thick plume of greasy black smoke into the blue bowl of the sky.

Ana felt the heat on her face, but she was still cold inside, even colder now that she'd done this awful thing. The fire on Jaime's boat had been bad enough, but this . . . and she had caused it. She felt that she'd had no choice, but it was still her doing.

She moved farther away, but the heat followed her as flames engulfed the car, incinerating everything not made of metal. The stench was awful, but she tried not to think about what inside the car was causing it.

Karen drove as close to the burning car as she dared. She lowered a window and said to Ana, raising her voice over the roar of the flames. "Come on. We've got to get out of here."

Ana heard her but didn't move. She felt hypnotized by the fire, as though something in it—or someone—were calling to her.

Karen leaned her head out the window and saw the growing black cloud above them. "Come on! This will bring the cops."

The mention of the police snapped Ana out of her reverie. "Sí, now we go."

She hurried to Karen's car, and they sped away.

CHAPTER TWENTY-NINE

Karen drove back to her house, Ana sitting beside her, neither woman speaking. When they got there, Karen opened the blue bag and took out four packets of bills.

She handed them to Ana. "Take this—you'll need it."

Ana shook her head. "No, I do not want any of the money. It got . . . it got him killed." She could not bring herself to say his name. "And Luis. Even my uncle."

"Don't be foolish. You can't get away without some cash. You'll have to pay that coffee-shop guy something just to get your driver's license."

"No!"

Karen paused. "Ana, Hal would want you to get away. Otherwise, he died for nothing."

Ana put her hand to her eyes, but she found she had no tears left.

She resisted for another moment, but she knew what Karen said was true—she had to have some money. "Ay, eso es verdad." She reluctantly took the packets from Karen.

Karen told her how to get to the shop where the counterfeiter hung out.

"I think I can find it, but I do not know what he looks like."

"That's okay. Just get some coffee, sit down, and wait. If he's there—or when he shows up—he'll recognize you from your picture. He wants the rest of his money, so he'll come to you."

Ana thought Karen sounded as though she had some experience with this sort of thing. "All right. What are you going to do?"

"Grab some clothes and a couple of pictures of Luis, take this money, and get the hell out of Puerto Rico. Go to New Orleans like I said. Where are you going?"

"I do not know."

"Well, you better make up your mind pretty quick."

That was also true. Ana nodded. "I will think of something. I will take the car we bought and go . . . somewhere." She paused, looking at Karen. "Thank you. And good luck."

Karen hesitated. She was still angry with Ana, but she realized that Ana had lost a man just as she had. "Good luck to you." She opened her arms, and the two women embraced.

Ana kissed Karen on the cheek and then turned and began walking down the street to where Hal had left the old car. Karen watched her for a few seconds, then hurried into the house to pack a bag—a different bag, one that wasn't blue.

□ □ □

Late that afternoon Ana parked the car near the guesthouse where they'd bought it. When she got out, she left the key in the ignition. She didn't think the manager or his brother would tell the police about the car's return. She checked her pockets to make sure she had her new driver's license and the remainder of the money and then started walking toward the cove where they'd left *Sun Chaser*.

It was possible, of course, that someone had stolen the boat, sailed it away. Ana had no idea what she'd do if that had happened. But when she got to the cove, she saw *Sun Chaser* floating peacefully at anchor. The slanting sunlight threw a long shadow from the boat but made her brightwork sparkle.

The boat's dinghy was there too, still hidden under a palm tree. Ana dragged it down to the water, got in it, and paddled slowly toward *Sun Chaser*. Her hands and arms were sore from the previous night, and she stopped halfway to rest.

She closed her eyes and imagined that Hal was there with her, that the two of them were swimming nude in the cool, blue-green water. Then she imagined them wading ashore and making love on the warm sand as the golden sun rolled down the deep-blue western sky.

Her eyes grew hot then, and she put a hand to her face. She sat there in the little dinghy, not moving, as she thought of him. That marred face with an eyepatch, a face that had scared her at first but that she had grown to accept, then admire, then love.

What had Jaime called him? "'This pirate'?" Yes, that was it. A strong, silent pirate who had saved her from the ocean, then from Jaime and his gang, and last from that man on the beach, a man who certainly would have killed her—and Karen too.

Hal had not been able to save everyone. Tío Paco was dead and so was Luis, but he had tried. He had done his best, and that was all anyone could do. She put the paddle back in the water and continued toward *Sun Chaser*.

When she got there, she tied the dinghy to a stern cleat and climbed aboard. Later she'd try to figure out how to hoist the dinghy back on deck.

Using the set of keys Hal had given her on Jaime's boat, she unlocked the main hatch. She went below and retrieved the paper chart that Hal had showed her. Then she sat in the cockpit and studied the chart.

They might still be after her. Maybe not, if they thought the money had burned up, either on Jaime's boat or in the gangster's car, but she couldn't be sure. And if they were still looking for her, the danger was too great. Identifying what was left of the gangster's car and the bodies inside would slow them down, but it wouldn't stop them. She'd heard stories about what Jaime and his crew had done to certain people . . . and she believed them.

No, she had to get away. Karen wasn't known to them, so she could risk using the San Juan airport. But they knew Ana and might recognize her as Jaime had, even with her changed appearance. She remembered Jaime had said they'd followed Tío Paco from the airport, so maybe some of his men were still there, watching. She wasn't going to bet her life that they weren't.

There was a better way to leave—on *Sun Chaser*. Between what her uncle had taught her when she was young and what Hal had shown her about this boat, she thought she might know enough to sail *Sun Chaser* to a nearby island. But which one?

She could head west to the Dominican Republic. She had friends there—but Jaime had had friends there too, and his friends would not be hers now. She could try go even farther west, to Cuba, but with Tío Paco dead, they'd probably put her in prison.

So those two places were out. She moved her finger to the right—eastward—on the chart, and then she had the answer. St. Thomas, in the U.S. Virgin Islands.

She'd find an empty beach or cove to bring *Sun Chaser* ashore or even anchor out and paddle ashore in the dinghy. Either way she'd be back in U.S. territory. She thought she was supposed to have a passport when arriving by sea, but if she didn't take *Sun Chaser* into a major harbor, that technicality wouldn't matter. They might be looking for her at the San Juan airport, but they wouldn't be at the airport in St. Thomas, and her new driver's license would be enough ID for her to buy an airline ticket to Miami.

There she could use her Spanish to get a job in some little shop run by Latino immigrants who wouldn't be too particular about checking on her citizenship. Go to night school and try to make something of herself as she'd told Hal she would do. Earn the life he'd died to give her.

She looked at the scale on the chart. She put her index finger next to the scale, noted the mileage that equated to the length of her first two joints, and then did a rough measurement of the distance to St. Thomas. Less than 150 miles. Two days' sailing, maybe three, if she took it in stages, sailing as far as she could and then anchoring near shore to get some sleep.

She was very tired from the horrific night before and the long day since then, but she was eager to get going. Plus she wanted to take *Sun Chaser* out of the cove while there was still some daylight. The moon would be up later, and she could sail for three or four hours before anchoring for the night somewhere east of Ponce.

But could she do it? Could she handle this big boat all by herself? What if another storm came up? There'd be no Hal to save her again.

But then she thought of all that had happened to her since then and all that she'd been able to do in that time. She'd stood up to Jaime Rivera and his men. She'd killed one with a broken piece of glass, saved Hal from drowning, and paddled a dinghy all night to get him and herself back to shore.

She'd done what she could for Karen—not enough, because nothing would make up for the loss of Luis, but all she could do. And she'd cremated the body of the man she loved and even used the fire to leave a trail of false evidence pointing away from her.

She imagined what Hal would say if he were there with her. "Yes, you do can do it—you can do anything you set your mind to." Then he'd look in her eyes and smile. "Don't let the bastards beat you."

The thought gave her courage, but she still wondered if she was up to the task. Could she really sail all that way by herself?

"Sure," she heard Hal saying. "Aren't you a pirate, just like me? And don't we pirates know how to sail? Now get going."

She sat still for a moment, lingering in her memory of him. Then she nodded to herself, put down the chart, and went to haul in the anchors.

THE END